The Mathematics of Murder:

A Fearne & Bracknell Collection

The Mathematics of Murder:

A Fearne & Bracknell Collection

Michael Gilbert

ROBERT HALE · LONDON

ISBN 0 7090 6723 2

Robert Hale Limited
Clerkenwell House
Clerkenwell Green
London EC1R 0HT

2 4 6 8 10 9 7 5 3 1

Typeset by
Derek Doyle & Associates, Liverpool.
Printed in Great Britain by
St Edmundsbury Press Ltd, Bury St Edmunds, Suffolk.
Bound by Woolnough Bookbinding Ltd.

Contents

1
The Mathematics of Murder

Friday, 18 March, was a date Hugo Bracknell was destined to remember. Having missed by two minutes the fast 6.30 train from Liverpool Street to Colchester, he had been forced to take, instead, the 6.55 train on the Braintree line. Anxious study of the timetable had shown him that it would, if it ran to time, reach Witham at 7.55. The snag was that it seemed to be a commuter special, stopping no fewer than nine times before it reached Shenfield; discharging at each of these stops a number of businessmen on the way back to their residences at Chadwell Heath, Gidea Park, Brentwood, and other portions of the suburban sprawl which separated East London from Essex.

After Shenfield it seemed to get a move on, stopping only at Ingatestone, Chelmsford, and Hatfield Peverel before reaching Witham.

It was important that it should run to time. He had been invited to spend the weekend with his aunt. She was a formidable old lady who liked to dine promptly at eight. If the train dallied, or there was any difficulty over picking up a taxi at the station, he was going to keep her from her grub. Unthinkable.

'Then don't think about it,' he said. 'Either you make it or you don't. So stop worrying.'

His thoughts reverted to personal matters; and there was much to think about.

For he had reached a milestone.

After leaving Oxford he had been allowed two years to widen his horizons, to enlarge his knowledge of human nature, to improve his mind; in fact, to enjoy himself, before plunging into the job for which he had been destined from birth.

He was now, and had been for the past ten days, articled to his father, Bob Bracknell, who, with Francis Fearne, constituted the partnership of Fearne & Bracknell, solicitors, in Little Bethel, an odd backwater near the northern end of Tower Bridge, flanked by the offices and warehouse of Ridolfi Brothers on one side and on the other by the Roaring Forties public house. When spoken of in the City – and for a small firm they were spoken of a good deal – they were naturally referred to as Fern and Bracken and strangers sometimes wrote to them under this name. It made no difference. The postmen all knew them.

Ingatestone was briefly stopped at, and left behind them. Three stations to go. Still only 7.45. Relax. Plenty of time.

Fearne & Bracknell was not a big firm. Far from it. But they had that mysterious, indefinable, unchallengeable something. Reputation. People said of them, 'Fern and Bracken. Very practical firm, that. Get on with the job, you know. No highfalutin law about them, but sound. Break the law? Of course not. They're not sharp. Just reliable.'

Hugo sometimes wondered how much of this reputation stemmed from their senior managing clerk, Horace Piggin. He had met Mr Piggin on many occasions when visiting the office in his school days and had sat kicking his heels in the waiting-room whilst his father dealt with some long-winded client. Mr Piggin had put himself out to entertain the boy.

He remembered one conversation which had taken place when he was in his last year at Rugby. Mr Piggin had set the ball rolling by asking him why he had decided to take up law. With a brashness which made him blush when he thought about it, he had said, 'Oh, I knew Dad would give me my articles here. And after all, being a solicitor isn't difficult. Look at some of the types you see doing it!'

Mr Piggin had agreed with him, gravely.

'Of course, I don't mean you, Piggy. And I don't mean this firm. We're different. I mean the stooges in Lincoln's Inn and Bedford Row who read it all up in books and copy it out!'

'That's one fault,' Mr Piggin had agreed, 'that you'll not find in this firm. We have hardly a law book in the place!'

'But surely, Piggy, you must want to look things up sometimes!'

To which Mr Piggin's memorable reply had been, 'If reference to the authorities is required, I trot along to the public library, scribble down the information, and trot back with it!'

The thought of Mr Piggin trotting up Tower Bridge Road with his white hair streaming in the wind had enchanted Hugo.

Chelmsford. A rather larger place. Might that mean a longer stop? But no. Quite a few men got off the now nearly empty train, but there were no passengers waiting to get on. Hatfield Peverel next. No one got off, no one got on. Excellent. Minutes were important.

It occurred to Hugo, who was in the rear coach, that he could save a little time on arrival at Witham if he moved up to a point nearer the centre. There was no difficulty about this. The train consisted of twelve coaches in three blocks of four, and it was possible to move from one block to the other. He passed two men, one at either end of the first carriage. The next two were empty. In the fourth carriage there were a woman with a dog and a man and a girl who were sitting close together and getting on with some very private business. Hugo skirted them and passed through the cubicle which joined the rear four carriages to the central four.

Again an empty carriage. In the next, there was one man slouched in his seat and blocking the door in the centre of the carriage that Hugo had been planning to use. As the train jerked to a stop, the man rolled over and lay across the two seats, staring up at the roof with a puzzled look on his face, and Hugo saw the narrow wound in the back of his neck with the dark blood oozing out of it.

It was instinct that led his hand to the handle of the door. Must have help. Must have air. Get the door open. He stumbled on to the platform and stood holding on desperately to the handle.

The guard shouted, 'Stand away,' an order which Hugo was unable and unwilling to obey. A louder shout brought out the station master, peremptory and indignant at the sight of a young man, apparently drunk, holding himself up by the door handle.

By this time the guard had come up. Hugo used his free hand to wave towards the interior of the carriage.

After that, things happened slowly.

First the arrival of a local constable. Then a more senior police-man. Then the business of evacuating the few remaining passengers and shunting the train on to a lay-by. Then the arrival of photographers and a police surgeon and a string of questions which Hugo answered as best he could while trying to control his rebellious stomach. Finally the body was moved and Hugo, his identity established and checked, was at last allowed to take possession of the taxi he had secured and to depart and endeav-our to placate his aunt.

He was able in the circumstances to excuse himself from carry-ing out his projected weekend visit, but he further disrupted his aunt's domestic arrangements by asking to be called at six-thirty. He reached his office at nine o'clock. Fearne & Bracknell – old-fashioned in this as in everything else – worked on Saturday mornings and he arrived, as planned, before either of the partners put in an appearance and made his way straight to the sanctum of their managing clerk. It was Mr Piggin's advice and support that he wanted.

'So you are the young man,' said Mr Piggin, 'described, but tactfully unnamed, whose exploits I have been reading about in the morning papers.'

'That's me, Piggy,' said Hugo. 'And I'll tell you something mighty strange. Nobody I encountered seemed in the least *surprised* at what I told them. Disturbed, excited, even shocked, but not surprised. The official people at Witham were clearly keeping something back, and my aunt, when she'd heard my story, simply closed her mind to it and discussed a problem she was having with the committee of the Women's Institute. But she knew something. I'm sure of it.'

Mr Piggin seemed to be faintly amused. He said, 'If you had opened a newspaper three or four months ago you'd have read little or nothing about indiscretions in Whitehall or massacres in Kurdistan. The front page of the paper and other pages as well would have been full of the activities of the creature they christened the Knifeman.'

'Are you telling me that yesterday was not the first—'

'It was the sixth known occasion on which he has struck. You have not seen one of today's papers? No. Well, I can assure you that he has regained his position on the front page. Was there nothing in the papers where you were?'

'The Italian press don't pay much attention to crime in other countries. They've got plenty of their own. Though now that you mention it, I do recall a brief comment about a serial murderer. When did it all start?'

Mr Piggin had been turning over the pages of his working diaries. He said, 'The first one was sixteen months ago, on Tuesday, November tenth. The next, near the beginning of last year, on Friday, February nineteenth. Then on June fifteenth, August thirteenth – which was also a Friday – and on Monday, October eleventh.'

'How did they know that these were all the same man?'

'It could not, of course, be *known*,' said Mr Piggin precisely, 'but the evidence that it was so was almost conclusive. His procedure in every case was the same. He waited until he was alone with one other man in the carriage, walked up to him as though

11

he was making for the door, and struck him on the head with a loaded stick or life preserver. As his victim crumpled up he produced his second weapon. This the pathologists, in every case, thought to be a long, slender surgical-type lancet. He drove this upward, through the back of his victim's neck, into his brain, killing him instantly.'

Although Mr Piggin was speaking flatly, as though he was explaining a legal problem, his words recalled the horror of the moment and Hugo found himself shuddering. He said, 'The man who does this – he must be mad – but he must also be wholly ordinary in appearance, so as not to excite any suspicion of his intentions.'

'Wholly so. And this agrees with the only description we have of him.'

'You mean – he was seen—'

'Exercise a little patience,' said Mr Piggin, 'and I will endeavour to explain. After five attacks, commuters – as you can imagine – became careful. They took precautions. They travelled, where possible, in parties. Then came this period of more than three months in which nothing happened. Precautions were relaxed – prematurely, you may think – but such is human nature.'

Mr Piggin was now studying his current year's diary.

'On Thursday, January twentieth a Mr Osbaldistone was travelling to Bures, where he planned to spend a long weekend with an old friend. This involved changing at Marks Tey. The train was slowing as it approached Kelvedon, the station before Marks Tey, when he suddenly realized that he was alone in the carriage with one other man *and that this man was advancing on him with his left hand in his overcoat pocket*. The consciousness of his peril deprived him, he said, of the power to move or shout. He was mesmerized. Most fortunately, at that moment a young man – the son of the house that he was visiting – came through the connecting vestibule into the carriage. He said, 'Mr Osbaldistone, isn't it? I guessed it might be you. You're spending the weekend with us.'

By this time the other man had opened the carriage door and departed. When Mr Osbaldistone related his experience, as he did, with some embarrassment, that evening, his hosts impressed on him that it was his duty to communicate with the police. Whether he was right or wrong in his suspicions, it was at least possible that he was the first man to come face-to-face with the killer and live to tell the tale. "You *must* describe him", they said.'

Because the first victim, a Mr Mathieson, had worked in Stepney and lived in Romford, both places being in No. 2 Area East, the case had been assigned to the head of that area, Chief Superintendent Oliphant. He had delegated the routine handling of it to Chief Inspector Mayburgh at Cable Street, and it was to Mayburgh that Mr Osbaldistone duly reported.

Mr Piggin said, 'I gathered from him – Osbaldistone is, by the way, a client of this firm and an old friend of your father's – that it was not a happy experience. I'm sure he did his best, but it amounted to very little. He said, quite reasonably, that he wasn't examining the man's face. His attention was fixed on his left hand, which appeared to be drawing some sort of weapon out of his coat pocket. He couldn't see more than the handle, but yes, it might have been a life preserver, something like that. "Or the whole thing might have been your imagination", says Mayburgh. "Yes, it might have been", Osbaldistone agreed. "But I was too worked up to notice precise details". All this was in answer to a series of bad-tempered questions and grunts. The inspector considered that Mr Osbaldistone had no right to get worked up. He should have been making a careful inspection of his assailant.'

'Mayburgh sounds a bit of a brute,' said Hugo.

'He's an old-fashioned rhinoceros who tries to arrive at the truth by butting at it, head first. His second-in-command, Inspector Barley, on the other hand, is what you might call – hum – a scientific policeman.'

Hugo gathered from Mr Piggin's tone that his description of

Inspector Barley was not intended to be entirely complimentary.

'In the end,' he said, 'he got nothing out of Mr O. except that his presumed attacker looked, in every way, like a normal City worker. Pale face, clean-shaven, indeterminate features, no distinguishing marks. When he said that the man was "ordinary" he had said it all. His failure on that occasion may account for the inspector's wish to question you.'

'For God's sake! Why me? I never even saw the man.'

'The working of the inspector's mind is a closed book to me. All I can tell you is that there was a message on our answerphone when I arrived that he would like to see you at ten o'clock. It's a quarter to ten now. Better not keep the rhinoceros waiting.'

When Hugo was ushered into Mayburgh's office he saw a man who could have been nothing but a middle-ranking policeman; one who had started at the bottom and crashed upwards not caring what toes he trod on. The red face, bristling hair, and angry eyes said it all. He barked at Hugo to sit down and opened fire with the observation that Hugo should not have disturbed the body.

'But I had to be certain the man was dead.'

'Were you in any doubt about it?'

'Not really, no.'

'Then why did you touch him?'

'If I hadn't, he'd have fallen on to the floor. You wouldn't have wanted that, surely.'

'It's not what I want, it's what the medical experts want. They can make useful deductions if they find the body *exactly* as it was at the point of death.'

This seemed like nonsense to Hugo, but had evidently gained the approval of the young man in glasses who was sitting quietly in the corner. The scientific Inspector Barley?

'Reverting to a point where you *might* be able to help us. It is fairly clear that the attack took place between Ingatestone and

Chelmsford and that the assassin left the train at Chelmsford. Did you take any note of the people who got off?'

'I was in the rear carriage at the time, but yes, I did look out. I was anxious about the possibility of the train being held up and I was glad to see that no one was waiting to get on.'

'It's the people who got *off* that I'm interested in.'

'Well, there were a fair number of them. All men. The usual home-going crowd, I thought.'

'Nothing more?'

'I'm sorry. No.'

'If members of the public kept their eyes open and their wits about them,' said Mayburgh, 'we might make some progress.'

This not being a question, Hugo did not feel called on to answer it, and five minutes later he had been bundled out of the room. As he closed the door, Mayburgh said to Inspector Barley, 'What did you make of that? Was he holding out on us?'

'I made nothing of it, because there was nothing to make.'

'He's old Bracknell's son. He's just joined the firm. And you know what they're like. Do anything they can to obstruct the police.'

'I don't think,' said Barley primly, 'that we can pin anything on to this young man if he only came back to England a fortnight ago.'

'I suppose that's right,' said Mayburgh.

It was evident that he was in some awe of his learned junior.

Hugo, meanwhile, had reported the outcome of this unsatisfactory interview to Mr Piggin.

'The man's a hog,' he said. 'If he'd been even remotely civil, I might have given him one useful piece of information. I'm fairly certain I recognized the man who was killed.'

'Did you indeed?' said Mr Piggin. 'That could be of major importance.' He sounded faintly aggrieved. His own sources of information were wide and various. It piqued him that a newcomer should know something that he did not.

'I spent six very enjoyable months at Perugia University and got to know a lot of the students and the younger professors. We used to meet for drinks in the evening and – well, you know how people talk. This particular man – an economics don called Carlo Frosinone – told me – I think he was three parts drunk at the time because the next day he denied that he had ever said it – that he had been approached by the capo of the local mafia to do a job for them and that he'd refused and was now in their black books. He sounded rather proud of this, as though it was a distinction.'

Mr Piggin, who had been listening carefully, had now extracted, from a locked drawer, his private address book. He was thumbing through the section under the letter A.

'Arbuthnot,' he said. 'That's the man. Colonel Arbuthnot. I'll give him a ring. I'm sure he'll be very interested in what you've told me. It may take a day or two to get hold of him. He's much abroad.'

On the surface, the next few days were uneventful, but there was a disturbing, undercurrent to them. The opposition, spearheaded by a claque of Members with constituencies in Essex, raised a number of questions in Parliament. The Home Secretary side-stepped them with practised agility, but was not as easy as he managed to appear; and his uneasiness was passed down, in a series of minutes, to the assistant commissioner, and through him to Chief Superintendent Brace, and, finally, to Superintendent Oliphant, who arrived at Cable Street with an ultimatum in his pocket.

'Bring me up to date,' he said. 'Particularly with regard to this last episode.'

'We've got a certain way,' said Mayburgh cautiously. 'We've circulated a photograph of the victim, which produced a number of identifications, none of them reliable, I'm afraid.'

'Had the man no papers on him?'

'Yes. He had an Italian passport. We passed the details to Interpol, who say that the details in it were false and the whole passport a clever piece of forgery.'

'And that's all?' said Oliphant.

'All except an enormous amount of routine work,' said Mayburgh rather bitterly. He indicated the six fat folders on a side table, rocks in a torrent of other documents. 'The real trouble is that the carriages concerned were of the open type, with thirty-two seats and a gangway down the middle. At the start of a commuter rush, all the seats would be occupied and a number of people standing in the gangway. As people got off, the standers would take over the seats and be replaced by other passengers coming in from even more crowded carriages. Our enquiry produced forty-one people who thought they might have been in the carriage concerned. All of them had to be questioned and their answers recorded.'

By the time he had finished this spiel Mayburgh was even redder in the face than usual. Oliphant said, 'I'm not suggesting that you haven't done your best with the resources at your disposal. But the official view is that the enquiry needs wider handling. I'm to tell you that unless you can produce concrete results in the next fortnight, the matter will have to be handed over to Central. Meanwhile, I'll alert all the other stations in the area to give you any help you need. So, if you do chance on a line, you can hunt it hard.'

When he had departed, it was Inspector Barley who broke the silence. He said, 'I feel, sir, that the first thing to do is to subject the case to a complete reassessment. If I might take all the papers home and be allowed a few days off routine duty. . . .'

'You'll need a pantechnicon to get that lot home,' said Mayburgh sourly. 'But go ahead.'

Barley was not dismayed. He foresaw days of a kind of work that was much to his taste.

On that same day, Hugo was summoned to the office of

Colonel Arbuthnot. It was in a building which overlooked St James's Park and seemed to be connected with the Ministry of Pensions. The colonel dismissed a pretty, dark-haired girl to whom he was dictating and listened with interest to what Hugo had to tell him. (The girl, who had managed to arrange things so that she could overhear what went on in the colonel's office, also listened with interest and spent some time that evening on the telephone.)

'What you say,' said the colonel, 'fits in with our information from other sources. You spent some time in Italy, I believe. Then I expect you know how the drug trade is organized there.'

'I know what every schoolchild seems to know. That the raw opium comes across from Turkey and is processed into morphia and heroin under the auspices of the mafia, who attend to its export and sale.'

'Remarkably well-informed schoolchildren,' said the colonel. 'The one point they may not have appreciated is that the mafia control the export of the hard stuff to North America and to many European countries – Belgium in particular. But they do *not*, at the moment, handle its export to this country, though they would much like to do so. If the victim of this latest killing was, in fact, Carlo Frosinone – equipped with a forged passport and having overcome his reluctance to help—'

'Or, more likely, been frightened into helping.'

'Quite so. Then it follows that the assassin was one of the London-based gangs which *do* handle the import and sale of hard drugs and would do anything to stop the mafia muscling in.'

'And the method of killing was designed to suggest that it was the work of the Knifeman?'

'Typical camouflage. And now that we appreciate the position, we can get the Metropolitan Police Drugs Squad and Customs and Excise Investigators – a very shrewd bunch – on to the killer. Working together they should soon be able to lay hands on him. And I am much obliged to you—'

'Different sort of man to Mayburgh,' said Hugo, reporting to Mr Piggin. 'Very pleasant, I thought.'

'So I've always found,' said Mr Piggin. 'I wound up his father *and* his grandfather. Talking of which, I've got a job for you. An old lady called Mrs Trumpington – a new client, so handle her carefully – wants to make a will. She is bedridden and cannot come to us, so you are to go round tomorrow and take her instructions. Here's the address. Carlton Mansions—'

As he surveyed Carlton Mansions Hugo surmised, from the appearance of the building, that Mrs Trumpington must be a lady of means. His surprise was increased by the appearance of the man who opened the door to him and ushered him into a handsomely furnished flat. Had he met him casually he would have taken him for a senior businessman, a man of authority, who would have taken the chair at board meetings. A second equally impressive but younger man was standing with his back to the fire.

Hugo, hearing the door click shut behind him, had the uncomfortable feeling that he had walked into something that it might be difficult to get out of.

Before he could open his mouth, the older man said, in a voice that matched his appearance, 'Let us cut all corners. There is no Mrs Trumper here.'

'Trumpington,' amended the younger man.

'Trumpington. Yes. She was, in any event, a myth. I am glad your father sent you, because it is specifically with you that we wished to speak. To discuss with you a professor of economics at Perugia University called Carlo Frosinone.'

Now how the devil, thought Hugo, would they know anything about *him*? Then he remembered the black-haired girl in Colonel Arbuthnot's office and ceased wondering.

'I understand that you identified the man who was killed on the train as being this professor and have accordingly alerted the security services to the possibility that he was murdered by one of the London drug gangs. Correct?'

Hugo nodded.

'Then let me clarify two points. First, Frosinone is still alive and it can only have been his heated imagination that led him to think that he was threatened by anyone. The man who died was Umberto Bardi, the son of Arturo Bardi and Janina Ridolfi, the youngest sister of Eugenio Ridolfi, whom I expect you know. His office is next door to yours.'

'Ridolfi Brothers?'

'Importers and Exporters,' said the young man with a half-smile.

'My immediate objective,' said the older man, ignoring him, 'is to convince you that I am telling you the truth. Have you made the connection?'

'He's ready and waiting.' The young man lifted the receiver and handed it to Hugo, who looked at it blankly and then said, 'Hullo.'

'Ullo, 'Ugo,' said a voice he recognized. 'Is that you? What can I do for you this fine morning?'

'I gather that the main thing is to assure me that you are alive and that there is no truth in your statement that you are being threatened by the mafia?'

'Whenever did I say such a thing?' The conversation was now in Italian.

'It was, I recollect, at a party with the Roncoronis.'

'Tony's drinks are always stronger than they seem. If I said any such thing I must have been – what is the expression? – talking out of the back of my neck. But what is all this about? Why does it worry you?'

'It only worries me because I thought you were dead.'

'If you were back in Perugia I could soon convince you that I was alive.'

'I'm sure of it.'

The older man, who had been listening on an extension, put out a hand and the young man killed the call.

'I apologize for terminating a reunion with your friend, but there is one further matter and time presses. Not only had we no hand in the killing of Umberto, but he was, in fact, our emissary, doing a job for us in this country. Consequently he was under our protection. Our honour is involved. We shall be taking steps to see that the killer is identified and punished. You follow me?'

Hugo nodded. The atmosphere in the room was so oppressive that he was finding it difficult to speak. Two things were clear. He had made a fool of himself, and he had upset some formidable people.

'You will appreciate that the activities of Colonel Arbuthnot and his friends make it more difficult for us to succeed in our task. So, in return for reassuring you about your friend, Frosinone, might we look to you to assure the colonel that we had no hand in the killing of Umberto and are ourselves seeking his killer?'

Hugo nodded again. All he wanted to do was to get out of the flat. The young man held the door open for him.

By the time he got back to the office he was on balance again. He found Mr Piggin deep in discussion with Eugenio Ridolfi, the older of the Ridolfi Brothers. He said, 'I asked Mr Ridolfi to call. As I suspected, he had *not* been shown the photograph of the murdered man – a curious omission on the part of the police. For as soon as he saw it he identified it.'

'As his nephew Umberto.'

'Precisely. You have just obtained that information from another quarter?'

'Yes.'

'From Mrs Trumpington, no doubt,' said Mr Piggin drily.

Hugo was saved embarrassment by Eugenio, who said, 'But certainly it is Umberto. He has dyed his hair and shaved off the handsome side whiskers that he usually wore. Although it is all of twenty years since I last spoke to him, I am in no doubt about it. My wife agrees. You must understand, Mr Bracknell, that my youngest sister, Janina – let us speak no ill of the dead – was a foolish girl, but not a wicked woman. On the other hand, the man she ran away to marry in Italy *was* a bad man. An associate of criminals. Since we learned of the marriage, I and my brother-in-law, Gino Alvaro, have had nothing to do with the Bardis!'

'Is it possible,' said Mr Piggin slowly, 'that Umberto was coming to England in an attempt to reconcile the two sides of the family?'

'It is possible. There are people who would like to see the Ridolfi and the Bardi firms working as a unit. But if that was his task, I do not think he would have been able to accomplish it!'

'Meanwhile,' said Hugo, who had lost his way in the intricacies of the Ridolfi–Bardi clan, 'I have to persuade Colonel Arbuthnot to leave it to the mafia to find the killer!'

'Nor must we forget,' said Mr Piggin, 'that an equally efficient body of people will be engaged on the same task. From what I have learned from my friends in the City, the police have embarked on an entirely new tack—'

The new tack had been the brainchild of Inspector Barley. After three days of study, he had propounded a novel solution to his superior officer.

He said, 'The science of psychological fingerprinting is still in its infancy, but if you apply it to the evidence in this case, an outline – you might call it a silhouette of the killer – appears on the screen. It is necessary to accommodate two widely different aspects. On the one hand, the pathologists who studied the body all arrived at the same conclusion: that the killer must have been trained – though not necessarily practised – as a surgeon. He used a surgeon's knife with a surgeon's skill. That is the left-hand aspect. The right-hand aspect is the nature of the persons selected – apparently arbitrarily – for slaughter. A bill broker, a stock jobber in a small way of business, an assistant bank manager, and two accountants.'

'And one Italian, now identified for us as Umberto Bardi, possibly a criminal, and sent here by the mafia.'

'The sixth victim,' said Barley severely, 'had nothing to do with the other five. His killing in that particular manner was a blind, calculated to deceive us.' He looked severely over his glasses at Mayburgh, who said, 'Please go on.'

'The picture of the killer must combine these two facets. A man trained as a surgeon abandons that profession for reasons we can only speculate on and sets up a business of some sort in the City. His business collapses. His bank manager refuses further credit. A receiver, probably an accountant, is appointed. Either he himself is adjudged bankrupt, or his company is placed in compulsory liquidation. Since the fury inflamed by these happenings was fresh and compelling, I deduce that the business collapse must have occurred shortly before the first of the killings. They were random, in the sense that the victims were not selected personally. They were chosen as types. Just as Jack the Ripper is said to have been revenging himself on all prostitutes, *he* was taking *his* revenge on the City.'

'Could be something in that,' said Mayburgh. 'But where does it take us?'

'Surely, if you accept my analysis, what we have to do is to study the record of business failures in the twelve months prior to the first killing. If the party involved has a background of surgical training – not a difficult matter to ascertain – then we have our hands on our man.'

Several weeks later Mr Piggin reported to Hugo, with some amusement, 'A business friend of mine tells me that Mayburgh is behaving – as he puts it – like a buffalo in a swamp. Raging to get out and attack, but too clogged to move fast in any direction. When he started he can have had no idea of the number of failures of small businesses. More than seven hundred in London alone in the year before the killings started. Nevertheless, he is plodding steadily forward, convinced that he will reach firm ground at last. He may do so. Inspector Barley is a clever young man. He may well, in fact, have arrived at the motive for the killings. But that only takes him halfway to the winning post.'

Hugo said, 'I have been doing some thinking myself and have made some calculations.'

'Excellent. Most problems in this life can be solved by mathematics.'

'Actually, I was calculating what forces the police would have to deploy to protect the public. If the killings continue to be confined to the seven commuter lines from Liverpool Street—'

'Yes,' agreed Mr Piggin. 'I think we can take that as a basis for calculation.'

'Then since many of the early evening trains consist of twelve coaches, eighty-four men would be needed. Suppose that this degree of cover is maintained for, let us say, three months. If you ignore the weekends, this would mean sixty-five working days, necessitating a total deployment of five thousand, four hundred and sixty man hours. It's a daunting total, but an effort of this magnitude wouldn't be out of place to trap a serial killer.'

Mr Piggin steepled his fingers and said, 'Allow me to correct your factors. In making your calculations you have fallen into the same error as the police and the mafia. You have studied the killer's method, but not his mind. So please think about him. He is a loner, sitting at home, working out his revenge on the City. Someone you might describe – odd though it seems in the circumstances – as an old maid, with an old maid's love of neatness and regularity. Just consider how methodically he has conducted his campaign. One killing on each of the seven available lines. Upminster, Southend, Southminster, Clacton, and Norwich. And – this was the one you were involved in – Braintree. Then we have the aborted attempt on Mr Osbaldistone – a most important episode. It took place on the Colchester line. *And it was a failure.* A man like ours abhors a failure. It upsets his pattern. Can we doubt that his next, and possibly his final effort will be a repeated attempt on the Colchester line which will round out the pattern?'

'Seems logical,' agreed Hugo.

'And since he always selects a latish commuter train I'd lay very heavy odds on the six-ten.'

'Well,' said Hugo, '*if* you're right, I agree that my first factor should be one, not seven. What about my other factors? Do you question them?'

'In mentioning twelve carriages you overlooked the fact that this man has always seated himself in the centre of the train, clearly in order to be as close as possible to the exit point on the platform when he leaves the train. I agree that he might choose either the fifth or the sixth carriage, so I'm prepared to allow you a second factor of two.'

'Thank you,' said Hugo. 'But even if you're right, two men on your selected train on every working day in the year – it's still quite a substantial total, isn't it?'

'That,' said Mr Piggin, 'is where you make your gravest error. I invited you to consider the *mind* of the killer. Lonely, methodical, introverted. Is it not clear that he would be a numerologist?'

'You've lost me.'

'A numerologist is a man who places such importance on numbers that he regulates his life by them. There are lucky and unlucky numbers. The unluckiest is, of course, thirteen. Some people carry it forward through the multiplication table and consider twenty-six, thirty-nine, fifty-two, and so on as equally unfortunate. I once had a client who believed so firmly in this that when I presented him with a bill for thirty-nine pounds he came round in person to protest. I could only pacify him by increasing it to forty pounds. On the other hand, there are lucky numbers. They are based on the number seven and all its multiples up to sixty-three, which was, historically, deemed to be the grand climacteric. A particularly lucky number in this series was twenty-one, additionally important as being the age of majority.

The law on that point may have changed, but the number has never lost its supreme power. And clearly it rules this killer absolutely.'

'How do you mean, Piggy?'

'You haven't seen it? Look at the dates he selected. November tenth, February nineteenth, June fifteenth, August thirteenth, October eleventh. Write them numerically: 10/11, 19/2, 15/6, 13/8, and 11/10. You see? The total, in every case, is twenty-one. The Osbaldistone attempt on January twentieth fits in also. One or two might have been a coincidence. Certainly not six. Quite impossible.'

Hugo, who was feeling breathless, said, 'Good God!' and 'You don't really think.' And then, 'And what about the one I was involved in? That was March eighteenth – 18/3.'

'Quite so,' said Mr Piggin. 'And it is significant in two ways. First, it means *that it was unquestionably one of the sequence we have been discussing*. I refuse to believe that chance could have dictated this particular date. Second, it means that your mafia acquaintances are quite wrong in supposing that the killing was anything to do with Umberto's mission for them in this country. He simply happened to offer an ideal chance for the Knifeman, whose opportunities had been much diminished as men tended to travel in groups. But Umberto, who had been living in Italy, would have known nothing about all this. Indeed, if the mafia had thought about it, they must have realized that their rivals in the drug trade would have had no time to organize the attack. Umberto had arrived from Italy, unannounced, that same day. No, no. It is quite clear that the man the mafia should be pursuing is not a professional rival but the Knifeman himself.'

Hugo had started scribbling dates on a piece of paper. He said, 'April seventeenth adds up to twenty-one. Why did nothing happen on that day?'

'Because it happens to have been a Sunday.'

'Oh. So it was. Well then, look here—'

'Yes?'

'The next one is May sixteenth.'

'Yes.'

'Which is next Monday.'

'Quite so.'

'And do you really think—'

'Either you accept the laws of mathematics or you reject them.'

'Then shouldn't we tell someone?'

'Can you imagine explaining it to Chief Inspector Mayburgh?'

'Perhaps not,' said Hugo. 'But we must do *something*.'

'Certainly. Next Monday we will catch the six-ten train to Colchester. I will occupy a seat in carriage number five. You will occupy one in carriage number six.'

Hugo said, 'Oh!' rather feebly. And then, 'I suppose it would be the logical way of doing it.'

His carriage, which had been crammed to start with, was emptying rapidly. Hugo's mouth was dry and he had an uncomfortable feeling in the pit of his stomach. Although he kept telling himself that Mr Piggin's theory was moonshine, one corner of his mind concentrated obstinately on the idea of a knife: long, thin, sharp-edged, with a needle point.

Shenfield, Ingatestone.

He stole another look at the man occupying the far corner seat. A very ordinary man. The only thing that had attracted Hugo's attention was his immobility. His evening paper was on the seat beside him, but he was making no attempt to read it. Nothing suspicious in that, surely?

At Chelmsford, most of the other passengers got out. Apart from this character in the corner, there was now only one other occupant of the carriage, a stout, red-faced man who was sitting in the seat beside the carriage door. The train lurched forward again. The next stop would be Hatfield Peverel and it was clear that both men were preparing to get out. The stout man had stowed his paper away into his briefcase. The suspicious character had got to his feet and was moving across. He was carrying no luggage and seemed to be feeling for something in the inside of his coat. For God's sake, thought Hugo, surely he daren't attempt anything with me watching him.

As the train stopped, the stout man got up and politely opened the carriage door. The suspect pulled out the season ticket he had been feeling for and both men descended on to the platform. They were laughing at something.

Hugo let out all the breath he had been holding. Then he sat back in his seat as his heart resumed its normal rhythm. Of course nothing had happened. Mr Piggin had been talking nonsense. He got up, strolled down the now empty carriage, and peered into the next one.

What he saw stopped him in his tracks.

Mr Piggin, apparently deep in the study of his evening paper, was occupying the seat next to the door. There was only one other man in the carriage, and as the train slowed he got up and started to move across. It was clear that his route to the door was going to take him very close to Mr Piggin, who looked up with a bland smile as he approached.

It was the sort of smile, thought Hugo, that might have illuminated the face of Pythagoras when, at long last, he saw the proof of something he had previously only suspected. He croaked out, 'Why, hullo, Mr Piggin. I didn't expect to see you on this train.'

Hardly pausing in his stride, the unknown man thrust the door open, climbed down on to the platform, and slammed the door shut behind him, without looking round.

Hugo said, 'Was that—?'

'Certainly that was our man. One hand was actually on the handle of the life preserver he intended to use. He had it half out of his pocket. I must confess that I was glad when you intervened. If I may say so,' – Mr Piggin sounded mildly reproachful – 'I thought you left it rather late.'

'I'm sorry, Piggy. It was just that, at the last moment, I couldn't believe it was really going to happen. What do we do now?'

'We alight at the next station and take the train back to London. I've no doubt that our man will be doing the same. He would only have to cross the footbridge and keep out of sight until the train arrived. There's an up train reaches Kelvedon at seven-fifteen. We should be in plenty of time to transfer to it. On this occasion, we'll spread our net a little wider. You get into the front carriage. I'll travel in the rear one. We'll get off when he does, but we can't plan further ahead until we see what he does. Fortunately, I have used this line so frequently that I know most of the station staffs well.'

Hugo's confidence in Mr Piggin was now so complete that it was no surprise to him when he saw their man come out of the little hutchlike waiting-room at Witham and climb on to the train. It would have surprised him if he hadn't.

It was a stopping train. And as station succeeded station without their man making a move, Hugo began to worry. Might he be going all the way back to Liverpool Street? Which could be awkward. But no. It was at Manor Park, three stations from the terminus, that they saw him emerge and watched him disappear into the ticket office. Mr Piggin seemed to be in no hurry to follow. He was deep in conversation with the ticket collector. As Hugo came up, he heard, 'That man who went out just now? That's Mr Appleyard. Lives along South Park Road. If you hurried you could catch him.'

Mr Piggin thanked him and as soon as they were clear of the station, said, 'They sell a very nice line of beer at the Green Man. I think this calls for a drink, don't you?'

'Seconded and carried unanimously,' said Hugo fervently.

It was when they were seated, with pint glasses in front of them, that Hugo started to see rocks ahead. He said, 'You've done a marvellous job, Piggy. An absolutely incredible job, and we now *know* who the killer is. But tell me this. How are we going to prove it? Think what a meal you'll be for defending counsel. "*How* did you identify the accused, Mr Piggin? By mathematics? Really, sir, if the matter was not so serious, I'd imagine you were joking—".'

Mr Piggin took a long pull at his beer, replaced the half-empty glass on the table, and said, 'It had not been my intention to trouble our overworked police force, or our notoriously inefficient prosecution service with this matter.'

'Then what—?'

'You have some means, I imagine, of getting in touch with your mafia acquaintances. I think, don't you, that once they understood that it was Mr Appleyard who killed their protégé, they would take appropriate steps.'

A week later the householder at 27 South Park Road telephoned the police to say that a dangerous escape of gas seemed to be taking place at No. 25 and no one seemed to he doing anything about it.

This brought Chief Inspector Mayburgh on to the scene. Normally he would not have become involved in such a routine matter, but he had received a telephone call earlier that morning from a man who had refused to give his name but had said, 'If you want the Knifeman, go to Twenty-five South Park Road. Don't forget to look in the desk.'

The coincidence of the address had stirred him into action. He brought Inspector Barley with him.

They found that the fire brigade, equipped with respirators, had entered the house, turned off the gas, which was pouring into the kitchen, and succeeded in clearing the atmosphere. They had not disturbed the body of the householder, a Mr Appleyard, which had been found on the floor beside the kitchen table, on which two pillows and a rug had been placed.

'Made himself comfortable, didn't he?' said Mayburgh.

'It's often the way they go,' said the police surgeon. 'When he finally lost consciousness he must have rolled off the table on to the floor. That would account, no doubt, for the bruising on the back of his head.'

When Mayburgh examined the desk, he was delighted to find in one of the drawers a surgical knife, a homemade life-preserver, and Mr Appleyard's private diary, which contained a full account of the difficulties and final collapse of the company selling medical equipment which he had founded when he left his post as assistant in the surgical wing at St Christopher's Hospital.

Chief Inspector Mayburgh was not a man who threw compliments around, but he felt that something special was called for on this occasion.

He said to Inspector Barley, 'I regard this as a triumph for the theory of psychological fingerprinting. Clearly what happened was that this man heard of our enquiries, felt the net closing round him, and took this way out. You must write it up for the *Police Gazette.*' The inspector smiled modestly and said that he would see what he could do.

Mt Piggin said nothing, He was too busy. Fearne & Bracknell had been instructed by one of their City clients in a particularly unpleasant case of blackmail.

2
Tiger Country

Clive Brocklehurst and his wife no longer shared a bed, but they shared everything else in their lives and had done so for more than thirty happy years. It was only after Laura's second, and more serious, attack of asthma that Clive had retreated to the dressing-room.

On that morning in early October Laura had been lying awake for some minutes when she heard her husband getting out of bed and leaving the dressing-room by the far door. Her sleepy mind registered two things. First, that it was unusually early for him to be stirring. Being the senior partner in the firm of Brocklehurst and Grampound, Accountants of London Wall, he normally got up for a leisurely breakfast at eight o'clock and was rarely out of the house before nine.

The second thought was that he had left his room so quickly that he could not have had time to do more than throw on his clothes. Usually he was a careful and meticulous dresser. Then she heard the front door of the house opening and shutting softly. Some minutes passed. Where could he be going? She remembered that on one occasion, when she had forgotten to replenish her asthma medicine, he had slipped out to the chemist in the village, who lived over his shop, and had extracted a new bottle from him. That was the sort of thing he did for her.

Then she heard the car starting up.

After listening for a few minutes she got out of bed, put on dressing-gown and slippers, went downstairs and out into the garden.

The car seemed to have been running for a long time. As she approached she could hear the engine thudding away. When she tried to open the garage door she found that it was not only shut, but seemed to have been bolted on the inside. She wasted a few minutes clawing at it. Then turned, ran back to the house and grabbed the telephone.

The local policeman – there was only one in the village – had been out most of the night before watching for poachers, but the panic in her voice ultimately stirred him into action.

'Come quickly, please.'

'Sounds as if the door's jammed. If it is, I'll have to bring tools to break it down.'

'Quick, quick.'

'Quick as I can, ma'am.'

When he had succeeded, twenty agonizing minutes later, in getting the door down, he was surprised that the garage was not full of exhaust fumes. Until he saw the piece of rubber hose, one end wired to the exhaust pipe, the other end tucked into the rear window of the car.

Francis Fearne said to his partner, Bob Bracknell, 'Of all the people in the world I should not have expected to take their own lives, I'd have put Clive Brocklehurst near the top of the list.'

'You knew him pretty well, didn't you?'

'Very well indeed. We qualified in the same year. Clive as an accountant, I as a solicitor. We were members of the same club and partnered each other in a lot of inexpert bridge. And we shared a rough – a very rough – shoot in Sussex.' He looked regretfully out of the window. It was a perfect day. With the weather like that, how often had they played truant from their offices and enjoyed themselves almost as much as the rabbits, pigeons, and pheasants whose numbers they never seriously diminished.

'You're his executor, of course.'

'Yes.'

'Have you seen Laura since it happened?'

'I telephoned her as soon as I heard the news. The doctor answered the phone. He said that she was in no condition to talk. I left it for twenty-four hours, rang again, and found that the telephone had been disconnected.'

'So?'

'So I'm going round to see what's happening. I'll get Tara to drive me. There are a lot of things I need to know. She can take notes. Addresses of relatives. Insurance details. Where he kept his private bank account. And – well—'

'And,' said Bracknell after a long pause.

'And some hint, some sort of clue to explain what can have driven a man who was healthy, as far as I knew – and comfortably off financially – I'm sure of that – to do what he did.'

'Yes,' said Bracknell. 'One would like to know that.'

When Fearne reached the Brocklehurst house he found the doctor on guard downstairs. His opening words were, 'It's a bad case. As bad as any I've had to deal with. I felt it my duty to get a second opinion. Since the trouble seemed to be more mental, than physical, I needed a neurologist or a psychiatrist. Fortunately I knew the ideal man and he happened to be available. He's with Mrs Brocklehurst now.'

Fearne's heart sank. Like all lawyers, he distrusted psychiatrists. He had heard too many of them contradict each other in the witness box.

'Which member of the tribe is this?'

'Dr Sampson. George Sampson. I believe he's generally considered—'

'No need to tell me about him,' said Fearne. The relief in his voice was apparent. 'You couldn't have anyone better.'

George Earle Sampson was a qualified doctor and a psychiatrist. He rarely appeared in court and, when he did, spoke the truth as he saw it in simple language. Fearne had briefed him more than once, was confident of his ability and his integrity. Later that morning he listened carefully to what Dr Sampson had to tell him.

'I gather,' he said, 'that Mrs Brocklehurst was not a very strong character, but there is no question that she was totally devoted to her husband. He was her prop. Without him she is, for the time being, helpless and adrift. It is not an uncommon case, but there are one or two things in it which are not usual: For instance, she seems frightened of authority. Particularly of male authority. Anybody who might seem to usurp the place of the husband she has lost. If she was questioned by a policeman or by a senior lawyer, even a good one like you—'

'Thank you,' said Fearne.

'—she would retreat at once into herself. If you persisted, she would probably break down entirely.'

'You mean she would become insane?'

'Temporarily. Yes.'

Fearne thought about it, unhappily. He said, 'Someone will have to talk to her sooner or later. I can get most of the information I need immediately from his secretary. But there are other things – more important things – that I can only get from her.'

'Then let me make a suggestion. Is that attractive young lady I saw in your car a member of your staff?'

'She is a member of my staff. She's a qualified solicitor. She is also my daughter. Why?'

'I have a feeling that Mrs Brocklehurst might talk to another woman – ultimately. Suppose that your daughter started with a few unimportant routine matters and then moved on, slowly, to a more personal approach. Is she capable of that sort of manoeuvre?'

'When she was younger,' said Fearne, 'she had no difficulty in twisting *me* round her little finger.'

'Good. Let's try it, anyway.'

'You said there were other things you noticed.'

'Yes,' said Dr Sampson. He seemed, for a moment, unwilling to go on. 'I'll tell you something, if I have your undertaking to pass it on to no one else. I have no clear proof of its truth, and if I'm wrong about it, it might have a terrible boomerang effect. But since it may help you, you shall have it. Somewhere, in her poor old muddled mind, there is a feeling of *guilt*. She thinks she was, or may have been, responsible for what's happened. Which means – if your Latin is up to it – *festina lente*.'

'Step at a time,' agreed Fearne. 'The secretary first.'

Mr Brocklehurst's secretary, Miss Sharpe, was a sensible middle-aged woman who had been with him for ten years and knew almost as much about his business as he did himself. She was able to supply, without difficulty, the details that Fearne wanted. It was only when he touched on the second part of his enquiry that her replies became hesitant.

She said, 'It's true. And I'd noticed it. He had been worried.'

'For how long?'

'I should say, perhaps, for two months. More or less.'

'Did it start with anything in particular? A letter. Something like that.'

'Most of his mail came to the office and I saw it before he did.'

'Might it have been a letter he got at home?'

Miss Sharpe thought about this. Then she said, 'I don't think it was a letter at all. I think it started with a telephone call. A man rang up, said it was personal, and I put it through to Mr Brocklehurst. A few minutes later he came into my room – he hadn't cut the caller off – and sent me out to get some cigarettes. Quite unnecessarily. He had a boxful on his desk. Then he must have gone back to continue taking the call.'

'An unusual precaution.'

'Unheard of,' said Miss Sharpe. 'I was completely in his confidence. Or had been until then.'

'And it was after this that he started worrying.'

'Yes. And there were more calls. Carefully timed, on each occasion, to take place when I was out at lunch. I asked the girl on the exchange to make a note of the caller's name—'

'Let me guess. It was Mr Smith.'

'Robinson, actually. You think someone was blackmailing him?'

'I certainly had the possibility in mind.'

'Then I can assure you of one thing. If it was blackmail, the blackmailer wasn't paid.'

'How can you be sure of that?'

'Mr Brocklehurst had only one personal bank account. As his executor, you'll need the account sheets, and I've got them out for you. They go back for six years. You can see from them that he was as open about money matters as about everything else in his life. Until—'

'Until he got that phone call.'

'Yes. But even after that, you'll find no sign of large or unusual transactions.'

'Thank you,' said Fearne. 'I'll take those sheets with me, if I may. One other thing. I'd like to look through his files.'

'All of them?'

'I don't mean client files. Personal ones.'

'I'm glad you didn't mean client files,' said Miss Sharpe, with the ghost of a smile creasing her severe mouth. 'Because we've three filing cabinets full of them. There are quite a few personal files, too.' She was opening a fourth cabinet. 'How far back would you like to go?'

'Three or four years will be enough to start with. If I want more, I'll let you know.'

To his partner, Bob Bracknell, Fearne said next morning, 'Clive might, of course, have had a second bank account somewhere, but I'm damned if I can see where it would have been funded from. His only income was his share of partnership profits, and as you can see, they were credited to this account every quarter. And it's quite clear that he has drawn no large sums out in the last four years.'

'But it's obvious these phone calls were threats of some sort. If blackmail wasn't behind them, what was?'

'I can think of one plausible motive. Hatred. Someone hated Clive so much that they didn't want money. They didn't want Clive to buy himself out of whatever mess he'd got into. They were going to watch him wriggle and enjoy every moment of it.'

Bob thought about this. He respected his senior partner's instinct, honed in a hundred skirmishes in the jungle of the law. He said, 'If you're right, it's going to be devilish difficult to locate this chap. And even more difficult to deal with him when you find him.'

'I'll deal with him. Be sure of that,' said Fearne. Bob thought he had never seen him looking so savage. 'However, I think the time has come to hand over to the second eleven.'

He referred, in this disparaging way, to his daughter, Tara, and Bob's son, Hugo, who, with their managing clerk, old Horace Piggin, made up the operative side of the firm.

To Tara he said, 'I've got one or two papers that need Mrs Brocklehurst's signature. That should enable you to get alongside her. And once you get there, stay there.'

Tara accepted this vague and irregular commitment without surprise or dissent.

To Hugo, he said, 'I want you to read through these personal files.'

'All of them?'

'You can start with the last three years. And check them against the bank statements. There'll be occasions when he bought someone a present and was thanked for it. Quite clear?'

'It's clear what you want me to do. But it would help if you'd tell me what we're looking for.'

'Hatred,' said Fearne.

A fortnight later Hugo turned over the last page of the third large file. He had to do most of his reading in the evening, after a fairly demanding day's work. The figure emerging from the files was an agreeable one. Hating nobody and hated by nobody. A man at peace with himself and his wife. There was a regular payment into her account, for household expenses. The only other sizeable payments were his club fees and his half share in the shoot. It was clear that he was earning more than he spent and there were regular transfers to his deposit account. The deposit bank sheets also were available. They showed only payments in. No with-drawals.

When he reported his lack of success, Fearne said, 'Go back three years more. There's something buried there. I can smell it.'

Tara was unsympathetic. She said, 'It's all right for you. You can do your work in the office or at home. You don't have to sit for hours holding an old lady's hand and wondering if she'll be alive when you go back next.'

'Alive? What makes you think—'

'I found that she'd got hold of two bottles of aspirin and a full bottle of sleeping pills and hidden them in the cupboard beside her bed. I saw them when she was out of the room for a moment. And something else with them. Her husband used an old fash-ioned cut-throat razor. That was there, too.'

'Good God!' said Hugo. 'Shouldn't you tell someone?'

'No. I don't think she'll kill herself. Not now. The shock's wear-ing off and she's getting more rational. But whatever you do, don't tell Dad. He'd have a fit. Promise me.'

Hugo promised. But very unwillingly.

During those weeks they both – Tara in particular – found Mr Piggin a great help in keeping an eye on their matters: dealing with occasional crises and keeping the wheels turning. He said to Hugo, 'Keep it up. It doesn't matter how long it takes – give the old man the lead he wants and he'll sniff out the truth.' He added, 'If I'd done something to upset him and I knew he was after my blood, do you know what I'd do? I'd emigrate.'

October died in glory and turned into a chilly November. Tara had established a friendly relationship with Mrs Brocklehurst's housekeeper, Mrs Vicarage, who attended to Laura's personal needs, while Tara herself dealt with business matters. This was largely a question of paying the household bills. There were not a great number of them, but she had come to the end of the current cheque book and suggested writing to the bank for a new one.

Laura said, 'Now you mention it, I remember on the morning – on the morning it happened – there was a letter from the bank. It was probably a new cheque book. I put it in Clive's desk.'

Tara went downstairs to Clive's study. She had never been in the room before. It was cold and dusty and seemed to be mourning for its previous occupant. She found the envelope from the bank in one of the pigeonholes in the desk. There was a new cheque book in it. Something else too, which came out with it. Bank passbook sheets for the last quarter. She looked at them for a moment, then picked up a piece of paper and started to scribble. Then she poked the sheets back into the envelope behind the cheque book and went upstairs, on legs that felt oddly weak.

'Do you think she knew you'd seen these bank-account sheets?' said her father.

'I don't think so. She got the cheque book out without looking at them. If I thought she had seen them – well, I can only tell you that I'd left the door ajar.'

'Why? Do you think she'd be violent? Her preparations, surely, were for suicide, not murder.'

'Then Hugo told you? He'd promised not to—'

'Of course he told me. As soon as he thought about it, he realized he had got to. And don't talk about promises. We're not playing nursery games. Now, about those statements. You got it all down accurately, I hope.'

'I think so,' said Tara faintly. She'd never seen her father in that mood before and it frightened her.

'On September first she drew a cheque for five thousand pounds in favour of stockbrokers Welsby and Grintham. There wasn't a lot of money in the account, so she must have deposited the share certificate, or contract note, or whatever, with the bank as security for a temporary loan. Then on September fifteenth, she paid in six thousand, two hundred and fifty pounds, discharged the loan, and was credited with the profit – one thousand, two hundred and fifty?'

'Can you do something like that?'

'Easily. If you have inside information. Now, let's think. You'd better keep clear of the Brocklehurst house for a bit. If we need anything, we'll send in Mr Piggin. He has a very calming effect on hysterical women.' Noting the look on his daughter's face, he added, 'Cheer up. I doubt if anyone could have done better than you did. Or as well.'

At eleven o'clock that same night Hugo closed the sixth personal file, which he had just finished, rubbed his eyes, and opened them again. Yes. Surely. There *had* been something. He had been so sleepy that, at first reading, he had missed it.

It was the carbon copy of a letter from Clive to Rupert Maxwell, the senior partner of the internationally known firm of City solicitors, Mayne, Maxwell, and Freemantle. They were evidently old friends.

'Dear Rupert, If you want my advice, as an accountant, I'd say no to Whillins. You say that he's a clever chap. All right, I accept your word for that. What makes me doubt whether he's really fitted to be finance manager to a firm of your standing

*is that he appears to be totally unqualified. He calls himself
an accountant. Anyone can so describe himself. But I'd prefer
to see the letters FCA or FCCA or even FCMA after a man's
name before I put him into such an important post.*

When he saw the letter next morning, Fearne said, 'Well played
the second eleven.' He told Bob what Tara had discovered.
'Plenty of grounds there for Whillins hating Clive. *If* he saw the
letter. Which he could only have done if he was working, in some
capacity, at Mayne, Maxwell, and Freemantle at the time. It's an
enormous outfit, with a rapid turnover of junior staff, so it's quite
possible that he was. We'll get Mr Piggin moving on that side of
it. Meanwhile, it's about time I had a word with Clive's partner.'

Sam Grampound said, 'You can count on me, of course. Any help
I can give you, you've only to ask. I'm still shaken when I think of
what Clive was driven to. Ghastly. Do you know, a few days
before it happened, we gave him a little party to celebrate the
fortieth anniversary of him joining the firm. And he seemed so
happy and relaxed.'

'He was a very self-controlled man,' said Fearne. 'I doubt if
anyone, even his wife, had any idea of what was happening. What
I want you to do now is to let me have a list of all the companies
your firm acts for, leaving out small private companies.'

'Even without them it will be quite a long list. But you shall
have it.'

'Right. Then I want you to mark on it any companies that have
had capital dealings in the last six months. I mean takeovers, or
being taken over. Increases or reductions of capital. Rights issues.
Bonus issues. Anything like that.'

'There won't be many of them.'

'Good,' said Fearne. He thought for a moment and then said,
'At that party you gave for Clive, were there any presents?'

Grampound said, with some surprise, 'Only two. The firm gave him a set of golf clubs, and his wife gave him a camera. A very fine modern one. He was a keen photographer and was mighty pleased with it.'

'It would have cost a lot of money?'

'A fair amount, yes.'

'As much as one thousand, two hundred and fifty pounds?'

'Could be. But, forgive me, I hardly see how this information is going to help you.'

'It fills out the picture,' said Fearne. He added, 'The fact is that I'm tracking a jackal, in very thick country. I can see his paw marks and I'm beginning to hope that with the help I am getting—' He smiled gratefully at Grampound. 'I may soon sight him. When I do, I'll skin him and nail his hide up on the wall.'

After which the pace slackened for some weeks, while Mr Piggin pursued his molelike activities.

He knew many of the managing clerks and senior office staffs in the City offices. He stood a great many drinks and, in important cases, a few lunches. He knew that it was no use being impatient. If he listened carefully and waited long enough, the great sounding board of the East Central district would transmit to him the message he wanted. It reached him in the bar of the Falstaff, when he was talking to a retired stockbroker's clerk.

He reported to Fearne. 'Whillins's your man. Not a shadow of doubt about it. Four years ago he had a temporary job with Mayne, Maxwell. He was being considered for a permanent job, but for some reason he didn't get it. When it was clear that he wasn't going to – that letter you showed me must have tipped the balance – he seems to have behaved like the unjust steward in the Bible. Feathered the nest he planned to occupy. He gave a number of useful tips to a not very large well-known firm of stockbrokers, Welsby and Grintham. When Rupert Maxwell heard about it and kicked him straight out, he got a job with them and has been there ever since. Not a patch on the job he lost, but better than nothing, I suppose.'

'So that's the truth of it,' said Fearne. 'He must have seen that letter when he was at Maxwell's – some secretarial indiscretion – and realized who had ditched him. So what does he do? Nothing, for a bit. Then he scrapes acquaintance with Laura Brocklehurst. She's a sociable type. Got a certain way into her confidence. Bided his time. The chance he'd been waiting for came when she wanted to give her husband an extra-special present. There had long been an idea in the City that Kadmack and Afro-Engines might amalgamate. He must have had a tip it was coming off. So he told her she could make a few hundred pounds – maybe a thousand – by buying and selling Kadmack shares.'

'The engineering firm?' said Bracknell.

'That's the one. Brocklehurst and Grampound acted for them. They were on the list Sam gave me. They were in the middle of the amalgamation with Afro-Engines. When it came off, both lots of shares were going to go up. I needn't say that Clive, who was organizing the amalgamation, wouldn't have touched the shares himself. And if he'd known that Laura was going to, he'd have warned her off. But that was where Whillins was so clever. Clive wasn't to be told. The whole thing was to be a surprise. And I guess he reckoned that the transaction was too small for the Stock Exchange Surveillance Department to worry about it.'

'Large or small,' said Bracknell, 'if it had come out, it would have been assumed that Clive had tipped his wife off and they'd both have been in dead trouble, every way round. Insider dealing is a social as well as a legal crime nowadays.'

Fearne said, 'It was the trouble coming to Laura that was in his mind when he switched on the car that morning. He knew that once he was out of the way, Whillins wouldn't move again.'

'Why should he? He'd done what he set out to do, the nasty little sod. So now that we know, what do *we* do?'

'We tell the whole story. To people we can trust.'

'Trust not to pass it on, you mean.'

'On the contrary, people we can trust to pass it on.'

'We'll have to ask them to be a bit discreet about where they got it from.'

'Yes. But not too discreet,' said Fearne.

And so, in the exclusive luncheon clubs, in the not-so-exclusive drinking clubs, and in the entirely inexclusive sandwich bars, the story spread. Most people knew about Clive Brocklehurst's death. Many of them had liked and respected him. When they heard the true story – on the unimpeachable authority of Francis Fearne – their indignation and their dislike for the perpetrator grew with each telling.

The City is a close community; in many ways as close and as prejudiced as a boarding-school. Physical retaliation was out of the question, but there were other, more subtle and equally hurtful ways of expressing their feelings.

The luncheon club to which Whillins belonged – it had taken him five years to procure his membership – had a simple method of preserving its tone and standing. Under the club rules, a fresh application for membership had to be made every year. Normally it was accepted as a matter of course. In Whillins's case it was refused. 'Very sorry. Pressure of new members,' said the secretary.

Whillins, his indignation mixed with a less comfortable feeling, spoke to Mr Grintham, the partner for whom he did most of his work.

'It's a scandal,' he said. 'Pressure of new members. Why should new members be preferred to me?'

Mr Grintham, looking at him over the top of his rimless glasses, said, 'Do you really not know why they ousted you?'

'I know that Fearne's been spreading some lying story about me. I didn't know that anyone believed it.'

'They not only believe it,' said Mr Grintham coldly, 'they're beginning to react to it. I suppose you noticed that we lost two of our best clients recently. Again, no reason given. Companies are free to choose what brokers act for them. But off the record and from remarks that have been made to me, I've no doubt at all. It's a sign of displeasure *because you work for us*. Also because it was through this firm that the purchase and sale were made, which is true, of course. We can't deny the fact.'

'It's quite true,' said Whillins. 'I handled it myself. Mrs Brocklehurst is an old acquaintance of mine. She asked me to do it. Explained that she wanted to raise a little cash for a present to her husband. I saw no reason to refuse.'

'Why did she choose Kadmack?'

'She said she had a feeling they were going up. A woman's instinct. You know what they're like.'

'Then the whole idea was hers, not yours?'

'Yes.'

'You're absolutely sure about that?'

'Absolutely. Why?'

'Because, as a measure of protection for the firm – and for you, of course – I have already spoken to George Capel. You know who I mean?'

'The QC.'

'Right. A specialist in defamation. I told him the whole story. And I asked him, if we brought an action for slander against Fearne, would we have a case that would stand up, and would he act for us. You know how counsel shy away from slander cases. In the end he said he thought we would have a convincing case and that he would act for us, subject to two points. The first was that there appeared to be no reason why you should have trapped Mrs Brocklehurst in the way Fearne is suggesting. What was the suggested *motive* for the steps you took? Had you any reason to dislike Brocklehurst?'

'None at all. I've never had any dealings with him, professional or social. Apart from the fact that he was Laura Brocklehurst's husband, I hardly knew of his existence!'

'Good. That should help a jury to make up its mind. Counsel's second point was a very simple one. Fearne is saying that you suggested the sale and purchase to Mrs Brocklehurst. You say that the suggestion came from her. Two different stories. Which of them is true?'

Before Whillins could answer, Mr Grintham leaned forward and said, 'If it was put to Mrs Brocklehurst, would she support you?'

Whillins said, picking his words carefully, 'She's not in a very good state of health at the moment. In fact, her mind's said to be going. If it was put to her, her first reaction might be to say that she'd forgotten all about it.'

'But if she was pressed – reminded of the precise circumstances in which the conversation took place—'

'Yes. I think she'd admit that the suggestion came from her.'

'Then ask her!'

'Personally?'

'Why not? You're an old friend. Even if she's bedridden, surely you'd be allowed in to see her!'

'I imagine so. Mrs Vicarage knows me. But if Laura says – what we want her to say – shouldn't I have a witness with me?'

'She'd be more likely to speak freely if you were on your own. But there's no reason you shouldn't take a tape recorder with you.'

When Albert Whillins was ushered into her bedroom by Mrs Vicarage and the door had closed behind her, Laura experienced such a feeling of relief and joy that it almost overwhelmed her. It was something she had hoped for and prayed for without really expecting it to happen.

Her hand slid down into the narrow space between the far side of her bed and the wall and her fingers caressed the stock of Clive's shotgun.

She drew it up quite slowly.

When Whillins saw it, his first instinct was to try to grab it. Then he changed his mind and made for the door. As he was trying to open it, Laura, resting the gun on the rail at the foot of her bed, discharged both barrels into the small of his back.

'Did you guess he'd come to see her?' said Bracknell. 'And did you know she'd got hold of Clive's gun?'

'No to both questions,' said Fearne. 'I'm not a prophet or a mind reader. One thing I do know: we shall have to get busy now organizing her defence.'

'She'll get a lot of sympathy from the jury,' said Bracknell.

3

The Lord of the Book

Robert Bracknell said to Hugo, who was his son and a junior partner in the firm of Fearne & Bracknell, Solicitors, 'I wonder if you know a man called Rupert Hay.'

'Rupert,' said Hugo enthusiastically, 'I'll say I know Rupert. The best lock forward we ever had in the Southwark team. Played regularly for Middlesex—'

'But, surely—'

'Shoulders like a blacksmith.'

'Surely he's a bit old to be playing Rugby football.'

'Well, it's mostly coaching these days. But he still turns out for the "A" team when they're short. And mighty glad they are to have him. Pushes in the scrum like a bulldozer, but give him the ball and he goes for the line like a wing threequarter.'

'Could we confine ourselves, for the moment, to facts? What sort of age is he?'

'Well, he must be all of forty, I suppose. His son's just left school. He plays for us, too. A very promising fly-half—'

'Hasn't he got a daughter as well?'

'I believe he has,' said Hugo, with a massive indifference that immediately aroused his father's suspicions.

'What does he do?'

'Oh, his job – something to do with building.'

'You mean that when he isn't chasing an egg-shaped ball up

and down a muddy field, he's carrying hods of bricks up a ladder.'

'No, no. He's not a labourer. I didn't mean that. He's got his own building firm. Not a large one, but very sound. If you want a repair job done—'

'My interest in Rupert Hay is purely professional. He intends, if I agree, to become a client of this firm.'

'Couldn't have a better one.'

'We'll see about that. General Crispin certainly gave him a good chit. The only thing was that when Hay spoke to me on the telephone he seemed a little confused about what he did want. All I could gather was that it was something about his daughter. Do I gather that you've never met her?'

'She came to our last rugger club dance.'

His father observed a slight but treacherous colour in his son's smooth cheek. He said, 'And did you dance with her?'

'When I could get near her. The chaps were round her like flies round a jam pot.'

'Then I gather she's attractive.'

'You could say that. Yes.'

'Have you seen her lately?'

'Now that you mention it, I haven't. No. Someone told me she'd gone abroad, to be finished.'

'Not so. I gathered from her father that she's been kidnapped.'

Hugo stared at him and then said, 'But surely, Dad, the police—'

'The police can do nothing. This is a strictly legal kidnapping. Now, don't ask me a lot of questions that I can't answer. He's coming to see me this afternoon. I'll tell you all about it this evening.'

When Rupert Hay arrived at the Fearne & Bracknell office, which is not easy to find, being tucked away behind the Tower of London, he stopped in the outer office to have a word with Mr Piggin, their managing clerk. They seemed to know each other, but then Mr Piggin knew almost everybody in the curious area, half City and half East End, that lies between Southwark Cathedral and Aldgate Pump. It occurred to Mr Bracknell that if he had wanted background information it would have been more sensible to have consulted Mr Piggin rather than his own son.

His new client came into his office cautiously, as though he were negotiating a minefield. Clearly not a man who had much to do with solicitors. He refused a cigarette, murmuring something about training, and seated himself on the edge of the client chair. Mr Bracknell, deciding that the normal preliminaries would be a waste of time, simply said, 'Tell me about it.'

'Well, it started with window cleaners.'

In the pause that followed, Mr Bracknell tried to adjust himself to this unexpected opening.

'They came – there were two of them – my wife and I were away for the day and Antonia was alone in the house. I think they must have watched us drive off. They knocked at the door and told my daughter that we had ordered them, so, of course, she let them in.' Feeling that some further explanation was needed, he said, 'They weren't a pair of scruffs. They were wearing camou-flage jackets and their hair was cut short, but they were quite personable and well spoken. Two of them, they explained. One to clean the insides, the other the outsides. It took them two hours and they made a good job of it. When they had finished Antonia offered them a cup of tea. "If it's not too much trouble", they said. Then they got talking. We heard all about this when we got back. It seemed that window cleaning was only a part-time job. They took money for it – quite a large amount, I thought – but it didn't go to them. It was all paid into a fund, run by a man who called himself the Lord of the Book. They were just his – I don't know the right word—'

'Acolytes?'

'Yes. That would be the word. A good deal of religion came into it, that much I did gather.'

Mr Bracknell now had a fair idea of where they were going, but he refrained from interrupting. Experience had taught him that when a client had something he wanted to get off his chest, the sooner he was allowed to do so the better.

'There's this book, you see. It's more than two thousand years old. It had been sealed up in a box and buried in the Gobi Desert. An explorer found it and brought it back to England. He couldn't read it, because it was in Latin – not straightforward Latin, more a sort of code. This man – the one the explorer showed the book to – his name's Hegler, Paul Hegler. He's a great scholar. He had copies made and worked on them for more than a year. He found that the book was full of wonderful truths which could be given a modern interpretation. Antonia told me one of them. I wrote it down.'

He opened the briefcase he had brought with him and after a search produced a rather scruffy piece of paper and read out: ' "Benign spiritual health is being constantly showered down on us from the ether. Like electricity, it can be captured and stored in batteries for our use." She thought that was remarkable. They gave her a book which had a lot of other pieces in it.'

'Gave it?'

'Well, no. She had to pay for it. It cost her ten pounds. When I heard this I began to think that the whole thing was a bit of a swindle. About a week later, when we were out, the same men came round again. This time Antonia didn't tell us what they said, or anything about it. One of our neighbours noticed them and told us. Then, for a month or more, nothing happened. There may have been letters, or telephone calls. She may have gone out to meet the men. We don't spy on our daughter. We just hoped the whole thing, whatever it was, would blow over. Then we found this on the dining-room table.'

This time it was a sheet of expensive writing paper that appeared out of his briefcase. On it, in a clear schoolgirl hand, was written: *I have decided to become a Maiden of the Book. There is no need to look for me. I am guite happy.*

There was a long pause while Mr Bracknell looked first at the paper and then at Mr Hay. He said, 'And so—'

'We didn't know what to do. Antonia is over sixteen and free to live her own life.'

'And was that all?'

'No. A short time after that we got another note. Here it is.'

This one was in block capitals. It said: I NEED SOME THINGS. PLEASE SEND £500 OF MY MONEY TO THIS ADDRESS.

'Well, that seemed quite possible. She may have needed any amount of things. When she left she had nothing with her but the clothes she stood up in. She had quite a large balance with a savings account we'd opened for her. Withdrawals had to be signed by her and me. There was a withdrawal form with the paper, which she'd signed. So I added my signature, withdrew the money, and took it round to the address she'd given us. It turned out to be a tobacconist's. I didn't much like the look of the man behind the counter, but he gave me a receipt.'

This was added to the other papers on the table.

'And then—' said Mr Bracknell gently.

'Next time it was two thousand pounds. There was just enough in the account to meet it.'

'And you sent it?'

'No. I decided I must get some advice. Your son had often mentioned your name. I was certain you'd be able to tell me what I ought to do.'

'First things first,' said Mr Bracknell. 'This sort of thing is rather outside our ordinary run of business. I shall have to consult my partners.'

'Hugo is one of your partners, isn't he? I'm sure he'd want you to help me.'

There was an undercurrent of desperation in his voice.

Mr Bracknell hardened his heart. He said, 'Hugo's only one of my partners. There are two others. If they agree, I'll accept you as a client. But I feel bound to tell you that I can't, at the moment, see how we can help you.'

That evening the partnership was in formal session. It was a tightly knit group.

Francis Fearne and Robert Bracknell had been in practice together for more than twenty years. Recently they had been joined by Bracknell's son Hugo – after he had been allowed to waste a couple of years skirmishing round Europe – and Fearne's daughter, Tara, who had taken a Law degree at London University, with First Class honours.

Fearne was in the chair.

He said, 'Viewing him as a person, I should have no objection to acting for Rupert Hay. I acted for his father when he formed the company which took over his building business. He is an honourable man, who would and could pay any charges he incurred.'

His audience nodded their appreciation of this important point.

'On the other hand, I doubt whether we are really equipped to handle this particular matter. It would be considerably outside the normal run of our business. I know this organization – if that is the right word for it. It functions from that large double-fronted building at the end of North Street. They purchased it six months ago, from the council. That they were able to do so argues that they are not short of money.'

'I've seen the place,' said Bracknell. 'They've turned it into a regular fortress. A high wooden fence round it, with lots of barbed wire on top and bars on all the windows.'

'It isn't a fortress,' said Hugo. 'It's a prison.'

'That's just an assumption,' said Tara. 'The only message we've seen from the girl says she is happy.'

'That was early days. She may, by now, be longing to get out.'

'On the other hand,' said Bracknell, 'she may already have been systematically brainwashed. If you were allowed to speak to her she might simply say, "I'm quite happy. Leave me alone".'

'I've read about this brainwashing,' said Tara. 'How do they do it?'

'Different methods with different subjects. With a young and suggestible girl it may just be talk. Talk and argument. With a tougher subject, shortage of food and deprivation of sleep can be combined with the attachment of a headset through which a stream of propaganda can be poured into the victim's ear, night and day.'

'You used the right word when you said victim,' said Hugo, who was trying to control his feelings. 'Not disciple, or adherent, or follower, but victim. Someone to be tortured into submission. Surely, surely, there's only one choice here.' He swivelled his gaze between his father and Mr Fearne. 'We must do something before it's too late. It's our plain duty—'

'Our duty,' said Fearne, drily, but not unkindly, 'is to practice the law. Not to enforce it. Enforcement is the role of the police.'

'Then we must alert the police to what is going on. If they knew that a girl was being refused access to her parents, squeezed out of her life's savings – surely they would take action. Drastic action, if necessary.'

'Storm the place, you mean,' said Bracknell. 'If any such suggestion was made, I fancy they'd remember the Branch Davidians. They wouldn't want to end up with a mass suicide on their hands.'

'You're missing the point,' said Fearne. 'No action of any sort could be taken by the police unless we can show that a crime has been committed. Our information, so far, shows nothing of the kind. This young lady, over the age of sixteen, has decided to spend her own money in her own way.'

'Mightn't it be possible,' suggested Tara, 'to have her made a Ward of Court?'

This suggestion produced a thoughtful silence. The silence of professional people who are being asked to take a course of action which they understand in theory, but of which they have no practical experience.

'It's a matter of Chancery practice,' said Fearne doubtfully. 'One has to set up a settlement in favour of the young person concerned. Some outside person has then to approach the Chancery Division and persuade them that the trust is not being administered to the advantage of the child. An application is then made for the child to be constituted a Ward of Court and possibly for The Public Trustee to be appointed.'

'And how long,' said Hugo, 'would all this take?'

'Chancery proceedings are never swift.'

'Jarndyce versus Jarndyce,' said Tara under her breath.

'There are forms and precedents that have to be followed. With help from counsel we might push it through in six months.'

'By which time,' said Hugo, 'the girl will be a mindless cabbage.'

Bracknell said, coldly, 'Tara has suggested a course of action. It might be slow, but if it came off it would be effective. Now let's have your idea.'

Hugo said, 'The last thing these people want is publicity. Any publicity. Anything that brings them out into the open. Surely it *must* be a breach of the law to keep a young girl from her parents and persuade her to hand over her money. If we threatened to bring in the authorities, to stir up the whole matter, they would see that giving up Antonia would be a small price to pay.'

'And how do you suggest,' said Fearne, 'that the threat should be made? In correspondence? A difficult letter to write, with more than a suggestion of blackmail in it.'

Bracknell said, 'It would clearly be more likely to be effective if the threat was made personally. And since it is your idea, Hugo, you are clearly the person to do it.'

Hugo said, 'Oh, certainly, yes.'

He had an uncomfortable feeling that Tara was laughing at him.

Hugo strode up to the large, double-fronted building in North Street with an assumption of confidence that he was far from feeling. He jerked the bellpull beside the tall, iron-latticed gate. It seemed to be working, for he heard a deep tolling inside the house, but it produced no immediate reaction.

After waiting for a full minute he pulled the bell again and was about to do so for a third time when the front door swung open and two young men stepped out, both about Hugo's age, both shaven-headed and fit-looking.

The Sons of the Book.

They walked up to the gate without making any move to open it. The taller of the two, speaking through the bars, said, 'Whatever you're selling, we've got plenty of it, so go away.'

Hugo said, 'I'm not a salesman and I have a message for your leader.'

'If you're not a salesman, who are you and what do you want?'

'I am a lawyer. And I will tell you once more, and only once more what I want. I want a word with whoever is in charge of this' – difficult to find the right word without being offensive – 'this institution.'

The two young men looked at each other. They were both smiling. The one who had spoken before said, 'I hope that you have something to say that is of interest and importance. If not, you are taking a considerable risk by forcing your way in.'

'I shall have to take a chance on that,' said Hugo. He looked behind him as he did so. North Street, being residential, was never crowded. At that moment it was completely empty. He had an illogical feeling that he would have been happier if there had been a few people about.

'On your own head be it.'

The second young man, who had not so far spoken, unfastened the gate – massive old-fashioned lock, Hugo noted, and bolts top and bottom.

The men stalked ahead of him up the path and opened the front door. It was an unremarkable front hall with a well-polished floor and furnished only with a prie-dieu in the corner. A gesture invited him to follow them upstairs.

At the top of the stairs they paused for a moment, as though listening. The house was almost entirely silent, but he thought he could hear a subdued murmur of sound from somewhere above, half recitation, half chanting, but so soft that it might have come from a great way off. Then a loud voice.

'He may enter.'

Hugo guessed that the room from which the voice came over-looked the front path and that he had been under observation from the moment he approached the house.

'Come in, come in,' said the voice impatiently.

'The Lord of the Book grants you audience,' said the young man. 'We hope you are conscious of the privilege that is being accorded to you.' The other young man nodded. Clearly he hoped so too. Hugo opened the door and went in.

It was a very ordinary study, or writing-room, and its occupant, whom Hugo had expected to be a long-haired prophet dressed in a robe of some sort, turned out, disconcertingly, to be a tubby middle-aged man in a well-cut business suit.

He said, 'I would invite you to sit down, but I have found, by bitter experience, that visitors who sit down tend to outstay their welcome. That is why I have had all other chairs removed. However, I am sure you will be able to deliver your message with reasonable speed.'

Hugo, who had rehearsed his opening carefully, said, 'I am a partner in the legal firm of Fearne & Bracknell. One of our clients is a certain Rupert Hay. You may have heard of him. He is very well known in these parts. A member of the borough council and chairman of the watch committee. He and his wife have consulted us on behalf of their daughter.'

'She is, then, a young girl.'

'She is sixteen years old.'

'Old enough to have a mind of her own. Why did she involve her parents?'

'She did not involve them,' said Hugo, conscious that he was being driven off his prepared track. 'They have simply behaved like responsible parents. I understand that they have made two attempts to contact their daughter. One by telephone, one in person. In both cases they were refused access. It is contrary to the laws of this country to deprive a child of the protection of its parents.'

'Being a lawyer, you will no doubt refer me to the precise statute or decided case which lays down this doctrine. A novel one to me.'

'I am speaking of natural justice.'

'Then you are talking nonsense. Natural justice is the last resort of the charlatan. You are wasting my time.'

He must have made some signal because the door opened and the young men came in. There was a third man with them. The Lord of the Book was now standing.

He said, 'This man is an impostor. Remove him.'

Hugo's arms were gripped and twisted behind him. He realized at once that resistance would be futile. Both men were as strong or stronger than he was. The Lord of the Book regarded him impassively for a moment and then said, 'You need not be gentle.'

What followed was undignified.

With the two men holding him and a third close behind him he was hustled down the stairs, out along the path, and into the road. There he was frog-marched along the pavement. A series of jolts, from the knees of his captors, into the base of his spine caused him such acute agony that he was relieved when they reached the main road and deposited him in the gutter. He felt thankful for the small mercy that no one who knew him seemed to have witnessed his undignified arrival.

His gratitude was, in fact, premature.

59

The scene had been observed by someone who not only recognized him but was carrying a camera that he knew how to use and had taken two rapid pictures. This was Bertie Dillon, a young man who had recently joined the staff of the *Southwark Herald*, and it was his first opportunity to capture an important picture. He abandoned his intended assignment (the festivities attending the third wedding of an important local tradesman) and hurried back to the office, bearing his spoils with him.

'You saw *what*?' said the editor.

'These three men had caught someone. I thought I recognized him. A man who works for Fearne & Bracknell. Fair hair and a broken nose.'

'That sounds like Hugo Bracknell. So what were the three men doing to him?'

'They were sort of hustling him along. Frog-marching, we used to call it at school. Then they dropped him in the gutter.'

'And you have photographs of it?'

'Yes, sir.'

'Then you will destroy them.'

'Destroy?'

'Burn them. Tear them up. Dump them in the rubbish bin.'

'Er – yes, sir.'

'The men who carried out this assault. What did they look like? Short hair and combat jackets?'

'Yes, sir.'

'As I thought. Sons of the Book, they call themselves. If they were honest' – the editor's face was by this time bright red – 'they'd be wearing swastikas on their arms. A new sort of *Sturmabteilung*. A private army. I'll have no picture glorifying *them*, in this paper.'

'I'd no idea, sir—'

'Not long ago a number of them pushed their way into the bar of the Black Prince, around closing time. Threw a Hitler salute – which the people in the bar, not unnaturally, objected to – and set about them. Not a fair fight, really. These people are trained in unarmed combat and the men they attacked had been drinking. On this occasion the butcher's bill was a broken arm and a fractured jaw.'

'Surely, sir, the police—'

'Yes. They were charged. Pleaded provocation. Got off with a fine. Which they could well afford to pay. They've got plenty of money, a lot of it extracted from old ladies they call on when they're alone in the house. Sons of the Book! Dregs of the earth. Rancid thugs.'

Having got this off his chest the editor cooled down a degree or two. He said, 'I'm sorry about your photographs, Bertie, but I can promise you this: get a picture showing *them* in a compromising or humiliating position and I'll not only print it, I'll let you write the story.'

Like all takers of pictures, Dillon considered himself an inspired writer of words. He said, 'Thank you, sir. Thank you very much. I'll keep my eyes open.'

When questioned by his father, Hugo simply said that he had had no luck. He had seen the prophet, who had refused to discuss Antonia. He said this with such firmness that his father, who suspected that something untoward had occurred, refrained from comment. Also, he wondered why his son was limping.

To Mr Piggin, as he usually did when in trouble, Hugo told the whole story.

Mr Piggin was a good listener. He said nothing until Hugo had finished, after which he remained silent for two whole minutes. Then he said, 'You *were* asking for trouble, weren't you? Talking about "natural justice". What did he call it?'

'The last resort of the charlatan.'

'Not bad. In fact, I rather agree with him. No, no. If you were going to base your argument on the law, you should have selected a more conclusive branch of it.'

'Which branch do you suggest, Piggy?'

'The most detailed and generally accepted legal code is the one which governs the purchase and sale of houses. Preliminary Enquiries, Local Searches, Requisitions on Title—'

'Conveyancing, you mean. How does that come into it?'

'The house in North Street that these people bought used to belong to the council. I was talking to old Stagg, their legal man, and he told me – I found it hard to believe – that the Lord of the Book, as he calls himself, did not employ a firm of solicitors. His idea seems to have been to save money. One of his young men' – Mr Piggin snorted – 'had taken a law degree and this was thought to equip him to deal with a simple matter like buying a house. If you were looking for a chink in his armour, that's the place to concentrate on. I'll have to make a few enquiries.'

Mr Piggin's enquiries seemed to be extensive and time-consuming and he was little in the office during the next two days. He renewed his dialogue with Mr Stagg and stood him lunch. The early part of the evening he spent at the headquarters of the Southwark Rugby Football Club, accompanied by Rupert Hay, whose presence secured him respect and attention. On the following morning he was observed, once again, at the borough council offices, ascending on this occasion to the top storey which was occupied by the planning department. Here he was among old friends, who were happy to enlighten him on a number of interesting points of procedure and practice.

By the afternoon of the second day he considered himself equipped for the contest.

When the Lord of the Book looked out the window and observed Mr Piggin ambling up the path, he was angry. He said to the young man who stood beside his desk, 'I thought that you and the others had succeeded in discouraging the legal fraternity. If I'd thought we were going to be bothered further, I'd have kept the gate locked.'

'We hoped we had, sir.'

'Then what does this one want?'

Mr Piggin had rung the doorbell.

'Would you like us to deal with him?' The young man's face was alight with pleasurable anticipation.

'Yes. But remember, this is a much older man. You must not damage him severely.'

'What I had in mind was that we might remove his trousers. Then, if he didn't take himself off smartly, we could use our towels.'

'Towels?'

'At school we used to strip the new boys and flick them with towels. It did no real harm, but if the towels had been dipped in water, they seemed to sting.'

'Very well. You and the other two can stand by. But do nothing until I give the word.'

When Mr Piggin was admitted to the study he walked in sedately. He noted the boys who were standing in the passage outside the door, but they seemed to upset him less than the fact that when he got into the study there was no chair for him to sit on. However, after moving a couple of files to one side he was able to seat himself on a corner of the table.

He said, 'It is kind of you to spare me a moment, Mr Hegler.'

'I have long abandoned that name. I am now addressed either as the Lord of the Book or, simply, as Prophet.'

'In law a man can change his name as often as he wishes,' said Mr Piggin agreeably. 'It is a fallacy to suppose that it requires a deed poll. However, that was not what I came to discuss. Allow me to put a few points to you – I think you'll find them interesting – about this spacious building that you purchased recently from the council. I'm told that you did not employ solicitors yourself.'

'I saw no reason to do so. One of my young men assured me that he could deal with any points which might arise.'

'Including planning matters?'

This produced a moment of silence. Then the prophet said, 'We were buying the house for our own occupation and use. We had no immediate intention of building on or adding to it – though our numbers are growing so fast that we may have to do so. In which case we should, of course, seek planning permission.'

'I was not thinking of development,' said Mr Piggin, 'but more of user.'

'User?' The word seemed to hang for a moment in the air.

'North Street is a very select area. The houses in it are high-class buildings. Mostly in single occupation. On the other hand, the functions carried on here seem to me to be well outside what would normally be considered as residential.'

'Perhaps. So what?'

'If you have, in fact, effected a change of user and consent has not been obtained, you could be in trouble. You could be forced to discontinue whatever is now being carried on here. And since you have been operating illegally for several months, there could be a substantial fine.'

Before the prophet could speak, Mr Piggin added, 'I should not wish to make too much of this. I have spoken, off the record, to certain members of the planning department. Their view is clear. Houses, they realize, are used for a number of purposes which are not strictly residential. They cannot inspect every house in the borough. Provided there is no complaint, from neighbours or members of the public, they are prepared to accept the position. But once a complaint is lodged, they are forced to examine the matter.'

'And when they find, as they will, that we are simply housing a number of residents—?'

'There is surely a little more to it than that.'

'We shall be prepared to defend any action that the planning authorities might bring.'

'It will be an interesting case,' said Mr Piggin with a smile.

He had moved from his perch on the table and was now standing by the window.

'No doubt,' he continued, the smile still lingering, 'when you made your purchase, you inspected the house.'

'Of course. It was empty and our surveyors were able to make a thorough structural examination.'

'Did it not seem odd to you that all of the upper-storey windows, but none of the ground-floor ones, should have been barred?'

'Odd, perhaps, but useful. As you see, we have added bars on the ground floor too. We discourage unauthorized visitors.'

'Then you made no enquiry as to what use the council had made of the house before you purchased it?'

For the first time the prophet looked uneasy. Angry, as well, but there was a worm of uneasiness under the anger. There was something upsetting in Mr Piggin's deliberate delivery.

He said, 'We didn't consider the matter important. And now, if you've quite finished—'

'But surely,' said Mr Piggin, 'if a complaint is made, you will be forced to argue – at a public hearing – that the use to which *you* are now putting the house is basically no different from that of its *previous* user. A hearing of that sort will be widely reported, and I cannot help feeling that such a contention may give rise to a certain amount of hilarity.'

'Oh, why?'

The word was spat out from between tightly closed lips.

'You were not aware then that the previous user was – if I may use the old term – as a lunatic asylum. What, as boys, we called a loony-bin.'

The anger which had been heating up as Mr Piggin proceeded with his leisurely disquisitions now boiled over.

'I've had enough of your impertinence. Standing there, lecturing me on the law. So we're in danger, are we? Have you any idea what danger you stand in yourself?'

Mr Piggin said, 'If you are contemplating treating me in the outrageous way you treated young Bracknell, I'd advise you to look out the window. The eight men you can see on the pavement are the larger, and rougher, members of the Southwark Rugby Football Club. They would, I am sure, resent any attack on myself and would be likely to respond in kind. I do not know who would come out on top in such a confrontation, but before you decide to provoke it, take a look at the ninth man. The rather smaller one, standing at the back. You see him? He is on the staff of the *Southwark Gazette* and he has brought his camera with him. A picture of a sanguinary encounter in this respectable street would sell a lot of copies of the paper, but it might also lead directly to the unfortunate results I mentioned earlier.'

It was clear that this final thrust had pierced the prophet's armour. He reverted promptly to the businessman. Returning to his chair he sat down, extracted a cheque book from the drawer, and said, 'How much?'

'I don't follow you.'

'I imagine you want money. How much do I have to pay to prevent you going to the planners?'

'Money doesn't enter into it,' said Mr Piggin, virtuously. I am not a blackmailer. I should be quite satisfied if you dismissed your recent recruit, Antonia Hay. I suggest you inform her that, in the short time she has been here, her character has demonstrated its unsuitability for her to be a member of your organization.'

'She was furious at the reason given for her expulsion,' said Rupert Hay to Mr Bracknell. 'Absolutely furious. But, in her heart of hearts, deeply relieved. Not only at getting clear, but at salvaging most of her money. When General Crispin mentioned your name to me, do you know what he said? "Not a lot of legal nonsense about them, but eminently practical".'

4
Rat's Castle

'They're a bunch of bloody crooks,' said Treadwell.

As a solicitor, Francis Fearne had often heard this said. Usually it only meant that someone had got the better of the speaker in a financial or legal deal. On this occasion he was inclined to take it more seriously. Bernard Treadwell was not only one of his oldest clients, but, as head of Treadwell, Rooke, and Boskett, a leading property firm, was a man of standing in the City.

'What makes it worse,' he added, 'is that my son, Tom, is one of the people who've been caught.'

'That does give it a sort of personal angle,' agreed Fearne. 'Do I assume, then, that your son was one of the unhappy tenants of Fifteen Porter Place?'

'He was. And all I can say is that it looked all right. A nice, old-fashioned doctor's residence, with plenty of big rooms below and smaller ones above. Not in the most fashionable part of London, but near enough to the centre for a businessman. It seemed to be an excellent development, and my son – who'd just got married – was glad to pick up a seven-year lease of the last of the flats that was going.'

'And the landlord was . . . .?'

'A man called Reuss-Roberts. He bought the house from Dr Lewin's widow.'

'Who acted for her?'

'She handed the whole thing over to Reuss-Roberts's solicitors, Chatterway & Duxford.'

'You mean they acted for both parties?'

'You don't like the idea?'

'It's not against the law, and it saves costs, but I certainly wouldn't advise it. Who did the conversion?'

'One of Reuss-Roberts's companies, the Scottbar Property Company. They also dealt with prospective tenants.'

'But Chatterway's drew up the leases.'

'Yes.'

'What were the rents?'

'The rents,' said Treadwell, choosing his words with care, 'were specified in the leases. In my son's case it was twenty-five hundred pounds a year. There was one larger flat and two others about the same size as my son's. I don't know the rents, but they were probably comparable. I happen to know that the small one at the top was fifteen hundred.'

Fearne, who had been scribbling busily, said, 'Seeing that you can't get a flat anywhere around London for much less than fifty pounds a week, the rents, if they were fixed for seven years, don't seem unreasonable.'

Treadwell uttered a curious sound, halfway between a snort and a growl. He said, 'Fixed. You did say fixed, didn't you?' He extracted a document from his briefcase and spread it on the table. 'This is my son's lease. I'm sure you'll find it interesting.'

After the usual rigmarole about paying the rent and keeping the property in repair, there was a clause that caused Fearne to remove his glasses, polish them, and replace them on his nose before reading the clause carefully once again.

Headed *Additional Rent* it ran: *Should the Landlord decide, at his discretion, to effect improvements to the property, such improvements will be carried out by a builder nominated by him. The cost, as certified by Messrs Selverman Buckling and Company, will be divided rateably between the flats and added to the rent.*

'Rather a one-sided arrangement,' said Fearne.

'If my son had shown it to me I'd have warned him. But he was busy getting married. I suppose the other tenants were so glad to get a decent flat at a reasonable rent that they overlooked the small print.'

'So what happened next?'

'The first year they seem to have rebuilt part of the roof, quite unnecessarily. It was a very good roof before they started mucking about with it. That added nine hundred pounds to my son's rent. The second year they started on the interior. Redecorating the common parts and replacing some of the softwood parts with hardwood. That was an expensive item. The result was a further twelve hundred pounds on to my son's rent.'

'Next year,' suggested Fearne, 'I suppose they'll start gilding all the woodwork.'

'Something of the sort.'

'A very cosy arrangement. Particularly if you happen to have the builder and the valuer in the game with you. What do you think will be the next move?'

'The next move has already been made. The landlord has offered all his tenants a new seven-year lease, with a fixed rent – really fixed this time – no additions, all maintenance and alterations to be paid for by the landlord.'

'At an increased rent, no doubt.'

'Of course. My son's rent – already jacked up to four thousand, six hundred – was to be fixed at five thousand pounds. The small one at the top – occupied by Miss Grahame, a retired schoolmistress – was to be four thousand pounds. I got that from my son, who's made friends with her. He's pretty certain she can't afford it. The other proposed rents were in line with my son's, I imagine.'

'Who are the other tenants?'

'In two cases, professional men who work in the City. The largest flat is let to a businessman, fairly wealthy. After the last rent increase he had a storming row with Reuss-Roberts and threatened to throw him out of the window.'

'And did he?' said Fearne hopefully.

'He couldn't. Roberts had a couple of plug-uglies in the offing. Called themselves private detectives. Private thugs.'

'Has he accepted the new lease?'

'Not yet. But I think he will.'

Fearne, who had been making further calculations, said, 'One flat at four thousand, three at five, and one at, say, six. That's a rent roll of twenty-five thousand pounds. So then?'

'Then he sells the freehold. He's asking for seven years' purchase, which is a hundred and seventy-five thousand.'

'How do you know that?'

'I know it,' said Treadwell, 'because he offered it to me at that figure.'

'Are you thinking of accepting it?'

'It goes against the grain. I happen to know that he paid Dr Lewin's widow fifty thousand pounds. A ridiculous price. If she'd consulted me I'd have told her to ask for a hundred and twenty and not settle for less than a hundred. The so-called improvements, mostly fiddling things, will have cost very little, which means that this crook, having contrived to swindle the widow over the sale price, now clears a profit of a hundred thousand on resale. Probably more.'

Fearne thought about it. He considered adding a word about Mrs Lewin's shortsightedness in bypassing her own solicitors – who would hane insisted on an independent valuation – but thought better of it. No point in preaching to the converted. He said, 'It seems to be legally watertight. I'll have to think about it.'

After which, as in so many legal matters, there was an interval of some months in which nothing much seemed to happen. Fearne had plenty of other things to think about – it was the time of the great City Bank scandal – and he relegated the problem of 15 Porter Place to the back of his mind. He thought, comfortably, that young Tom Treadwell would get help from his well-heeled father to meet his increased rent. The other tenants were businessmen and capable of looking after themselves.

He had forgotten about the small flat at the top.

On a dull morning in September, one of the second-storey tenants smelled the escape of gas. He went upstairs, found the door of Miss Grahame's flat unlocked, and went in. Fortunately he was a man of decision. He ran down to his own flat and telephoned the fire brigade, the police, and the local hospital – in that order. Within a very short time the firemen, forewarned and wearing masks, had extracted Miss Grahame, whom they found in her living-room with her rent book in one hand and a Bible in the other, and packed her off in an ambulance to the hospital. Here the doctors fought for her life, pulling her back, inch by inch, from the unknown country she had been heading for. When she found herself back in this world she did not seem greatly pleased, but she did promise her one close friend, Tom Treadwell, that she would not embark on that journey again without consulting him.

It was Tom's father who brought the news round to Fearne & Bracknell.

He said, 'This made up my mind for me. I wasn't going to have a life on my hands. I paid Reuss-Roberts the price he was asking. As their new landlord, I've reduced Miss Grahame's rent to its original figure and I've lowered my son's rent, which was immaterial as I was subsidizing him anyway. The other rents I've left as they are. The tenants can afford them. So in the end I shan't be greatly out of pocket. All the same—'

'All the same?' said Fearne, when Treadwell seemed unable to go on.

'I can only repeat what I said when I first came to see you. Add Reuss-Roberts to the Scottbar Property Company, and throw in Chatterway & Duxford, solicitors, and Selverman Buckling, valuers, and you've got a gang of stinking crooks. And seemingly there's nothing anyone can do about it.'

'I'm not sure. My managing clerk, Mr Piggin, has been looking into the matter. If there's an avenue to be explored or a stone to be turned, be sure he'll find it. But don't read that as a promise.'

And that was all that Fearne would, or could, say.

Mr Piggin, being a bachelor, made lunch his main meal of the day. He belonged to two City lunch clubs and was a welcomed attender at three others. His table companions were usually from the middle ranks of professional firms: solicitors, accountants, estate agents, surveyors, and such. It was by talking to them that he tapped into the City network of personalities, feuds, and prejudices, governed by an almost schoolboy code of behaviour. On this occasion, whatever facts may have surfaced, he kept to himself.

Meanwhile, Reuss-Roberts, having concluded one satisfactory campaign, was looking for other fields to conquer. He and his partner, Maurice Lignes, made a perfect pair. Reuss-Roberts was the corsair who scanned the main for victims. Lignes was the careful man, the accountant, who weighed up figures and prospects and made sure that the answers came out right.

His partner's latest activity had worried him somewhat.

He had snapped up the freehold of a dilapidated property, 16 Bridewell Lane, at an advantageous price, from its owners, the Abel-Baker Property Company. Having heard, on the City grapevine, that they were in financial difficulties, he had stepped in with a prompt offer, cash down of £150,000.

'It's a snip,' he said. 'A good position, eighty-four hundred square feet on four floors. All four let, of course. When I saw the leases – fourteen years without any breaks – I could hardly keep a straight face. Do you know what the tenants are paying? One pound fifty a square foot for property that needs only a spit and polish and it could be let for at least eight pounds – possibly ten.'

'Are you sure about those figures?'

'Lutters have confirmed them. You'll admit they're reliable people. Most of the banks use them. They put the value of the freehold, even encumbered by those ridiculous leases, at a figure of around two hundred fifty thousand.'

'So now we sell and pocket the profit. Right?'

'Chicken feed, Morry. Chicken feed. No, no. What we do now is clear out the tenants. Buff up the offices and relet them at a proper market figure. *Then* we might think of selling.'

'And the tenants have all got leases with several years to run. So—?'

'We use method B, of course.'

Business tenants could not be dealt with in the same way as residential ones. Being businessmen, they had read and considered their leases. More direct tactics were called for. Lignes knew about method B and disapproved of it, but on financial rather than ethical grounds, since it involved a further outlay of cash.

The first step was to undertake a complete refurbishment of the outside of the building. No one could object to this.

Did not the leases stipulate that all exterior repairs were the responsibility of the landlord? So up went a scaffolding, all round the building.

Then the existing plaster had to be stripped. This was done with a machine that banged and clattered and belched out fumes. Naturally the windows had to be boarded up whilst this was going on, to keep out the debris of the old plaster and the water the exposed brickwork had to be sprayed with before it was replastered.

It all seemed to go on for a very long time.

The ground-floor tenants were the first to give in. Soon after they departed the lift went wrong. This appeared to knock the stuffing out of the tenants of the upper storeys. When they raised the question of surrendering their leases, the landlord was sympathetic. He would not charge them anything for dilapidations – which, strictly, he was entitled to do – since, as he explained, he intended to strip and repaint the offices as soon as they had departed.

'All out,' reported Reuss-Roberts two months later. 'Next step will be to put our builders in.'

'*Our* builders?' said Lignes. 'I suppose you read that article in the *Sunday Monitor*. They couldn't make out that we were doing anything illegal, but they latched on to the fact that the whole operation was carried out by what they called "a small clique of firms".'

'Certainly I read it,' said Reuss-Roberts. 'I cut it out and put it in my scrapbook with other stupid effusions. It did, however, make me decide that on this occasion we'd employ an outside firm for the actual redecoration. Carstones. Independent, I think you'll admit.'

'And expensive.'

'Maybe. But I've tied them up with a contract. They do the job, all in, for forty thousand pounds. A quarter payable in advance, the other three-quarters at monthly intervals. With a penalty for delay, which means they won't hang about.'

'So we have to find another forty thousand before any rentals start coming in.'

'No difficulty. The bank has offered us a standing credit of fifty thousand at a fixed rate of eight and a half per cent.'

'So,' said Lignes unhappily, 'we shall be paying out more than eighty pounds a week until the job's done.'

'A tiny sum when we've got our hands on one of the biggest plums in the market.'

He looked as happy as Little Jack Horner.

Lignes said, 'I'm still puzzled that Abel-Baker let you have the property at such a low figure.'

'They accepted it because they were hard up.'

'I wonder. They're such shy people that it's difficult to get at any real facts about them.'

'A search in the Companies Register—?'

'Of course I searched. They have a nominal capital – of a hundred pounds and were formed by the accountants, Renishaws. The directors and shareholders are all partners in the firm. Nominees, of course.'

'That's common form, surely!'

'Maybe. What isn't so common is for a hundred-pound company to have acquired that particular building. There's someone behind them and I'm going to find out who it is.'

'How?'

'I'm in touch with a low-level employee of Renishaws.'

Reuss-Roberts understood by this that he had managed to bribe one of the secretaries or typists. He said, 'You're pissing against the wind, Morry. This is a straight legal deal. No one can unstick it. For God's sake, stop worrying.'

Meanwhile Mr Piggin, having concluded his arrangements in the City, had been briefing his faithful and unquestioning follower, the firm's office boy, Michael Donovan.

He said, 'I expect you've got a friend who wouldn't say no to a little extra cash.'

'Dozens,' said Mick.

'One will be enough, as long as he can get plenty of time off and can hold his tongue.'

'OK. So what are we going to do?' He hoped that it was something exciting, like burglary or arson.

'It's a watching brief. You can take it in turns, or you can do it together, whichever suits you. But one or both of you are to be there, where I put you, all day, and keep your eyes and ears open. Ears particularly. Do you know how to use a mobile phone?'

Mick awarded Mr Piggin the sort of look that a modern boy reserves for his elders when they ask stupid questions. He said, 'When do we start?'

'When I tell you,' said Mr Piggin.

Maurice Lignes irrupted into his partner's office and said, without sitting down, 'I've got the answer.'

'Answer to what, for God's sake?'

'To who's behind the Abel-Baker company.'

'So who was it? The Archbishop of Canterbury, or the head of Scotland Yard.'

Lignes ignored the flippancy. If his partner was happy, he was not. He said, 'It's Bernard Treadwell.'

After a short pause Reuss-Roberts said, 'What's so exciting about that?'

'You took him to the cleaners three months ago. He won't have forgotten about it, even if you have.'

'Sit down, Morry. And take a deep breath. There's nothing strange about his name cropping up. He's always buying and selling properties. He's well known for it. But tell me this: what harm can he do us? We've bought the freehold and removed the tenants. And we've put in a well-known and independent firm of builders. They moved their stuff in last week. Yes – what is it?'

His secretary said, 'I know you weren't to be interrupted, sir, but it's Mr Robert Carstone. He seems to be upset about something.'

'Then we'd better have him in.'

To say that Mr Carstone was upset was an understatement. The first coherent words he managed to get out were, 'What-the-hell-are-you-playing-at?'

Reuss-Roberts said, 'I'm not playing at anything.'

'If you aren't, someone is. Our foreman had left all his stuff, ladders and paint and equipment, outside each flat, so that he could get straight on with the job. When he arrived this morning he found it had all been moved into one of the flats. *And the door had been locked.*'

'Who the devil—'

'There's no secret about who did it. It's a man called Joy.'

'Never heard of him.'

'You're going to hear a lot about him. He's your top-storey tenant.'

Lignes said, 'Tenant? I thought you'd dealt with all the tenants.'

'So I did!'

Carstone said, 'Well, you overlooked this one. Quite easy to overlook. He's only got the one room. Tucked away, right under the tiles. A sort of attic. He showed me a copy of his lease. I've got it here. Help yourself to an eyeful of Clause Seven.'

The Landlord undertakes that the staircases and passages between the demised premises and the front door of the building shall be kept clear at all times of obstructions.

'That's why he moved all our stuff away, and what's more, he said, he's not going to have our men tramping up and down the stairs.'

Reuss-Roberts said, 'I'll deal with Mr Joy. I'd better have a word with Duxford first. He seems to have slipped up.'

Lignes said, 'In view of some of the – er – transactions we've had with that firm in the past, I should advise against starting a quarrel with them.'

'I wasn't thinking of quarrelling with Duxford. I just want an explanation.'

When he reached his solicitor's office, Duxford leafed rapidly through the file and said, 'I see that we asked for full details of the tenancies of the ground, first, second, and third floors. Those being the floors you told me were occupied – it's in your letter, here. So those were the leases I saw. I had no idea there was another tenant. It would have been friendly of the landlord's solicitors to have warned me, but if challenged, I suppose they'll say they didn't mention the fourth floor because they weren't asked about it.'

'And who 'are these' – Reuss-Roberts swallowed the adjective that had occurred to him – 'these singularly unhelpful solicitors?'

'It's a firm called Fearne & Bracknell.'

'And if they mean to be really obstructive, what can they do?'

'Well, they might apply to the court for an injunction restraining you from interfering with Mr Joy's quiet enjoyment of his office. Whether they succeed or not, it would make it impossible for Carstones to get on with their work until the court had decided the matter!'

'Leave it to me,' said Reuss-Roberts. 'I'll settle this right now!'

The lift being out of action, he had to climb three main sets of stairs and a fourth much smaller flight before reaching the door which, according to the brand-new plate screwed on to it, led to the premises of Norman Joy, Agent. The door was opened by a mild-looking, bespectacled man who waved him to a chair on the other side of a desk which was clear of papers. The only things on it were a pen set and a china ashtray.

When his visitor was seated Mr Joy also sat down and waited, with folded hands, for him to state his business.

'I've come,' said Reuss-Roberts, speaking as though the words choked him, 'to find out on what terms you'll surrender your lease.'

'Why should I surrender it?' said Mr Joy. 'I'm very happy here. Excellent prospects. Plenty of fresh air!' He indicated the window, which was wide open, though the October day was far from warm. 'I keep it like that so that I can hear the birds singing.'

'Then I must tell you quite frankly that I'm not prepared to have you here. And I'm prepared to pay a reasonable sum of money to get rid of you. I had in mind a thousand pounds.'

'I couldn't consider it. It took me months to find this delightful place. So quiet, so easy to work in.'

'Do you want more money?'

'No, no. Money doesn't enter into it. The quiet, the birds—'

'Then what the hell do you want?'

'Just to be left in peace.'

'That is something that I can't guarantee. I mean, you're so isolated here. Has it not occurred to you that you might not be able to summon help, if anything should happen?'

'Anything?' Mr Joy leaned forward, as though anxious to hear what his visitor was going to say. 'What sort of things had you in mind?'

'Who can say? These are violent times.' As he rose to go, he added, 'In the circumstances, I'd go as high as two thousand.'

'The money is quite unimportant. And as for these premises being secluded' – Mr Joy smiled gently – 'that is their main attraction. That and the birds.'

'I hope you will find it so,' said Reuss-Roberts. And, later, to his partner, 'I went up to two thousand pounds, but I couldn't budge him.'

Lignes said, 'I hope you realize that five thousand – even ten – wouldn't have been excessive. Have you *any* idea what this delay is going to cost us? Seven hundred pounds a week is my estimate. Penal interest on our overdraft and stand-off payments to Carstones. They're bound to claim that. They'll have turned down other work to oblige us. And if the matter does come to court, the delay may last for six months or more.'

'Then there's only one thing for it. We'll have to take a short-cut.'

'As long as you know what you're doing,' said Lignes.

It was on the following day, at four o'clock in the afternoon, that Lou and Jake, employees of Tramplings Detective Agency, arrived outside the door of Mr Joy's office. When they had rung the bell and rapped repeatedly on the door without result, Lou said, 'We saw him go in. Can't have got out. Unless he's grown wings and flown out of the window.'

'Perhaps he's asleep,' said Jake. 'Have to wake him up.'

The door was a rickety affair and Jake had only to kick it twice to carry away the lock. Then they walked in.

Mr Joy was sitting behind his desk. He looked more surprised than upset at this forceful entry. He gazed mildly at Jake, who advanced to the table and laid a paper on it. 'Something for you to sign, squire.'

Mr Joy said, 'Now what might that be?' He leaned forward as though anxious not to miss the answer.

'Simple. It's a paper that says you give up your lease in return for two thousand in cash. We've got the money here.'

'But suppose I don't want to give up my lease?'

'In that case, squire, you might be in trouble.' He put one finger under the small table beside the desk and tilted it until it fell over, bringing down the telephone that stood on it. Jake said, 'Look what I've done! Clumsy me.' In picking up the telephone, he seemed, somehow, to have detached the wire. 'See what I mean? Accidents happen. Telephone out of order. You can't send for help.'

'I could always shout.'

Lou, who had been standing by the open window, peering down into the dark little courtyard far below, enclosed by the walls of the building, said, 'You'd have to shout bloody loud and bloody long to bring anyone up here.'

'Always supposing,' said Jake, 'that whoever it was came in allowed you to go on shouting. They might be rougher than we are. One of them might hold you down while the other one trampled on your face. That wouldn't be agreeable, now, would it?'

'Certainly not,' said Mr Joy. As though fearful that action might start at any moment, he removed his glasses, polished them carefully, and laid them down on the desk. Jake, who was finding Mr Joy's placidity hard to take, stepped forward, grabbed him by the lapels of his coat, and shook him.

'Stop mucking about, you old coot,' he said. 'Sign up or take the consequences.'

Lou, who had moved away from the window, was now standing in front of the door to block any thought of escape that their victim might have. He said, 'Get a move on. We haven't got all freaking night.'

'In that case,' said Mr Joy, 'I must give you my answer at once.'

He picked up the heavy china ashtray and threw it straight out of the open window. In the silence which followed this unexpected move they all heard the explosive sound as the ashtray hit the flagstones of the courtyard far below and disintegrated.

'Now, what was the object of that?' said Lou. He had moved back to the window and was peering down. He could not see Mick Donovan, who was behind the open door of the coal shed, talking busily into his mobile telephone.

The number he had called was Leaman Street Police Station, which Mr Piggin had found more co-operative than Cable Street and better organized. Having been alerted to the possibilities of the situation, they had expected the call and reacted promptly. One of their patrol cars was within a few streets of Bridewell Lane and Jake was just saying, 'I don't know what the old coot's up to and I don't like it,' and Lou had agreed with him, reluctantly, that it was time to leave, when the three-man crew of the police car reached the office, out of breath from their rapid climb, but ready for action.

'Glad to see you,' said Mr Joy. 'Well now, I'm charging these men with breaking and entering, with assault, and with threats of bodily harm.'

'It's a lie,' said Jake. 'We never threatened him.'

'And the door was broke when we arrived,' said Lou.

'Natcherly we looked in to see if we could help.'

'Just happened to be passing, I suppose,' said the police sergeant genially. 'Try it on the judge. He might believe you.'

'When the matter comes to court,' said Mr Joy, 'I'll let the prosecution have an interesting tape. Not liking their appearance, I turned the recorder on when they came in. So we'll be able to hear exactly what they did say, shan't we?'

'I suppose you realize what you've done,' said Lignes speaking in tones more savage than Reuss-Roberts had ever heard before. 'I've spoken to those two oafs. They're on bail for the moment and haven't opened their mouths. But as soon as the court proceedings get under way, you know what tune they'll sing, don't you? It wasn't *their* idea. *They* were obeying orders. Whose orders? Why, naturally, the orders of the man who wanted so desperately to get Mr Joy out of his office. And when the police see which way the wind's blowing they'll suggest that it might pay them to change sides. To help the prosecution, with a suitable indemnity for any part they played in the matter. Then *they'll* be in the witness box, but *you'll* be in the dock.'

Reuss-Roberts opened and shut his mouth. The fight had gone out of him. Eventually he said, 'Is there nothing we can do?'

'Maybe. But you'll have to give me *carte blanche* so far as expense is concerned.'

Reuss-Roberts nodded. He said, 'How would you set about it?'

'I'd offer Mr Joy, who's clearly in it for what he can get, a really substantial sum if he not only clears out of the office, but also tells the police that he can't help them. The tape he mentioned has unfortunately been wiped. And, now he comes to think of it, the lock on the door was broken. It's true that the men, who had come on business, had burst in uninvited, but they had not been threatening. Of course, the police will realize that he's been bought off, but there's nothing they can do about it. Without his help there's no case. Right?'

'Go to it,' said Reuss-Roberts between clenched teeth. 'And the sky's the limit.'

*

'Then it was a trap,' said Fearne.

'That's right,' said Mr Piggin happily. 'A great big lovely rat trap. Mr Treadwell did most of the work, but I was able to help him from time to time. I introduced Reuss-Roberts to the possibilities of the property. At third hand, of course. And I made the arrangements with Mr Joy. He has been helpful to me in one or two little matters. But Mr Treadwell did everything else. The tenants were friends of his – big people whose toes Reuss-Roberts had trodden on. They had no objection to a small part of their business being carried on for a few months from Bridewell Lane. He offered to pay them disturbance money, but they wouldn't take it. They said that hearing Reuss-Roberts squeal was all the pay they wanted.'

'Schoolboy justice,' said Fearne. 'All the same, it was risky.'

'There are risks in all business transactions. What particular one had you in mind?'

'The obvious one. That Reuss-Roberts might discover, before completing the purchase, that there was a cuckoo in the nest.'

Mr Piggin smiled. 'They'd have been very smart and very quick to have found out about Mr Joy. We only installed him on the evening before completion. No. There was a much bigger risk than that. Reuss-Roberts had to be persuaded that he ought, on this occasion, to employ an independent, and preferably an expensive firm to carry out the redecoration. The article in the *Sunday Monitor* was a great help. We arranged for copies to reach him from three independent sources. Once he had signed up with Carstones, we knew that we had him by his scaly tail.'

'So who gets the money? How much, by the way?'

'One hundred thousand pounds. Not an enormous amount, but satisifactory. The bulk of it, of course, to Mr Treadwell, to compensate him for such losses as he suffered over Porter Place.

Then Mr Joy had to be paid – danger money – the police might not have arrived in time. And our costs. We're not a charitable institution.'

'That's right,' said Fearne, as though the point had occurred to him for the first time. 'We're not a charitable institution.'

5
The Message of the Stars

In spite of the fact that he was one of the senior partners in that well-known firm of East London solicitors, Fearne & Bracknell, Bob Bracknell's elder sister, Felicity, still contrived to view him as a younger brother, improving, but not yet to be trusted entirely. When she spoke to him on the telephone that morning it was in her Roedean voice.

'Louella Firebrace is an old friend of mine. A very old friend; General Firebrace's youngest daughter. I'm sending her round to see you. She needs advice – and help.'

The way in which his sister stressed the last word alerted Bracknell to the possibility of trouble. Once before she had sent him a young man who needed help. The young man had since been detained in a criminal lunatic asylum and seemed likely to remain there.

He said, 'What particular sort of help do you think she needs?'

'She's afraid that she may be going mad.'

'Oh dear!'

'It's too soon to be certain. With help and sympathy she may easily recover her balance. In the past she has certainly shown herself to be a good businesswoman. Do you read the *Message of the Stars*?'

'Not knowingly.'

'Then you don't follow racing?'

'I venture a pound or two on The Derby and the Grand National.'

'If you were a serious student of racing' – Felicity managed to make it seem blameworthy that he was not – 'you would certainly have run across the *Message of the Stars*. It is clearly designed for people whose idea of picking a winner is to do it with a pin.'

'Is there any other way?'

'Now you're being facetious. You know very well that serious followers of racing study the blooodlines on both sides of any horse they fancy, follow its current form, and weigh up the odds very carefully.'

'And which method – the arbitrary or the painstaking – do the stars favour?'

'It was to prevent you making remarks like that when you see Louella that I telephoned you. She needs assistance, not mockery. You must see her today. There's no time to lose.'

This was midday on Monday, and Bob's diary was already fairly full, but he had realized, at an early age, that it was no use saying no to his sister once her mind was made up.

'Tell her to come along at two o'clock,' he said resignedly, 'and I'll be able to give her half an hour.'

One thing he had decided; he would have Mr Piggin in with him when the lady arrived. His old managing clerk had a notably calming effect on hysterical girls.

But Louella was a surprise.

When Felicity had said 'the youngest daughter', he had pictured her as a flippant young female whose mind had been captivated by astrology. The woman he shook hands with was of roughly the same age as himself and had the look of a housewife used to controlling a husband and a brood of children. Troublesome children, maybe, which would account for the lines that framed a pair of gentle brown eyes.

She got down to the business in hand with a speed that Bob appreciated.

She extracted from her bag and laid on the desk a collection of printed papers. Reading them upside down, Bob saw that they were all headed, in capital letters, THE MESSAGE OF THE STARS, followed by a date. Louella smoothed them on the desk with loving care.

'My life's work,' she said. 'Felicity tells me that you are not interested in racing, so they will not mean very much to you.'

'I fear not.'

'These are my last two dozen. They go out each Monday with tips for the racing at the weekend. I've been doing this for nearly five years. When I reached number two hundred my club subscribed for a brooch. Wasn't that kind?' She indicated a small silver horse's head with eyes that might have been rubies.

'Your club?'

'That sounds rather grand, doesn't it? When I started, most of my readers were friends and acquaintances. They paid ten pounds a year each, which gave me enough to cover my expenses. Some of my early tips came home at good odds, but it wasn't until I picked the winner of the Queen Mary Stakes at twenty-five to one – no one else fancied her – that things started to snowball. I got so many applicants that I raised the entry fee to fifty pounds, thinking it would choke people off.'

'And naturally,' said Bob, 'this simply increased their keenness.'

'New members now have to pay one hundred pounds and still they come. I award the horses one, two, or three stars – three stars denoting a special favourite. And – if there are horses which I feel are absolute duds, I give them a black mark. Occasionally a black-mark horse wins and the laugh is on me. It doesn't happen often. It's easier to pick losers than winners.'

'And if you nominate a three-star horse, does that affect the market?'

'Shorten the odds, you mean. Yes, I think it must. Members are supposed to keep my tips to themselves, but you can't prevent them talking to their friends. On King Cophetua, for instance, in the Saint Hilda Handicap, my club members were able to get ante-post odds of twelve to one, whilst by the day of the meeting he'd been marked down to five to two.'

'And he won?'

'Yes. By a short head.'

'And can you remember how you arrived at that inspired tip?'

For the first time, Louella looked worried. She said, 'Really, I can't explain exactly how I did it. A bit of it was because I fancied the jockey. You might say that I was following people more than horses. Then again, I got a certain amount of help from my son, Malcolm. He's a major in a cavalry regiment, so he ought to know about horses.'

Bob nearly said that a modern cavalry man was more interested in horsepower than in horses, but refrained. He divined that his client was coming to the matter that had upset her.

She said, 'That was how it went, for a long time. I had one or two pieces of good luck and a few of bad luck. But now, suddenly, it's changed. Here's where you have to promise not to laugh.'

'I promise.'

'You described my tips as inspired. Until recently I shouldn't have used that description. I'd have said that they were partly the result of a careful study of form and partly of sheer guesswork. But recently, they have been, in fact, inspired. It happens at night. A little man stands by my bed and whispers. Just the name of a horse followed by a suggested ranking. One star, two stars, or three stars. He repeats it in an urgent whisper, until he sees that I'm awake. Then he disappears.'

Bob had promised not to laugh, but it needed all his professional training and experience to keep a straight face. He said, 'And how often has this – er – manifestation occurred?'

'So far, three times. Always on Saturday night. In good time for my circular to club members that goes out on Monday.'

'And you adopted the suggestions which came to you in this way?'

'I felt so strongly that they were inspired that I was quite unable to depart from them. The first one – a three-star choice – was Sovereign, in the Trouville Claiming Stakes. He was the favourite and came home an easy winner. In the second case the horse I was told to give three stars to, Suvlac, was joint favourite before I tipped him and he won at very short odds. On the third occasion, I was told to give only one star to Hushaby, in the Middlehampton Maiden Stakes. He came in second, but at long enough odds to make an each-way bet profitable.'

'What about last Saturday?'

'Once again I was told to give my three stars to a favourite, Barnabas, and a black mark to Tittup, who was already an outsider at twenty-five to one. If I condemn him, he will probably go down even further.'

'And that's what you're going to do?'

'I haven't sent out my weekly sheet yet. I wanted your advice before I did so.'

Bob said, speaking slowly, to give himself time to think and hopefully, to give Mr Piggin a chance to chip in, 'So on three occasions your dwarf's advice has enhanced your reputation. And if you follow it this time you should certainly come to no harm.'

'That's right.'

'And you've still got to tell me what's upsetting you.'

This produced a long pause. Then Louella said, 'It's not easy to explain. But before this – this visitation – I was my own master. I'd done the things I ought to do, studied the pedigrees and the previous form of the runners, and made my own mind up. Now I'm having my mind made up for me. I am in someone else's hands. I don't like it.'

'I appreciate that,' said Bob. 'May we start from one firm supposition? That your visitor is a figment of your imagination.'

'I certainly think he must be. I occupy the top floor of a pretty solid Victorian building. There are two flats below mine. We all have a key to the front door. When we come in at night the arrangement is that we ring through to the caretaker, who lives in the basement, and tell him we're back. When we've all reported in, he bolts the front door. And I always bolt my own door as well.'

'Doesn't sound easy for anyone to get in,' agreed Bob. 'Bolts are safer than locks. They can't be picked. What about windows?'

'The ground-floor windows are barred. That was done by the tenant, who's an art dealer and has a lot of valuable pictures. All the upper-storey windows have window locks. The insurance company insisted on that. But locks or no locks, I sleep with my bedroom window open. I've done so all my life and see no reason to change my habits.'

'Drainpipes?'

'Nothing like that. There is a lightning conductor, but it's something you could hardly get the tips of your fingers round.'

'Everything you tell me,' said Bob, 'strengthens my view that the messages you get come from inside your own head.'

He looked at Mr Piggin, who had been sitting quietly in the corner. He looked up from some notes he had been making, and said, 'It certainly seems so. But I would like to borrow those predictions. And if I'm to understand them, I shall need some publication which gives details of the runners and the results.'

'The *Racing Calendar*. You'll find it in the reference section of any public library.'

Mr Piggin thanked her gravely and accompanied her downstairs and out into the street, standing in the doorway for some minutes after she had left. When he got back to his own room he found Mr Bracknell there.

'What do you make of it?' he said.

'Difficult,' said Mr Piggin.

'The way I see it – here's this lady – seems a sensible sort of person—'

'By no means hysterical,' agreed Mr Piggin.

'She's been handing out racing predictions for four or five

years. Now her mind has become so fixed on them that they follow her into her sleep.'

'Quite possibly. There's just one thing that doesn't fit into that picture. Could you explain why Louella Firebrace should have been followed when she came here?'

'Followed? By a dwarf?'

'No. By an unpleasant character, known in criminal circles as Knocker Bates. An ex-boxer – very much ex – and a hanger-on of a racecourse gang.'

'Are you sure?'

'Michael Donovan spotted him. And had him under observation for some minutes.' Michael was their office boy and general factotum, who worked under Mr Piggin and admired him greatly.

'He described him as having cauliflower ears and a broken nose – common enough in a pugilist – but also as having a totally bald head with a scar running across it from ear to ear. Which means it was Knocker, all right. He had evidently been following Miss Firebrace. When she came in he seemed to be interested in our plate. Mick could see his lips moving as he spelt out the words "Fearne & Bracknell, Solicitors and Commissioners for Oaths". When he'd digested all that he backed off and hasn't been seen since.'

Bob said, 'That certainly is odd. What's behind it do you think?'

'It's too soon to jump to any conclusion. When I've studied all those papers and made one or two enquiries, I might be able to suggest something. At the moment I can only agree with you. It's odd.'

For the next three days Mr Piggin was exceptionally busy, even by his standards. He spent long hours reading and rereading the predictions of the stars and comparing them with the records in the *Racing Calendar*. This was followed by a round of visits to off-course bookmakers who all informed him, with surprising unanimity, that business was bad; a fact which did not seem to inhibit them from driving expensive cars and smoking large cigars. After which, by arrangement with Miss Firebrace, he paid a visit to her flat and inspected the back of the building, from below and from above, and had a talk with the caretaker, a grizzled ex-policeman.

His next move was less predictable. His interest appeared to shift to small theatres, music halls, and touring circuses, and he took a certain Levi Lexington, who seemed almost to monopolize bookings in these affairs, out to a liquid lunch at the Falstaff. By Friday morning he was able to present the four partners with an interim report.

'You must appreciate,' he said, 'that most of what I am going to say is theory. Very little hard fact. Though more may arrive on Saturday night.'

'You mean,' said Fearne, 'when this dwarf next visits Miss Firebrace.'

'That's what I hope. Indeed, what we learn then could clinch the matter.'

'Then the dwarf really exists?'

'Very possibly. I have my eyes on a circus performer known as Little Al. Big Jim and Little Al: they're a duo who specialize in gymnastic feats, one of which is a version of the Indian Rope Trick. Big Jim throws what is, apparently, a rope into the air and Little Al swarms up it. He climbs like a monkey, and would regard the scaling of the wall behind Miss Firebrace's flat as an elementary feat. The bars on the ground-floor window would give him an excellent start and the two windows above it would just be steps in a ladder. The top one, Miss Firebrace's sitting-room, would be shut and locked. But he could reach across one finger behind the lightning conductor, get a knee on to the open bedroom window sill, and be inside in a matter of seconds. Incidentally, as a cross-reference, Big Jim was, at one time, a strong-arm member of the same racecourse gang that employed Knocker Bates.'

When he had finished speaking, there was a moment of silence, broken by Bob Bracknell's son, Hugo. He said, 'If this dwarf exists, and you've certainly made a case for it, ought we to allow him to get into Miss Firebrace's bedroom? Shouldn't he be stopped?'

'The difficulty is that we shall have no real confirmation of my theory until we know what the dwarf is going to say. Let me explain. I think that what he and his backers are up to is what bookmakers call a two-horse trick. Suppose that an owner has two horses running in the same race. Probably a race with a smallish field. Horse A is the stable star, and in view of the modest opposition will start at very short odds – possibly odds-on. Horse B has never won a race – at least, in this country. He may have notched up a success or two on the Continent, but in this country his form has been dire. If you have both the trainer and the jockey in your pocket, it is easy enough to ensure that a good horse runs badly. So Horse B is quoted at fifty to one. He has a modicum of support, because his pedigree is good and he is handled by an expert trainer. No one, except the people who are behind the ramp, knows one salient fact: that in a number of very privately conducted trial runs, *Horse B has consistently beaten Horse A*. Nor are they to know that in the hour before the "Off" very large sums of money have been staked, with half-a-dozen out-of-town bookmakers, on Horse B.'

'I follow that,' said Bob. 'But it's obviously a ramp that needs long and careful working up. So how can you be sure that they're planning to bring it to a head this week?'

'They'll have been told that the lady on whom they've been relying to crown their efforts – three stars for Horse A, a black mark for Horse B – has consulted her solicitors. So, no time to waste.'

Fearne's daughter, Tara, said, 'All the same, I don't think we ought to allow our client to run any risk.'

Her father said, 'I agree. A decision in the matter will have to come from her. We must ask her round and put the facts, as we see them, before her.'

'In which case,' said Mr Piggin, 'might we not offer her a measure of protection? If she invites her soldier son, Malcolm, to sleep in the flat over the weekend, he could rig up a simple alarm system. A bell or buzzer that sounds in her son's room, connected to a switch by her bed. She could have her hand on it when the dwarf appears. But not press it until after he has delivered the *Message of the Stars*.'

'I can't tell you how deeply relieved I am,' said Louella.

'Relieved?' said Fearne. It was the last reaction he had expected when he had explained Mr Piggin's ideas to her and had invited her to act as the cheese in the trap they were setting.

'Deeply relieved,' said Miss Firebrace firmly. 'If this dwarf really exists, then the whole situation is changed. He's not just a figment of my fevered and unbalanced imagination.'

Fearne, who felt, by now, a considerable admiration for the lady, thought he had rarely seen anyone less fevered and unbalanced. He said, 'If you're willing to co-operate, it will certainly narrow the field.'

'I can narrow it even further. You spoke of a smallish number of runners and of long odds. The two things are not consistent. For instance, if you examine last week's results at Brighton, where there were never more than seven runners in each race – I am speaking from memory – no horse was quoted at longer odds than ten to one.'

'Correct,' said Mr Piggin, who was elbow-deep in paper.

'You only really get odds of 50-1 or 100-1 in races like the Grand National. If you're looking for odds around 25-1, you'll have to concentrate on the larger fields. There were two at 33-1 at Ripon last week. In both cases a sizeable number of starters.'

'Sixteen in one case, eighteen in the other,' murmured Mr Piggin.

'The predictions I send out every Monday are for a meeting either on the Friday or the Saturday. When we see what the dwarf has to suggest we can easily see which meeting and which race he has in mind.'

'Hopefully you're right,' said Fearne. 'And you must pass the information to us at once. Then we can make up our minds what your Monday message to your club members is to be.'

For the first time it seemed to occur to him, but to no one else, that this might be the most difficult step in an operation that was tricky enough already.

For all her cultivated calm, Louella was finding it difficult to get to sleep. It was a comforting thought that her resolute, fifteen-stone son was sleeping one room away. She hoped that he was not sleeping too soundly. She passed her fingers over the switch beside her hand.

The quarter-past one from St Barnabas Church sounded clearly through the wide-open window. The sky outside was blue-black, lit by an army of stars. Remote points of crystal light. She stared at them, wondering how she could have been so presumptuous as to suppose that they could interest themselves in mundane matters.

Half-past one.

The stars were blotted out by a shape that slid silently through the window and came sidling across the moonlit floor like a huge and horrible crab.

Miss Firebrace summoned her soldier ancestors to her aid and held her breath.

'Three stars for Sir Dominic, a black mark for October Lad.'

As the urgent whisper sounded, inches from her ear, she contrived to grunt and roll away, pretending not to hear.

Then the words came again, more clearly and urgently than she had ever heard them before. Not advice now, more a command. She moved her hand over the switch and pressed it.

The sound of the bell was clearly audible. A few seconds' pause was followed by the pounding of steps in the passage as her son burst into the room.

She said, 'You'll see him better if you don't turn the light on.' They crowded into the window. 'There he goes,' said Malcolm. 'What a mover. Did you get the message?'

'Yes,' said Louella, choking back a feeling compounded equally of outrage and relief. 'I got it.'

Louella brought the news to the partners herself, after breakfast on Sunday morning. Her son had refused to come with her. He was angry at his failure to catch the dwarf after a breakneck descent of the stairs and an eruption through the back door.

Louella was inclined to be philosophical. She said, 'I'm just glad that we've cleared it up. I wouldn't care to go through all that again.'

'Nor should you,' said Tara warmly. She had been opposed all along to Louella running risks.

Bob said, 'So now we know. It's the Sedgefield Handicap at Southwell that they've got their eyes on. Horse A is Sir Dominic: and Horse B is October Lad.'

'Different owners,' said Hugo. 'Sweeny – Clark.'

'But not all that different,' said Mr Piggin, 'when you consider that Charles Sweeny is Bill Clark's nephew.'

Bob said, 'And the odds have worked out in the way we expected. Sir Dominic a clear favourite at five to two; twenty-five to one currently quoted on October Lad. If your message tomorrow blacks October Lad he may go out still further. Maybe thirty-three to one.'

There was a short silence. All eyes were on Fearne, who was the only one who had not spoken. Finally he said, addressing Louella, 'Have you, in fact, considered what your Monday message is to be?'

The question seemed to surprise her. She said, 'To tell you the truth, I was so relieved that you'd identified that horrible dwarf that I hadn't really thought about it. I suppose – well – it's not going to be easy, is it?'

'It's an extremely difficult problem.'

'I suppose you could always—' and she stopped, realizing that she really had no sensible suggestion to offer.

Fearne said, speaking slowly, 'If you analyse the position you'll see that you have three courses open to you. Each of them has its own, quite serious, drawbacks. Number one, you could do exactly what the dwarf has told you to do. Three stars for Sir Dominic, a black mark for October Lad. This will be the clincher that the men behind the dwarf have been playing for. It will confirm and support the misleading picture that they have been carefully painting. However, if you do so, particularly now that you have every reason to suspect what is going on, you will have made yourself an accessory to the scheme. Not a comfortable thought, is it?'

'It certainly isn't,' said Louella.

'On the other hand, you could reverse the order. Give three stars to October Lad and black Sir Dominic, which might, now, be a more honest statement of your opinion. Your recent successes must have made a number of punters prepared to follow you blindly. Though I doubt whether you could reverse the odds, you could certainly affect them dramatically. But by doing so you will have earned the enmity of a powerful and unscrupulous set of men. The dwarf will have told them what happened last night, and they will be on the lookout for trouble. If crossed, they can be extremely unpleasant.'

'Oh dear,' said Louella. 'What am I to do, then?'

'As I said, there is a third course open to you. Rather than making any prediction at all, you could simply announce your retirement. If you do so, I fear that the newer members of your club, who joined at a hundred pounds, will be disappointed. They will feel that they are not getting their money's worth. They may even be tempted to sue you.'

'Oh, no. That, at least, is impossible. When the fees started to mount, I took Felicity's advice. She said that any new member should sign an agreement that I was under no obligation to continue advising. That was a condition of his membership.'

'And you got that, in writing, each time?'

'Signed and witnessed.'

'I always knew my sister was a better lawyer than I was,' said Bob. 'It looks as though course three is the winner.'

There was a general murmur of agreement.

Louella gave a great sigh of relief. 'I can't tell you how grateful I am. That's just what I'll do. Announce my temporary retirement. Then, if things straighten out, I can always start again.'

On the Saturday at Southwell, October Lad led the field of fifteen runners in the Sedgefield Handicap and ran out an easy winner at twenty-five to one.

On the Monday morning the partners met to discuss the work of the week ahead. This looked like being heavy. Captain Burd's wife had finally made up her mind to divorce him, and the Rumpole estate was coming up for auction. Then an awkward case of assault on a schoolboy had arrived, in the form of a distraught headmaster, at an early hour that morning.

When these matters had been fully discussed, Mr Piggin coughed and said, addressing Mr Fearne, 'If I might revert, for a moment, to a problem which we managed to solve last week, to the satisfaction, I think, of all parties. When you, sir, presented an admirable analysis of the three courses open to us, it did occur to me that there was a fourth, and additional, step that might be taken. In pursuance of this idea I managed to raise the sum of one thousand pounds and placed it, through a number of bookmakers known to me, on October Lad.'

The deep silence which this statement produced was broken by

Bob.

'Then – good heavens – you made yourself twenty-five thousand pounds.'

'Not for myself,' said Mr Piggin gently. 'Since the facts about the horse had come to me in the course of the firm's business, I naturally considered the winnings belonged to the firm. I felt that I was entitled to what you might call a commission, so after deducting five thousand, I have transferred the balance of twenty thousand to the distributable profits of the partnership. Tax free, of course.'

'Well,' said Fearne, 'that's extremely handsome.'

'Very handsome,' said Bob and Hugo in unison.

Tara said nothing. She was busy spending her share.

When they had got their breath back, Bob said, 'It was a daring coup. But if October Lad hadn't won, I hope you will accept that the partnership must have repaid you your stake.'

'My confidence in you is such,' said Mr Piggin, 'that I am sure you would have done so. But the possibility hardly arose. After all I was only following the advice of the stars. I was therefore in no danger of losing your money.'

In view of the outcome, no one felt inclined to niggle and it was only that night as he was lying in bed composing himself to sleep that the thought occurred to Mr Fearne.

If Mr Piggin *had* followed the advice of the stars he would have backed Sir Dominic, not October Lad.

The thought did not keep him awake for long.

6
The Good Shepherd

Being twenty-two years old, and unmarried, Hugo Bracknell, junior partner in the firm of Fearne & Bracknell, Solicitors, found it convenient to lodge, for the time being, with his parents. Matrimony or bachelor independence would eventually move him to a home of his own, but until that happened he was content to enjoy, and be thankful for, his mother's housekeeping skills.

Feeling that the small sum which was all that his father, Robert Bracknell, would accept for board and lodging was insufficient, he had got into the habit of supplementing the cash by gifts in kind. This involved early morning visits to Covent Garden, where he bought fresh fruit and vegetables off the overnight lorries, and fishing trips down the river to the sea in the tub dinghy with its outboard motor, which was his pride and joy. These expeditions produced pollack, whiting, and, on one occasion, a huge eel, which had been devilish difficult to kill and which his mother had refused to accept. ('Can't stand the slimy creatures.')

On this particular Friday, having crammed a day's work into the morning, he had set off at two o'clock. The last of the ebb tide and the current combined to take him quickly and smoothly towards his chosen fishing ground off Royal Oak Point, where the Medway joins the Thames and the two rivers run out, arm in arm, to the North Sea. It was crisp October weather, and if he had listened to the local wiseacres he would have learned that it was what they called a weather-breeder, but he was too young to listen to greybeards.

He had slid past Lower Upnor and was approaching the Hoo Salt Marsh when the advance guard of the mist rolled in from the sea. Before he could take two deep breaths, visibility was down to a few feet. He was keeping a course a little to the left of mid-stream and making no more than four knots. He gave vent to his feelings in a navy-blue expletive and throttled down still further, keeping one finger on the klaxon.

Then everything happened at once.

The loom of a high-cut shearwater, the deep coughing of a powerful engine, a fast-moving grey bulk – then a single raucous shout.

He swung the rudder wildly, but his way was so small that his little craft hardly responded.

A glancing thud and an ominous splintering crash.

No lights and hogging it on the wrong side of the river were Hugo's last thoughts as he found himself underwater.

It was not the first time that he had suffered violent immersion, and he had the sense to keep his mouth shut and not to struggle. He had no desire to come up under the propellers of that launch. When he surfaced he could tell by the feel of the wash that the immediate danger was past. He shook the water out of his eyes and swam towards the dinghy, which he could see bobbing in the tideway. When he reached her, he splashed round to the side which was higher out of the water and dragged down on it. This brought the further side into view and he was able to make a quick estimate of the damage.

A rib and two stretchers, he thought. The launch which had run him down had disappeared into the mist and the silence was now unbroken. Bloody swine. Not coming back to see what he hit, I don't suppose.

He hung for a few minutes, thinking. He was too experienced a waterman to be put out by any consideration of personal danger. He knew that he could reach either bank by swimming and the water, though cold, was not numbing as it would have been midwinter or early spring.

His concern was for the boat.

He had another look at the damage.

He noticed that as long as he had his weight on the undamaged side no more water was coming in. It seemed to him that something might be effected, particularly as the tide was on the turn.

He splashed round to the stern and hoisted himself up – not an easy feat, but he knew what he was about – and a mighty heave landed him on the stern seat. This manoeuvre had put the dinghy dangerously low and the water was coming in fast. He shifted his weight until he was crouching on the undamaged side. This was sufficient to raise the hole above water. He then got out the dipper and started to bale. He had nothing to plug the hole with. Even a temporary caulk would have helped, and water was still coming in, but the intake was manageable.

One of the oars had gone overboard with the shock of the crash. Hugo took his stand in the stern and using the remaining oar – gondolier fashion – he propelled the boat slowly towards the Essex shore.

Twice he had to stop to bail, and by the time the shore loomed he was heartily glad of it. The situation had got beyond his vocabulary and he had stopped swearing. He was beginning to feel the effect of the cold and the limited movement possible in the tilted craft was doing nothing to restore his circulation. Nevertheless, when he had finally run the boat ashore and lugged it as far as he could up the shelving beach, he stood for a long moment, looking around him.

He was seeking a landmark.

A tiny breeze had sprung up, as happened sometimes at the turn of the tide, and despite the fact that dusk was now deepening into night, visibility was a little better than it had been. When he caught a glimpse of the chimney of the oil refinery looming through the mist, he knew that he must be close to one of the two bankside villages. Hoo St Osmund or Hoo St Lawrence. He thought it was St Lawrence, the nearer of the two. That church, he knew, had been shut up, but even an abandoned church meant an old rectory and someone who might be helpful to a shipwrecked mariner.

He twisted the painter of the boat round a wooden stump, so old and so gnarled that it might have been there since the time of the Armada, and set out across the salt ooze, sinking deep at each step.

A stone wall loomed, low enough to climb. Once over it, he was in a wilderness. The long grass, laced with tilia bushes, was difficult to push through, but at least the ground underneath was firmer. He was beginning to be thankful for this when he tripped over a hidden obstacle. It was a gravestone. This must be the churchyard of Hoo St Lawrence. As he picked himself up he thought he could make out the loom of the church ahead of him. He remembered his father telling him that although it had been abandoned it was necessary, for some ecclesiastical reason, to reopen it once a year and hold a service. It must be an eerie affair. What echoes of old hymns sung and old sermons preached might the intruders hear; what ghosts might they see of past weddings and forgotten funerals.

The breeze was strengthening now and the yew trees were starting to whisper.

Suddenly he found that he was shaking. It was not only the damp clothes, which were clinging uncomfortably to his body, there was something disturbing and unpleasant about this little church, crouching among the encroaching jungle of thorn and elder; awaiting the second coming, when all graves would be opened and the dead would rise from their long sleep.

Get out of it, he thought. The quicker the better.

He started forward at a stumbling run, until another obstruction brought him to his knees. Be careful, slowly now. Stupid to break an ankle. When, after a minute or two of cautious progress, he found himself up against the wall of the church he stopped to think. If he kept on round the outside, circling the west end, he must come to the porch. What would he find there? If ghosts could pick locks, might he find the church door standing open?

What he did find brought him up with a slamming heart. Someone was crouching in the darkness of the porch.

'Hullo,' said Hugo. 'What are you doing?' He spoke sharply, to get over the shock. He could see now that it was a small hunch-backed man, almost a dwarf.

'Nothing,' said the man. 'What's more to the point, what are you doing?' A semi-educated voice.

'I've had a ducking. I'm looking for somewhere to dry off. Is the old rectory still inhabited?'

'Aye,' said the man, and seemed to have no more to say. Then, sensing Hugo's impatience, he added, 'Cathcart bought it when the church shut up.'

'Not Mr Donald Cathcart, by any chance?'

'We're not on Christian-name terms,' said the man sourly.

Could it be Cathcart, four years older than him, captain of cricket, in the fifteen; god of the house, whose football boots he had cleaned so diligently? He had heard that he had come to live in Essex and had sometimes wondered whether he might run into him.

'How do I find it?'

'Find what?'

'The old rectory,' said Hugo patiently.

'You'll see the light.'

He would have liked more precise directions, but the man was clearly unanxious to help him. He wondered why. But in fact, when he reached the wicket gate the way was clear enough. A beaten track led to the building ahead. In five minutes he was ringing the bell, and twenty minutes later he was in a hot bath and his clothes were drying in the airing cupboard. A long shot had come home. This was the Donald Cathcart he had known, now in his late twenties, with a charming wife, Celia, and an impertinent six-year-old son called Max.

With only a token show of resistance, Hugo accepted the offer of a bed for the night. He telephoned his father, who seemed to know the Cathcarts and approve of them. Over a late supper, Max having been removed, protesting, to bed, he was able to give his hosts an account of the events that had landed him at their door.

'That little hunchback,' he said. 'He'll be a local character, I imagine.'

'Albert Revill. Revill the devil, the village children call him. I don't think there's anything actually satanic about him. They don't like him because if he catches them near the church, he chases them off.'

'I got the impression he didn't care for me being there. Why should he want to keep people away?'

'Maybe a sort of residual authority. He was one of the late vicar's churchwardens. The only person who stuck by Kenneth Blacking to the end. It's a sad story. In the old days there may have been enough people to fill both churches. When church attendance fell it seemed sensible to concentrate on one of them. And there was no doubt in anyone's mind which to choose. Raymond Truelove at St Osmund's was – and still is – a very popular character. A typical old-time parson. People enjoyed his sermons. Blacking's, on the other hand, were intolerably dull, and I found out why. When we moved in here we bought some of the furniture. All Blacking's personal stuff was moved out. Only the movers missed this cupboard in the attic. And guess what I found in it?'

Hugo made one or two light-hearted suggestions.

'No. It was a set of twelve volumes of sermons. Fifty or more in each volume. Six or seven hundred; one for every imaginable text.'

'No wonder his congregation trickled off.'

'It started as a trickle. Finished as a torrent. The trouble was that the defections only made Blacking more uncompromising. He antagonized even people who were prepared to wish him well. In the end, his congregation was reduced to two. The people's warden, old Colonel Enright, and the vicar's warden, Bert Revill. When Enright died, it was Revill alone. Blacking still wouldn't give up and he couldn't be moved. One evening, on the last day of June, when something kept Revill away, he conducted the whole service to an empty church and concluded it by cutting his own throat on the altar steps. He must have done it inefficiently, because his heart kept on beating and pumping out blood in a long stream as he crawled to the west door, which is where he was found when people looked in to see why the lights were burning.'

'Since when,' said Celia, 'you won't be surprised to learn that the church is haunted. Particularly at the end of the month. That's where lights are seen and footsteps are heard.'

'Twenty-fifth of September today,' said Hugo. thoughtfully. 'Might that be why Revill was lurking in the porch? To scare off ghost hunters.'

'Could be,' said Cathcart, and switched the conversation to cricket.

Next morning he drove Hugo to Upnor to talk to the boatyard about rescuing and repairing his boat. Sam Curling, who ran the yard and knew Hugo well, listened to his account of the accident and said, 'Big grey boat with a high waterline. Real seagoing craft.'

'That's the one,' said Hugo. 'If you happen to know who owns it—'

'Nobody don't know that,' said Curling. 'Though many'd like to. All they know is he's seen in the estuary, after dark and always towards the end of the month. You're the only one he's actually sunk, though other craft have had narrow escapes.'

'A mystery boat,' suggested Cathcart.

'A mystery bloody nuisance,' said Curling. 'Howsoever, she don't seem to have done too much damage to your little treasure. Two ribs and a stretcher, you said. We'll soon have her patched up.'

On the way back they stopped at the church and walked down through the churchyard to make sure that the boat was safe. Cathcart had brought a length of rope with him and they used it to supplement the painter.

'Can't be too careful,' said Cathcart. 'The river and the tide play odd tricks.' Coming back, he stopped to light his pipe and when he had it going to his satisfaction he sat down on one of the tombstones. Guessing that he wanted to talk, Hugo selected another tombstone as a seat for himself.

Cathcart said, 'Are you thinking the same as me?'

'Allow me to read your mind,' said Hugo agreeably. 'You've noticed the coincidence of times and places.'

'Right.'

'Here's this launch. A big and powerful boat, well able to cross the Channel.'

'Or the North Sea. Or the Atlantic, come to that.'

'Which means that it's probably based outside this country. It turns up towards the end of the month, after dark, and is spotted cruising in the estuary. After which it departs. Having deposited its cargo, shall we say, in this deserted and unvisited church.'

'Right. And even if people did happen to see lights in the church, they'd be too frightened to make any close inspection. Then someone or other—'

'Stop beating about the bush. You mean Revill!'

'All right, I mean Revill. He picks the stuff up and passes it on to its real recipients. What do you think it is? Drugs?'

'Very likely. So what do we do about it?'

'We make an examination of what you lawyers call the *locus in quo*.'

'How do we get in?'

'Actually,' said Cathcart, 'I've got a key. I found it tucked away behind those sermon books I was telling you about.'

By daylight the church looked harmless enough. An hour of patient prodding and searching convinced them of one thing: even a small church offered a hundred hiding places. Under font or pulpit, around or in one of the many tombs, under the altar, in and under the pews. When they had finished with the church itself, the vestry offered dozens of further possibilities.

'What we need is a team of professional searchers,' said Cathcart.

'Or a bit of common sense. That launch was running a regular service. It was coming upstream when it hit me – on the way to the drop. The accident meant that it couldn't complete its run. Because I was between it and the church. But it'll be back, sooner rather than later, that's for sure!'

'So what do you suggest?'

'All we need is a couple of sacks of dust!'

'Ask Celia. She fills a sack every time she hoovers the house. What are we going to do with them?'

'We go in quietly, this evening. Take a sack each and spread it, working backwards, down the aisles and transepts towards the door. From now on Curling and all his friends will be keeping their eyes open. As soon as they report the arrival of the launch we go in, quick.'

'Before Revill can remove what the launch has brought him.'

'Right. When we find out what it is, we can decide what to do next.'

'And talking about moving quickly, if we don't stir our stumps we're going to get ticked off for keeping lunch waiting.'

This was one ordeal they did not have to suffer. As they drove back they were hailed by a cheerful, red-faced clergyman. He said, 'I've fixed it with your wife, Donald. You're all coming to lunch with me. I've been given a couple of pheasants by one of our local poachers – he sings tenor in the choir – and my house-keeper cooks them to perfection.'

So, for two hours, they were able to forget their plans and problems. The pheasants had been expertly cooked and stuffed with chestnuts. A bottle of Chambertin formed the perfect accompaniment.

On the way back, Cathcart said, 'Raymond Truelove is an example of a nearly extinct species. An eighteenth-century village clergyman. A bachelor, unambitious, happy in his job, friends with everyone. A good shepherd.'

Hugo said, 'Also, I imagine, a man with income.'

'Must be. That bottle of wine would have cost him most of a curate's weekly stipend.'

Celia said, 'Do you think it's wrong that he should have so much?'

'Certainly not,' said Hugo. 'If he does a good job.'

'He does a first-class job,' said Cathcart. 'Not only the routine stuff, but all the unpaid chores we land on our parish clergy. Visiting the sick, organizing collections for the needy – collections to which he makes generous contributions out of his own pocket. And he's particularly good with the kids. Persuading them to sing in the choir, preparing them for confirmation, and generally keeping them in order.'

'If he can keep Max in order,' said Celia, 'that alone will justify his income.'

Two days later, in the early evening, the call came. Hugo drove to Hoo St Lawrence at a dangerous speed. Armed with a torch apiece, he and Cathcart traced the footsteps which could be picked out, with perfect distinction, in the dust they had spread. They led towards the font, but they found nothing in it or under it.

Hugo, who was examining the footsteps more carefully, said, 'It looks as though he was standing tiptoe here just behind the font.

You can see scuffling marks and the points of both toes. You're taller than me. Try and see if you can reach that little shelf.'

It was there all right, the object of their search. Cathcart brought it down carefully. A neatly taped package, about eight inches square and ten inches deep. They carried it back to the house, where Celia produced scissors and a long-bladed paper knife. In the box were six 180E video cassettes. As they fixed one of these into the television set, Cathcart said, 'If these are what I think they are, darling, I suggest you don't look at them.'

'Don't be so Victorian,' said Celia. 'I'm enjoying this as much as you are.'

All the same, after ten minutes, she took herself off, saying that supper needed looking after. The two men allowed the tape to run for a further ten minutes before Cathcart switched off the set.

He said, 'It passes my comprehension how they can induce the actors to do such things. Particularly the boys.'

'Pay them handsomely, no doubt,' said Hugo. 'What do we do now?'

Cathcart had brought down a stout volume with black covers. 'Fifty sermons,' he said. 'I hope the men who come to collect the tapes appreciate what we're doing to improve their minds!'

After supper, helped by Celia, they made up the book into a package closely resembling the one they had lifted and took it back to the church.

'No visitors yet,' said Cathcart, examining the dust where the two previous sets of footprints could be distinguished. 'Of course, it may be days – weeks possibly – before Revill ventures in to pick up the stuff. We shall have to set up a proper watch. When a light is seen in the church I come out, assisted by a stalwart gardener, and we catch the little bastard red-handed.'

'And then?'

'Then we make a citizen's arrest. The curtain comes down. House lights on. God save the Queen!'

'Quiet,' said Hugo.

They stood looking at each other. They had both heard the noise. Without speaking, they slipped back into the shadows behind the font and stood there with their hearts thumping.

The door of the church, which they had relocked when they came in, was being opened and footsteps were coming towards them. The intruder was carrying a torch, which he used sparingly. When he reached the font it could be seen that he was carrying a heavy leather hassock out of one of the pews. Standing on this, he was just able to reach the ledge where the package lay. Having taken it down, he moved off.

A pause, whilst the hassock was being replaced in the pew, then the footsteps continued down the aisle. After that the sound of the church door being opened and relocked. Only then did the watchers move.

Hugo said, 'For God's sake. What are we going to do?'

'Let's have a word with Celia. She may have some idea.'

Celia said, 'Are you sure?'

'Quite sure. The back-glow of his torch showed his face absolutely clearly.'

'It was Raymond Truelove. No doubt about it.'

Neither man sounded happy.

'Then what are you waiting for? Tell the police. Now. Without wasting any more time.'

'I suppose we must.'

'If you don't,' said Celia coldly, 'and no one does anything, I suppose you realize that in a few years time this – this peddler of filth – will be preparing our son for confirmation.'

Cathcart, at whom this broadside was directed, nodded unhappily.

'The police won't be best pleased with you for removing the original packet. Give them the tapes and tell them the whole story.'

'I think,' said Hugo slowly, 'that before I do anything else, I'll have a word with my father. He usually sits up until I get back. I'll show him the cassettes. He'll know what we ought to do. You come too.'

They found Hugo's father sitting in front of the fire smoking his goodnight pipe. He listened impassively to what his son, interrupted from time to time by Cathcart, had to tell him.

When they had finished his father said, 'What you've been up to may have been fun to start with, but it's ceased to be amusing. You're not a policeman, you're a solicitor and an officer of the court. And both of you' – swinging round on Cathcart – 'are members of the public, with the obligations which that implies. You'll hand the tapes – I'll take your word for what's in them – to Chief Inspector Mayburgh and explain how you got hold of them.'

'You mean, go round now.'

'Certainly. You've wasted too much time already. I'll telephone the station to tell them to expect you.'

Hugo didn't know how Cathcart was taking this. He himself felt about two foot high. They got into the car and drove, unspeaking, through the silent streets to the police station.

His father's telephone call had caught Chief Inspector Mayburgh on the point of going to bed. He had vented his exasperation by calling his assistant, young Inspector Barley, from his bed, and the two of them now faced Hugo and Cathcart in a silence that seemed more hostile than any amount of questioning. When they had finished and switched off the recorder that Barley had brought with him, Mayburgh said, 'If you've nothing more to say, we'll have your statement typed out. You can sign it in the morning.'

After they had departed, he sat for a full minute in silence before giving expression to his feelings.

He said, 'Trust a pair of bloody amateurs to make a bloody mess of it. If he'd left the stuff where it was instead of that silly caper with the sermon book, we could have up Truelove with the cassettes in his possession. Then he'd have had some explaining to do. As it is – I suppose you realize – we've got nothing at all. As incumbent of both parishes, he'd every right to a key of that church. He saw a light and went in to investigate. Noticed this package, wondered what it was, and took it away to examine it.'

Barley, who was a fair-minded man, said, 'That doesn't explain two things, sir. Why he went straight to where the package was, and why he brought that hassock with him. Doesn't it show that he not only knew where the stuff was, but that it was somewhere high up?'

'Try it on the jury. You know what the defence will say. That he spotted the package up on the ledge, realized he'd need something to stand on to reach it, and fetched the hassock *after* he'd spotted it.'

Barley nodded agreement. He'd seen juries bamboozled often enough.

'Right,' said Mayburgh. 'Let's think how to clear up this mess. We've been getting reports from time to time about that launch, haven't we?'

'From Thames Division. Yes, sir. And from Revill. He's been watching the church.'

'So suppose Truelove is what these people clearly think he is. A middleman in a smuggling operation. We're not so interested in him. The men we want are the ones who are going to pick up the cassettes. We want them badly. And it wouldn't do any harm to identify the people they sell to. A few sharp lessons there would frighten off other prospective purchasers. What we have to do now is set a carefully organized watch on Truelove's house for the next few days. We'll need co-operation from the specialist squad at Central who deal with this sort of thing. I'll see to all that. You get the posts organized and the lines laid. If we move smartly we should have everything in position by tomorrow night. That should be soon enough.'

They had underestimated the speed of the men they were hunting.

Next morning Truelove's housekeeper, who slept in a separate annexe, ran screaming to the telephone.

'Horrible,' she sobbed. 'The things they've done to him.'

Mayburgh examined the crumpled and contorted body on the bed. Professionally unmoved, he said to Barley, 'They must have turned up soon after he got back from the church – may even have been waiting for him. Checked the parcel on the spot. Found they were being swindled. Suspected that Truelove was party to it and tortured him to make him tell them what he'd done with the cassettes.'

'Which he couldn't,' said Barley. 'Because he had no idea what had become of them.'

Mayburgh, who had been examining the body more carefully than Barley cared to do, said, 'The police surgeon will tell us, but my guess is that he died of shock. He was an old man. And when you see what they did to him—' He stared round the room that had been wrecked in a futile search for the tapes.

Barley said, 'Hopefully they may have left some signs behind which will help our people to trace them. Fingerprints, footprints, things like that.'

'I doubt it,' said Mayburgh sourly. 'They were professionals, not bloody amateurs.'

When he heard the news, Bob Bracknell said to Francis Fearne, 'Not really one of our successes.'

'Not really,' Fearne agreed.

7
On a Dead Man's Chest

Storm warning, thought Inspector Flower.

He was a bright young man, and in this case reading the omens called for no great skill. His boss, Chief Inspector Mayburgh, had been out all morning, talking to, or being talked to, by Superintendent Oliphant, the head of No. 2 Area East. Nor was Mayburgh a man who troubled to conceal his feelings. Mr Piggin, the managing clerk of solicitors Fearne & Bracknell, had once described him as an old-fashioned rhinoceros who tried to get at the truth by butting it head first. When the chief inspector got back to his headquarters that morning he was clearly in a mood which called for butting someone or something.

He growled at Flower, 'Would you say we were idle here? Would you perhaps suggest that we spent our time lying on our backs thinking beautiful thoughts?'

'Certainly not, sir.'

'Under-worked, with lots of time on our hands to chase any red herrings that District choose to throw at us?'

At another time Flower, who was a precision in speech as well as in dress, might have demurred at this grandly mixed metaphor, but not with Mayburgh in that mood. No, sir.

He said, 'We've got more than enough on our plates.'

Drugs, shop-lifting, juvenile delinquency, arson, vandalism, mugging. You name it, they had it.

'So guess what happens?'

Flower, unable to guess what additional burden might have been laid on their shoulders by District, could only grunt sympathetically.

'I'll tell you what happens. Interpol. Yes, bloody Inter-bloody-pol sends a report to Special Branch, who forward it to Chief Superintendent Brace, who takes a quick sniff at it and hands it on to Oliphant, who skims through it and passes it down to us – for action. Action! They don't need action. They need a crystal ball to tell them what to do, and the Brigade of Guards to do it.'

Having got this off his chest and paused for breath, Mayburgh condescended to produce some details.

'What the report says is that Interpol have had reliable information – reliable you understand – that a contract killer has arrived in London, charged with an important mission by the Rome mafia. He has been seen on one or two occasions – that's where the information gets a little less reliable – in this part of London. Would we therefore locate him, have him watched, and forward all information to Special Branch, since they have the responsibility for protecting the person, whoever it may turn out to be, that the mafia are threatening. That's the job which has landed on our plate, at fifth hand, and which I'm now passing on to you.'

'At sixth hand,' murmured Flower.

'What was that?'

'I said it sounded sticky.'

'Then it's up to you to unstick it.'

'Have we *any* information about the victim?'

'Only guesswork. You'll have read in the papers that the Italians are trying to cut the mafia down to size. A job they should have tackled long ago in my opinion. The case has been dribbling along for nearly five years. But when it seemed, at last, to be approaching its climax, with the betting fairly level between conviction and acquittal, a new and important witness was unearthed. *If* he was prepared to face the publicity, his evidence could very well tilt the scales against the mafia. This man, it seems, has been in England for some time and has therefore been comparatively safe – until the importance of what he has to say was suddenly realized. Upon which the mafia decided that he must be liquidated.

'I understand that,' said Flower patiently. 'What I really wanted to know was whether we had anything definite to go on – about the killer or his victim.'

'Since Interpol themselves didn't know the name of the victim, they could give us no help. In fact they were asking *us* to help them.'

'And the killer.'

'One of the men they think it might be goes under the name of Luciano the Limper. To distinguish him, no doubt, from Luciano the Lucky. Not a young man apparently. In his forties or fifties. But a very experienced operator.'

'With a limp.'

'So it seems. That should assist you.'

Flower wondered how many men there were in London who limped. But he was not disheartened. He had worked on more slender information and had reached a solution. Had he not recently located a serial killer by the application of the science of psychological finger printing?

It seemed that the information had come to Chief Superintendent Brace from the Head of Special Branch. A lofty exchange between chieftains. His own connections with that curious, semi-political police force were at a much lower level. One of its junior officers, Martin Medhurst, had been at school with him and they had kept in touch.

Having sorted out his thoughts, he arranged to meet Martin at a well-known Fleet Street watering-hole and explained the job he had been landed with.

'Typical buck-passing,' agreed Martin.

'I don't see much chance of locating the mafia killer. They've got a dozen crafty ways of getting into the country and friends to hide them once they're here. I'm only surprised he allowed himself to be spotted hanging round in our neck of the woods.'

'Over-confidence?'

'Maybe. But what I thought was, if we couldn't pinpoint him, we might at least be able to identify his victim.'

'Would be a step in the right direction,' agreed Martin.

'The way I've worked it out is this: first, if his evidence is going to be all that important he must be an important man himself. Both sides have been trotting out shady informers, men whose evidence could be bought for twopence a yard. One more like that wasn't going to make any difference.'

Martin lowered some of his drink thoughtfully and said, 'With you so far.'

'Next point. This trial started five years ago.'

'It was five years ago when they started pulling in the minor characters.'

'Right. Then I'm guessing our man must have been in England for around five years. Not much longer, if his information is going to be current enough to hurt. And not much less, or he'd have been picked off before he left Italy.'

Martin said, 'So you want me to look through our records and find an important Italian—'

'Or, more likely, a well-known Englishman living in Italy.'

'Right. One who came back here – around five or six years ago. It could be a longish list.'

'We can cut it down further. The man must have a house in our part of London. That would be the reason for the killer to be hanging around. We're told he is a thoughtful operator. He is probably making a reconnaissance for the job.'

'See what I can turn up,' said Martin.

It was more than a week before he produced his answer. An anxious week for Flower, when he reflected that the killer must be poised to strike. On the other hand, he had been described as middle-aged and experienced. A man who had learned to take no chances, who planned his approach march carefully; his retreat even more carefully.

The information, when it did arrive, seemed so promising that Flower took it straight to the chief inspector.

He said, 'I expect, sir, that you recognize the name Raeburn Bentley.'

'Rings a bell. Well-known artist, isn't he?'

'He is indeed. He's spent most of the last twenty years in Italy, living it up with a Bohemian crowd in Rome, painting for his living, portraits mostly and not making a lot of money until he came back here four or five years ago and did that thing which created such a sensation in the Academy. Called it *The Gamblers*. A crowd of men and women round a roulette wheel, with faces that people had no difficulty in identifying. Just enough indistinction about them to save him from a libel action. A clever piece of work. He sold it for a very large sum to a firm of playing-card manufacturers. Financially he's been up in the stratosphere ever since. When I add that he has a tiny house on Thameside, behind Southwark Cathedral – really only a studio, with an office behind it and a bedroom over it—'

'And no family?'

'There's a woman somewhere in the background and two kids. But they live separately.'

Mayburgh, a puritan at heart, snorted his disapproval of this irregular arrangement. He said, 'I fancy you may have spotted the right man. Living among the riff-raff in Rome he could well have picked up information.'

'And is important enough for anything he said to sound convincing.'

'Yes, worth following up, certainly. Do we know anything else about him?'

'Only,' said Flower reluctantly, 'that his legal business is looked after by *that* firm.'

He needed to say no more. At Cable Street Police Station 'that firm' meant only the partnership of Fearne & Bracknell, whose office was visible from their own top window, and with whom they had had, in the past, more than one difference of opinion.

Another branch of British officialdom was showing interest in Raeburn Bentley.

IRSID, The Inland Revenue Special Investigation Department divides London geographically. North, south, east, west and City. IRSID (E), which covered Southwark, Stepney and other parts of the East End was headed, at that time, by two industrious taxation ferrets; Albert Schwan and Leslie Jimpson. They were discussing, for the twentieth time, with frustration bordering on fury, the affairs of Mr Raeburn Bentley.

'He never answers letters,' said Schwan, 'and when we invited him to an interview he talked all the time and we got nowhere.'

Jimpson said, 'The fact is that until he came back to this country he was dealing with Italian taxmen.'

'Italians, yes.'

'Quite so.'

The two revenue officials looked at each other. Their views, though unstated, were plain.

'However, now he's here, he must be brought to heel.'

Schwan studied the thinnish folder on the table in front of him. 'In four complete tax years, and part of a fifth, he has made no returns at all.'

'Claiming that since he has no income, there is nothing to be returned.'

'Which is patent nonsense. I have it on reliable authority that he got a hundred and twenty-five thousand for the Academy picture and he must have painted and sold four or five since.'

'Well, we know how to deal with *that*.'

'Enrichment.'

'Precisely.'

The procedure which had been devised to cope with a person who claimed to have little or no income was simple. His style of life was examined and an estimate was made of the sort of income which would be necessary to sustain it. He was then assessed to tax on that amount. If he appealed, so much the better. The matter was now out in the open. The court would probably increase the levy.

'We know,' said Jimpson, 'that he maintains two households. The little studio on the river which he owns outright. And a flat which he leases for the Italian woman and two children. All in all it can't cost him less than forty thousand a year. Probably more. But we can use that for a start.'

'Right,' said Schwan. 'We'll collate the figures and institute the relevant procedure.'

Unconscious of the fact that one of his clients was attracting the attentions of the mafia, the Police *and* the Inland Revenue, Mr Piggin, the managing clerk of Fearne & Bracknell, was working happily in his sunlit office. He was engaged in constructing a crossword puzzle, so large and so abstruse that it seemed unlikely that anyone would ever complete it.

He heard the ring of the bell, and shouted out 'Mick.'

This produced Michael Donovan from a back room, a tall, thin boy whom Mr Piggin had installed to run errands and look after such important matters as the purchase of stamps, tea, milk and sugar. He had spent the first week of his employment concluding that he could not swindle Mr Piggin and since then had behaved beautifully.

'See who it is,' said Mr Piggin as the bell rang again. 'Tell them none of the partners is in.'

When Mick came back he was looking excited. This was unusual, since he modelled himself on Mr Piggin who never looked excited. He said, 'It's a box. A n'iron box. A chest, sort of.'

Mr Piggin abandoned his puzzle unwillingly and went to the

front door. In the street outside was a flat cart, drawn by a resigned-looking pony. On the cart, in solitary splendour, visible to a crowd of onlookers, was the chest.

'All right,' said Mr Piggin. 'If it's for us better bring it in.'

'Take two people,' said the driver.

'Give him a hand, Mick.'

It was as heavy as it looked. Attaching themselves to the handles on each side, the driver and Mick dragged the chest off the cart and carried it into the front office where two girls suspended their typing to stare at it.

'Anything to pay?' demanded Mr Piggin.

The driver said there was nothing to pay, but he had a letter for Mr Fearne.

Mr Piggin took the letter, the cart departed, typing was resumed and the onlookers drifted off.

Francis Fearne and Bob Bracknell arrived back at the office that evening within minutes of each other and Fearne found his partner examining the chest, with Mr Piggin in attendance.

'Fine piece of iron-work,' said Fearne. 'Might be medieval. Valuable I expect.'

'What are we supposed to do with it?'

'The letter may tell us,' said Mr Piggin.

There was silence while Fearne read it. Then he said, 'Good God!' and read it again. 'It's from Raeburn Bentley. Listen to this. "I'm sending this chest to you for safe-keeping. This letter authorizes you to deal with it and its contents on my behalf in whatever way you consider most beneficial to me, my two children, Meta and Frederico, and their mother, Antonia. One word of warning: When you do decide to open it, do so with *great* care".'

'And that's all?' said Bracknell.

'Raeburn was never a man to waste words.'

'You knew him well?'

'He was my father's client. I took him over when Dad died. Whilst he was in Italy there was nothing much to do. Since he came back, my main efforts have been to persuade the Revenue that he's not subject to British tax.'

'Five years. You'll have had your work cut out. Our tax people don't give up easily.'

'They're hard on his heels. But Raeburn was always remarkably light on his feet. An exceptional man. Blessed with that perfect co-ordination between hand and eye that makes him such a fine painter. Particularly as a portraitist. His eye can pick out, in a flash, the essentials of a face and his fingers can transfer it to the canvas. Incidentally, it made him, in his youth, a superb player of court games like tennis and racquets. He was also a fine target shot.'

'An all-round man.'

'Indeed,' said Mr Fearne, 'but whether a good all-round man, or a bad all-round man, I was never quite able to decide. Well, it's been a long day. I'm for home, supper and bed.'

Mr Piggin was normally first at the office and on this occasion he arrived shortly after half past seven. He only defeated Mayburgh by five minutes. The chief inspector apologized for calling so early, but explained that he, himself, had been up for most of the night. Had Mr Piggin noticed the fire?

Mr Piggin said, sourly, that he had been nearly run over by a fire tender swinging round a corner at speed. 'I could have forgiven him, if he was hurrying to a fire, but I imagine that by that time he was on his way home. How can we help you?'

'Bad news, I'm afraid. One of your clients, a Mr Bentley—'

'Raeburn Bentley.'

'That was the name. The fire was at his place. His bedroom was over his studio. Quite a small building on Thameside.'

'And that was what was burned last night?'

'Its owner, too, I'm afraid. The fire people found him – what was left of him – in his bed. They were far from satisfied that the fire was accidental and sent for us at once.'

'What made them suspicious?'

'For a start, the smell of petrol. The bed Bentley was in – indeed, the whole room – seemed to have been soaked in it. Happily the wind was blowing off the river and the front part of the building, mainly a ground floor office, was preserved. It was when we were going through such papers as had survived that we came on a number of letters from your Mr Fearne—'

'And here he is,' said Mr Piggin thankfully.

He retired to his own room. Not having known Raeburn Bentley well he was not unduly upset by the news of his death. What was exercising his mind was the question of what they ought to do about the chest which had been so fortuitously deposited on them the day before its owner's death. Or was it fortuitous? Were the two matters somehow connected? He was still wondering about this when Mr Fearne came in.

He said, 'The inspector was quite civil for once. He seems to have heard about that box. I wonder how.'

'I know how,' said Mr Piggin. 'The people who saw it arrive will have been gossiping and Mick will have told all his friends, who will have told all their friends. I'm only surprised the *Herald* hasn't been onto us.'

His surprise was premature, but only by a few hours. One of their first visitors that afternoon was Bertie Dillon, star reporter of the *Southwark Herald*. Dillon, who knew Mr Piggin, approached him cautiously.

He said, 'I'd like to do a piece on it, if it wouldn't embarrass you.'

'Since half London knows about it already, I can't see that it'd do much harm.'

'I thought of referring to it as a mysterious coffer.'

'Coffer,' said Mr Piggin thoughtfully. 'Isn't that a little limiting? Coffer suggests money. Now if you call it a box, or, better still, a chest, it might contain anything from a dead girl to a sack of rubies.'

Bertie accepted the correction gratefully.

On the following morning Mr Piggin brought Antonia Bentley into Tara Fearne's room. He said, 'Mrs Bentley wants to talk to someone, and I'm sure she'd prefer that someone to be you.'

It was one of the moments when he was glad that Fearne & Bracknell had a female partner.

Tara saw a little lady, perhaps in her late thirties, who looked like the sort of flower you might find in a hedgerow without being quite certain what sort it was. She was wearing a black band round the right arm of a spring-like dress.

Tara said, 'I am afraid my Italian is only schoolgirl standard. Perhaps we could talk in English.'

'English. Yes. I have been learned it well. For instance I know that if I say something I should not say, which I often do, then I should start by saying, "Parm me". Is that not so?'

'Quite correct.' Tara was finding it difficult to open the matters she wanted to establish. She said, 'You have come to see us about Mr Bentley. You were his' – how on earth should she put it? Girlfriend – ladyfriend – both impossible. She compromised. 'You were his friend?'

'I was not Ray's friend. We were living in Sinne.' She awarded the last word a capital letter and pronounced it with evident pleasure. 'That is what you say, is it not?'

'I shouldn't say it myself. Because I don't think there's any sin involved. If I had to be formal I should refer to you as Mr Bentley's common law wife.'

'Common ... law. I don't like that at all. I prefer Sinne. But let us, by all means, be correct. I will tell you that Ray asked me, many times, to marry him. I said "No". If we are married we shall always be quarrelling. Sinne is better. Then we are comfortable.'

The ice once broken Tara soon extracted the facts she wanted.

'Twenty-seven Blenheim Mansions. That would be the flat Ray took for you and the children?'

'For Meta and Freddo, yes; you shall meet them. You will like them, I think.'

'I'm sure I shall. Now, what about money?'

'For the present, I have no need of money. Ray placed five hundred pounds into my account in the bank. He did so three days ago.'

For a moment, the thought that Ray had been alive three days ago and was now no more, seemed likely to be too much for her and her face started to crumple. Then, with an effort, she pulled herself together.

'If I want more, I can come to you?'

'Of course.'

'But if I come, I would like to talk to you and not to the terrible Mr Fearne.'

'Is that what Ray called him?'

'He called him many things,' said Antonia, and started to laugh.

This made Tara laugh too. After that they got on well.

When she reported all this to her father she said, 'I can understand Raeburn falling in love with her. She has everything that would appeal to an artist. Colour, shape and spirit. When she has spent the five hundred pounds Raeburn left in her account, shall we be able to help her?'

'I have got what amounts to a power of attorney. I expect we shall be able to find a way.'

Meanwhile Mayburgh and Flower were studying the pathologist's report.

'Not that the fire left much for him to report on,' said Mayburgh. 'I see he concluded that the intruder surprised Bentley in bed, probably knocked him unconscious where he lay, soaked him and his bed and the floor round it with petrol, and set fire to it.'

'Typical mafia savagery,' agreed Flower. 'Does he give us anything on identification?'

'Not a lot. He goes into some detail about what was left of the teeth. A number of stumps and some places where the heat had melted a metal crown. If we could see his dental record.'

'From Italy. Would there be one?'

'They do have dentists in Italy. I suppose we could make enquiries through diplomatic channels.'

Weed-grown, sluggish channels, thought Flower.

'Then there's this bit about the leg bones. These pathologists have got some clever formula for calculating the height of a corpse by measuring the arm and leg bones. The legs were saved to some extent by being wedged under the bedclothes. He estimates a height of five foot ten inches.'

'About right,' said Flower. 'I remember standing behind Bentley in a crowd at the Academy and I'd have put him as two inches shorter than me.'

Flower was a gangling six footer.

'There's a note about a rib being cracked. Could have been by a revolver bullet.'

'Why should he shoot him lying in bed?'

'Could be lots of other ways for a rib getting cracked,' agreed Flower. 'Are we going to let his solicitors have a copy of this report?'

'If that fellow Fearne' – Mayburgh did not say *fellow* but used a word starting with the same letter – 'would take a step out of his way to help us, instead of doing everything possible to obstruct us, I might consider doing so.'

On the morning that this conversation took place, Mr Schwan arrived. He had telephoned for an appointment and Fearne had agreed, reluctantly, to see him. It appeared that he, too, had heard about the chest, though he did not refer to it directly.

He said, 'I understand that Mr Raeburn Bentley was your client.'

'We acted for him,' agreed Fearne. He was in one of his most unhelpful moods.

'Then it is in order for me to inform you that, immediately prior to his unhappy decease, the Revenue had a claim prepared for understatement of income during the last four completed tax years.'

'A claim which you cannot now proceed with.'

'Not against him. No. The claim now lies against his estate. For which, also, I imagine, you act.'

'Perhaps you will explain exactly what you mean by "his estate".'

'I mean, of course, his executor. If he left a will.'

'I know of none.'

'Then, of course, there will have to be letters of administration.'

'That is a matter for his family and the Probate Court. It is nothing to do with me at all.'

This was clearly a signal of dismissal and Mr Schwan rose to his feet. Then, summoning up a smile which was so clearly false that it hardly rose from his mouth to his eyes, he said, 'I am right, am I not, that you were a close friend.'

'No. His closest friends, recently, were all Italians.'

'I meant, of course, his closest English friend. Or so I gather from something I read in the papers.'

'If you are referring to the chest he deposited here, it should not be regarded as anything out of the way. Clients often deposit articles with their solicitors.'

'Of course,' said Mr Schwan. 'Of course.'

The next thing to arrive was a letter from Messrs Chatterway & Duxford, Solicitors, of Cannon Street, E.C. Its opening paragraph expressed the horror and regret – presumably of both Mr

Chatterway and Mr Duxford – on hearing of the tragic circumstances surrounding the untimely decease of the celebrated artist, Raeburn Bentley.

Then it got down to business.

We are instructed by Mr Desmond Bentley who is, we understand, the next of kin and the nearest surviving relative of the deceased. Since you had been acting for the deceased, our client has been in daily expectation of hearing from you. We appreciate that the suddenness and unexpectedness of the tragedy will have left you with many points to attend to, but we feel that some formal matters will now have to be disposed of. We refer to the probate of Mr Bentley's will. If it exists, we have no doubt that it is in your safe-keeping. If Mr Bentley died intestate, then our client would be the natural person to take out letters of administration.

One further point: we do feel that a careful inventory should be made of the deceased's effects. Much will have been destroyed by the fire at his house, but a man of his standing must have had assets of all sorts.

'So *they've* been reading about the chest,' said Mr Fearne when Mr Schwan had departed. He had had it moved into his own office, where it stood in the corner, covered by a brightly coloured blanket. 'The first thing is to make sure of this next-of-kin business. Could you slip round to Blenheim Mansions, Tara, and have a word with Mrs Bentley. She won't herself have any claim in intestacy, but I've no doubt she knows all about the family.'

On her return Tara was able to produce the necessary details. Raeburn's father and mother were dead and Desmond was the only son of his only brother, Brian Bentley. Brian, who had practised as a stock-jobber, had died of heart failure when his main client lost all his money in Lloyd's.

Robert Bracknell, who had wandered in when Tara was report-ing – in that firm the partners spent as much time in each other's rooms as in their own – said, 'I only met Desmond once, but he seemed to me to be a vintage example of a four-letter man.'

'In any event,' said Fearne, 'we're not going to be hustled into making lists of assets for him. Why should we?'

It was, possibly, a coincidence that he should have been eyeing the chest as he said this.

That same morning Mr Piggin emerged from the street door of the Fearne & Bracknell office and stepped out into the small square which also housed the offices of Ridolfi Brothers (General Agents), the Roaring Forties public house and two or three tall buildings, once the houses of City merchants, but now divided and subdivided into flatlets and single rooms.

The recessed doorway of one of these was immediately across the square from Fearne & Bracknell and Mr Piggin, after inspect-ing it, stepped in and accosted the man who was standing there.

He said, 'Surely they could have provided you with a chair.'

The man said, 'Whaddyer talking about?'

'I'm talking about you. You were here yesterday and have been here since ten o'clock this morning. Bad for your ankles, all this standing about. I've no idea why you're watching our office—'

''Oo said I was watching your office?'

Mr Piggin ignored this. He spoke briskly, as one who had not a lot of time to waste. He said, 'Your name is Gibbons – correct me if I'm wrong. You are one of the junior employees of Smedley & Co, private detectives. Captain Smedley is a very old friend of mine and when I tell him that you've got such a limited idea of how to carry on observation that you're in danger of becoming a nuisance, he'll be very upset about it, and I think you'll be look-ing for another job.'

'I'm not upsetting anyone,' said the man, but he sounded upset himself.

'Not yet,' said Mr Piggin. 'But if you become a permanent fixture in the square, people will start wondering what you're up to. And if they see that you are watching our premises, they might start wondering what *we* are up to. So might I make a suggestion? Go back to headquarters, explain the position to Captain Smedley – you can mention my name, Piggin – and tell him from me that there's an empty room in the next door building which you could have for a modest weekly rental. You'll be no bother to anyone there and much more comfortable.'

The man had nothing to say to this. After trying, unsuccessfully, to outstare Mr Piggin he swung round and shuffled off.

As was his custom, when important decisions were called for, Mr Fearne summoned his three partners and Mr Piggin to a conference.

He said, 'This Raeburn Bentley affair seems to be coming to some sort of climax. At least, I deduce as much from the fact that somebody has thought it worth paying money to have this office watched.'

'Chatterway & Duxford,' suggested Hugo.

'Possibly. But it would be so entirely unprofessional that I doubt it. It could be their client, Desmond Bentley.'

'More than capable of it,' said Bob Bracknell. 'I hear he's been asked to resign from his club. Something about dubious tactics at the bridge table.'

'But there are other possibilities. It's a curious fact that ever since we acquired that – thing,' – he glanced at the blanket-covered object in the corner – 'we seem to have become a focus of interest for a number of different parties. The police are the most straightforward. They think that Raeburn, fearing the worst, put some documents into it which would indicate the name of his killer. It might even contain specific evidence which would enable them to prevent the killer leaving the country, or would justify asking for extradition if he had got back to Italy.'

'I don't think the police could force us to open the chest if we didn't want to,' said Hugo. 'But you mentioned other parties.'

'Two at least. And they are thinking on the same lines. They are both sure that this box is crammed with money.'

'They have some reason for thinking so,' said Mr Piggin. 'I've been making enquiries in the City and it does seem that, for some months, Raeburn has been liquidating his assets.'

'The Inland Revenue. Basing themselves on a highly fictitious income of forty thousand a year for five years and assuming a tax rate of fifty per cent have raised an assessment of a hundred thousand. It is clearly very much in their interest to find a fund of ready money to discharge this liability.'

Hugo said, 'The other party I take it is Desmond.'

'Certainly. If he makes good his claim to his uncle's estate it is comforting for him to suppose that it consists of ample and easily realizable funds.'

'In short,' said Bracknell, 'all of them want you to open the chest.'

'Bearing in mind,' said Hugo, 'the suggestion that it might be dangerous to do so. Some sort of explosive device, do you think?'

'Possibly,' said Fearne. 'But it doesn't worry me, because I've no intention of opening it. Unless they can think of some way of forcing me to do so, I'm in favour of a policy of masterly inactivity.'

His four listeners considered the point. They were all trained lawyers. It was not easy to see what any of their opponents could do in the face of Fabian tactics.

'A necessary first step,' said Mr Piggin, 'would be to apply to the court to presume Mr Bentley's death. But that is a Chancery proceeding.'

'However,' said Fearne, 'there is one matter in which we can, and I think should, assume the offensive. The insurers are contesting the claim which I have put forward on behalf of the estate. This is in the sum of nine hundred thousand based on the value of the house and of six paintings which were in the studio. Mrs Bentley has supplied us with a list.'

'Are they really fighting,' said Hugo, 'or just being awkward?'

'Their refusal seems to be based on the supposition that Raeburn committed suicide, driven to it by the mafia threat. And that he set fire to the house himself. Not a very plausible defence. I have a feeling that if we stick to our guns they will pay up, or compromise.'

'Of course we must stick to our guns,' said Tara, speaking for the first time. 'Insurance companies are bullies. If the insured is a small man, they hope that he'll be too poor or too scared to litigate and will run away.'

'Not in this case,' said Mr Fearne. 'I assure you.'

'It's a bloody scandal,' said Desmond Bentley, 'a flaming bloody disgrace. There's that old bastard, Fearne, sitting like a dog in the manger on a heap of stuff and snarling when anyone comes near it. There *must* be something we can do.'

He was addressing Aubrey Duxford, the senior partner in the firm of Chatterway & Duxford. The only other person present was their most recent acquisition, a clever lad called Samuel Bax. So far he had offered no contribution to the discussion. Most of the talking had been done by Desmond.

'What we've got to do,' he said, 'is to get old Fearne in front of the court. When the judge starts asking him awkward questions, he'll have to answer up, won't he? Isn't there something called contempt of court? I was reading the other day of a case where a man refused to answer up and he was sent down for six months.'

He was clearly delighted at the thought of Mr Fearne chipping stone in a quarry.

'The difficulty,' said Duxford, 'is that to get someone into court, you have to commence an action of some sort against him. And I can't see how any action can be begun until we have obtained a legal presumption of Raeburn's death.'

133

'For God's sake,' said Desmond, who was fast losing his last vestiges of self-control. 'Surely the dumbest lawyer would agree that when a man's burnt to death he ceases to exist. Where do they think Raeburn is now? Flying round somewhere with a harp in his hand and a halo round his head? Though if half the stories of what he got up to in Italy are true he's more likely to be sizzling down below.'

'We did consider the possibility,' – Mr Duxford looked at Bax, who gave a fractional nod of the head – 'of saving time by instituting a form of double action. It would begin with an application before a Master in the Chancery Division to presume death. But we could join it with a further application. In the event of no will being produced, we would ask for an order recognizing you as the proper person to take out letters of administration.'

'And how long would this rigmarole take?'

'Chancery proceedings are never speedy. If we were lucky, we might get our order in six months.'

Mr Duxford feared for a moment that Desmond was going to have a fit. His face was scarlet and he seemed to be having difficulty in breathing. Then he managed a single tortured breath and said, 'You may not be aware of this, but I have been having that office watched. And it has been reported to me that that bitch Mr Bentley picked up in Italy has been round there three times – three times – in the last fortnight. And it doesn't need much guessing what she went there for. And got. A hand-out from the money in that chest. In other words, whilst we've been sitting round doing Sweet Fanny Adams, money that should be coming to me, has been dribbling out of the estate like water out of a leaking tap.'

'If I might,' said Bax gently.

The interruption brought two heads round towards him.

'As I understand the problem,' he said, 'what is wanted is some speedy action to bring this deplorable state of affairs into the open.'

Both listeners nodded.

'What I am going to suggest may sound unusual, but I believe, from what I have heard, that you would have the backing of both the Metropolitan Police and the Inland Revenue, which must add weight to your contentions.'

As he outlined his idea Mr Duxford had the look of a man who is doubtful, but is prepared to be won round. Desmond was, quite simply, delighted.

Whilst their opponents were planning their next move, the partners of Fearne & Bracknell were quietly carrying on their practice and dealing with a wide variety of matters; a variety which arose from the location of their office, on the borderline between the City and the East End. 'On one side,' Fearne used to say, 'legal crooks; on the other, simple crooks.' He much preferred the simple variety.

Tara found herself devoting an unusual amount of her time to Antonia Bentley, of whom she had become very fond. As for Mr Piggin, he seemed to be occupying such leisure as he had, in a search through old files.

Solicitors are unwilling to throw anything away, and the storage of old files presents a permanent headache. When there was no more room for them in the office they had purchased an unused drill hall, equipped it with shelves and loaded the shelves with forgotten matters. Among them Mr Piggin browsed happily, evening after evening.

He had now delved back to the time of Mr Fearne's father and had unearthed a number of facts about the young Raeburn, then at the outset of his painting career. One yellowing letter of thirty years ago had interested him so much that it took him on a visit to Southend-on-Sea. He was there when a letter arrived at their office which was so important that it was delivered by hand.

It was from the Law Society's headquarters in Chancery Lane. It came quickly to the point.

A complaint has been lodged with us which alleges that, in the case of R. Bentley deceased you have so conducted yourself as to obstruct the normal process of law. In particular that, although it was clearly open to you to do so, you have not, in the two months intervening since the death of the above deceased, made any approach to the court to presume death and that you have ignored a number of letters from the complainant, Mr Desmond Bentley, the nephew of the deceased, requesting you to assist him in the taking out of letters of administration and in listing the assets of the estate. You are invited to give such explanations as you wish to the Disciplinary Committee sitting at 34 Carey Street at 10.00am on 2 November.

By the time Mr Piggin returned from Southend, the partners had discussed this bombshell in all its aspects.

'It's not a bomb,' said Robert Bracknell, 'it's a torpedo. An underwater, underhand, unjustified attack.'

'I don't know,' said Mr Fearne. 'I suppose we *have* been a bit dilatory, but all the same . . . .'

When Mr Piggin was shown the letter, he said, 'One thing's clear, we must get a copy of that pathologist's report.'

'In the light of this development the police can hardly refuse it,' said Fearne. And, in fact, on the following afternoon several copies arrived with Inspector Flower's compliments. Mr Piggin studied the one that had been handed to him with great care, and underlined two sentences in it.

The Disciplinary Committee of the Law Society is both a statutory body and a domestic tribunal, which writes its own rules and follows its own, often informal, procedures.

On this occasion an unusually powerful trio had been summoned, to deal with what was clearly an unusual charge. It was headed by Mr Charles Grey QC, supported by two well-known City solicitors, Mr Archibald and Mr Lyon-King.

One result of informality was speed. Cases rarely took more than a few hours. On this occasion Mr Grey had presented Desmond's complaint – very fairly Fearne considered – and various statements in support of it had been read before the lunch break.

When the tribunal reassembled Mr Fearne was invited to address it.

He said, 'I am well aware, sir, having served here on one occasion myself, that it constitutes an unhappy and unproductive interference with the work of a lawyer as busy as, I am sure, all you gentlemen are.'

He distributed a polite smile round the table.

'I will therefore be brief. First, I should wish this report by Dr Vinelott, the county pathologist, to be accepted as it stands. I can call the doctor to prove it formally if you wish.'

Having collected nods from his confrères, Mr Grey said, 'You may proceed on that assumption.'

Fearne said, 'Then I invite you particularly to consider the study of the leg bones – final paragraph on page two – and the dental details – second paragraph on page four. After which I will, if I may, call my only witness.'

There was an interval while the tribunal looked at the report. Mr Piggin was pleased to observe Mr Lyon-King underlining the same sentences that he had himself picked out.

The chairman said, 'We are ready for your witness, Mr Fearne.'

The witness was an elderly man, bald, but showing few other signs of age. He perched sedately on the chair offered to him. Fearne said, 'To start with some matters of record, which will not be in dispute. Your name is Patrick McClellan. You are a qualified dental surgeon and were in practice in Southend for forty-five years.'

'Quite so.'

'One of your earliest patients was the artist, Raeburn Bentley.'

'The celebrated artist,' amended the witness.

'Oh, certainly. Since that time he has become very well known indeed. I have taken the liberty of photocopying that section of your notes which you kindly entrusted to me. They are notes you made, at the time, in the course of your practice?'

'Certainly. Copies of them had to be available to the District Dental Committee. You will observe the signature of their secretary in the margin.'

'Thank you. But before going further into the matters dealt with in these notes I would like to clarify one important point. Did you attend to Mr Bentley at any time *after* his return from Italy?'

'There was no reason for me to do so. But I did, in fact, see him once. I had, by that time retired, but he asked me to attend to a small adjustment of the plate which I had inserted after that major operation more than twenty years before. As an old friend, of course, I agreed.'

During this exchange the tribunal had been trying to do two things at once: to listen to what was being said and to decipher the page of handwriting which had been placed in front of them. The writing was not as bad as the average doctor's, but needed care.

'And what you describe as a major operation is the matter referred to in these notes, is it not? Perhaps a word of explanation'

The tribunal nodded gratefully.

Mr McClellan said, 'When I originally examined Mr Bentley I found, as you will see, that he was suffering from advanced and serious pyorrhoea – or, to use a lay expression, gum rot. It should have been attended to much earlier, but' – this with a dry smile – 'like many people he deferred his visit until the pain had become intolerable. I saw at once that it would be necessary to remove all his teeth and, after treating his gums with an injection to accelerate the hardening process, I fitted him with a complete set of false teeth. Successfully, I think, since they only had to be adjusted twice. Once in Italy and once, as I mentioned, after his return here.'

The tribunal, whose eyes were flicking between the pathologist's report and the dentist's notes, were beginning to understand what they were being told.

Mr Grey said, 'Has the witness seen the pathologist's report?'

'Yes, sir.'

'Then I will ask him one question which may resolve a number of our difficulties. I take it that you are certain, sir, that the body referred to in that report was *not* that of Raeburn Bentley.'

'Oh, quite certain. The reference to roots of some teeth and other teeth whose capping had been melted by the fire, makes it impossible to suppose that the same man was the subject of both reports.'

'And that,' said Fearne, 'was that.'

Bob Bracknell said, 'I understand that the chairman actually congratulated you on resisting an application to the court which might have resulted in an embarrassing series of errors.'

'Indeed. He was so grateful that he even invited me to explain – although the matter was not really in front of them – what I thought had happened. In measuring the leg bones the pathologist made a comment the significance of which seems to have been overlooked. He said that one leg seemed to have been two inches shorter than the other. I was able to suggest, therefore, that the man found in the bed might have been Luciano the Limper. This led to the further suggestion, which the tribunal was able to accept provisionally, that Bentley had rolled out of bed without being seriously burnt and had knocked his assailant into it. He was, after all, a powerful and active man.'

Hugo said, 'Anyone who had seen him play racquets would certainly agree with that.'

Tara was not interested in racquets. She said, 'Surely there's something more important. The tribunal's conclusion disposes of Desmond. Wipes him right out. Excellent. But didn't it do something even better? It knocked out the main plank of the insurance company's defences – that Raeburn committed suicide. If the facts surmised by the tribunal are accepted, the insurers will have to pay up.'

'That aspect of the matter had not escaped me,' said Fearne.

The week that followed was a busy one for the partnership. The conclusion of the Disciplinary Committee left the insurance company with no real defence. However, having admitted the claim they proceeded, as usual, to haggle over the details, particularly about the value to be attributed to the lost paintings. Ultimately, in order to avoid a full-scale dispute with art experts on both sides, Fearne agreed to accept £750,000 against his claim of £900,000. Armed with this sum he had tackled Albert Schwan and Leslie Jimpson. Aware that the Revenue case was based on theory rather than fact they had been glad to accept a cash payment of £80,000 in discharge of all unpaid tax.

'Which leaves us,' said Fearne, 'with a very handsome balance that we can use to assist Mrs Bentley. A substantial interest-free loan perhaps. Tara, you have her address. You'd better call on her and explain the figures.'

When Tara returned it seemed there was a snag.

'She's gone,' she said. 'Pulled out, with the children, two days ago. Paid up the rent and anything else that was owing and vanished.'

'Is there no end to the complications of this matter,' groaned Bob Bracknell. 'Just when I thought we'd got it all straight.'

'This isn't a complication,' said Fearne. 'It's a signal that I've been waiting for. Now we can open the chest. In view of Raeburn's warning, I think I'll get Mr Hamlet to do it for us. He understands these things.'

The opening took place in the presence of all the partners and Mr Piggin. Michael Donovan, who attempted to insert himself, was summarily expelled.

Mr Hamlet had brought a quantity of apparatus with him in his van, including an outsize weighing machine. The chest was hoisted onto it and its weight was recorded.

Mr Hamlet's next move surprised them. Attaching an electric drill to one of the office power sockets he proceeded to make a hole, in the lid, and in each of the four sides. Then he had the chest turned over and drilled a hole in the bottom. After which he proceeded to measure the chest, minutely, in every direction.

He said, 'As you can see, this chest is a simple piece of work. Four sides, a base and a lid. If you look closely you can see there was a handle on the lid originally, which has been removed. The lid is now kept in place solely by its weight and the tightness of its fit. It will need a bit of rough work to get it open, but first I have to complete these calculations. Perhaps you would like to check them with me.'

The paper was covered with figures, which meant nothing to his audience.

'Before I came here I obtained a piece of this type of iron – known in the trade as second-milling-pig – and was able to calculate its size-weight ratio. By drilling these six plates to discover their thickness, and measuring them externally, I have been able to calculate the weight of each. Added together, with an allowance for the two side handles, they must clearly be equal to the weight of the chest.'

While the partners were staring, in total incomprehension, at the figures, Mr Hamlet had armed himself with a steel chisel. This he positioned at the edge of the lid and proceeded to give it a succession of powerful blows with a hammer.

His audience drew back.

'Don't be frightened,' said Mr Hamlet. 'If you have followed my calculations you will see that there is no possible cause for alarm. The two totals correspond so closely that one can only conclude' – he inserted a steel claw in the gap he had made, pressed on the end of it and raised the lid – 'that the chest is entirely empty.'

Hugo said, 'Well, if you understand it, I don't. I think you might explain it.'

'Compose yourself in patience,' said Mr Fearne. 'I am awaiting a letter. It must come quite soon.'

The letter arrived three days before Christmas. It had clearly passed through many hands and gave no clue as to the country it had come from.

My dear Francis, wrote Raeburn, in his beautiful artist's script. *I really was sorry for Luciano. He was on a hiding to nothing. I had more friends in London than he did. They kept an eye on him from the moment he arrived. He, naturally, made all preparations for a quick exit when he had done his job, and it was these preparations that themselves indicated the day, almost the hour, of his visit to me. He was totally ignorant of the sophisticated alarms which I had installed. They announced his approach, his entry into the house, his ascent of the stairs to my bedroom. I was using my favourite .22 target rifle with supercharged ammunition. I had only to fire once. The bullet must have entered his heart bag, been deflected by a rib and emerged from his back. Since he had brought ample supplies of petrol with him, I cremated him on the spot.*

So far, so good. But there were many other matters to be attended to.

Most of my money was on its way from my Swiss accounts – your Mr Piggin has details of them – to the country I had selected for my retirement, but there were still some arrangements to make there. More importantly I had to conclude my negotiations with the authorities of that country to persuade them to accept Antonia and the children. Money opens most doors, but it all took time.

Above all I wished to divert the British authorities, if they suspected that the body was not mine, from taking steps which might have shown them the truth. They could, for instance, have made a painstaking search of the ashes and discovered the .22 bullet. They could have monitored my Swiss accounts and, worse, could have kept a watch on Antonia, hoping she would lead them to me.

I did not wish them to take any of these steps.

When I played racquets, I found that if I could induce my opponent to take his eye off the ball I could probably defeat him. I therefore organized a diversion which would, I hoped, take the eyes of the police, the Revenue and my unspeakable nephew, Desmond, off what I was doing. In short, I presented them with an attractive alternative. A treasure hunt.

The chest was one I bought some years ago as a prop in a picture I was painting. I felt sure that if it was delivered to you, with maximum publicity, they would be round it like wasps round a jam jar.

I knew, too, that I would gain all the time I wanted. I knew that whatever pressure might be brought to bear on you, the most obstinate and obstructive solicitor in London, you would hold them off and give me the time I needed to tidy up the loose ends I mentioned above.

Please submit an appropriate bill and pay yourselves out of the money you hold before remitting the balance to Switzerland.

'Well,' said Hugo. 'Isn't that splendid? Everything tied up, *and* our bill paid.'

His father said, 'What are you looking so upset about, Francis? Is it the fact that the insurance company has been induced to pay a large sum of money under a misapprehension?'

'Certainly not,' said Fearne. 'They paid as a result of what *they* concluded had occurred. It wasn't for us to put forward an alternative version. Indeed, by instituting proceedings we gave them the opportunity of having the whole matter thrashed out in court. But they ran away.'

'Then what is bothering you?'

'It's the last sentence in Raeburn's letter. Would *you* describe me as obstinate and obstructive?'

'Certainly not. Never. The idea's absurd,' said his partners.

8

Halfway House

'But, my dear,' said Lady Fiennes, 'you can do both. Enjoy your Midsummer Ball, it sounds great fun, but remember the excellent example set us by Cinderella: leave the ball when midnight strikes. And drive straight down here.'

'What a super idea,' said Elizabeth Tallis. 'However good the party is, the last hour always seems to drag. Tell me once more how to get to your new place.'

'Simple. When you get out of London just follow the A5 past Teynham – head for Faversham. Fork left at Boughton-under-Blean. That gets you to the A290. Once you're across it, you'll find more than one signpost to Honey Hill.'

'How long ought I to allow? I don't want to keep you all up.'

'At that time of night, with very little traffic about, you should do it in an hour easily. And we none of us go to bed before one.'

'I'm already looking forward to it.'

'As you're shutting up your flat I imagine you're all packed up.'

'Surely. I've got all my things in the car. Originally I was planning to drive straight down to my brother's place in Devonshire.'

'You can go on there when you get tired of us. We're not a grand party. Mostly students from Kent University and army people from Chatham. We can offer you riding in Clowes Wood, and Colonel Calcott lets us use his big open-air pool.'

'Sounds lovely.'

'We'll aim to keep you happy for a fortnight at least.'

'A night drive in my new car with the hood open seems to me the perfect finish to a stuffy evening of eating and drinking.'

'Not too much drinking, love. The Kent Police are pretty hot on drink-driving.'

'Two glasses of champagne shall be my limit,' promised Elizabeth.

But somehow, as so often happens on these occasions, it became three glasses and a small liqueur brandy to keep the champagne in its place. No matter, she had a good head for drink and it was more the fresh air than the alcohol that made her sleepy and accounted for her uncertainty about the way.

The first part was easy. She knew her way out of London, across Blackheath and onto the A2. The trouble was that she could not remember whether her godmother had said that it was 'Before Faversham', or 'After Faversham', or even 'In Faversham' that she must look for a turning to Boughton. All she was certain about was that it was after Teynham.

Never mind. If she got it wrong she could always turn back. She had made good progress and there was a lot of the night still left.

When she took the first fork after Teynham she could feel the sea breeze on her face and knew that she was heading north.

After ten minutes' drive, with the breeze freshening all the time, she arrived at a point where the road forked. The full moon gave her a clear view of the signpost. Left fork, Connington; right fork Upton.

She had taken a quick look at the map before she set out, but neither of these names rang a bell. She decided that the right-hand fork was the more likely. Also, by taking further right-hand turns she could circle back ultimately to the main road. And anyway, when she reached Upton she could surely knock someone up and get directions.

The surface of the road had deteriorated into something not

much better than a track, but it was perfectly motorable, and the springs of the Milano were one of its best features.

As she bumped along she encountered a strange animal, about the size of a badger, with a tapering snout. It had emerged from the ditch, and was standing, gazing up at her car, curious, but seemingly unfrightened by this scarlet and black creature with its glaring eyes that had invaded his domain.

Swerving to avoid it and nearly going into the ditch herself, she continued, cautiously, on her way.

She seemed to remember her godmother telling her something about a nature reserve and smiled at the idea that she might encounter a giraffe or a hippopotamus on this midnight jaunt.

The next thing she noticed was not so amusing.

She had meant to fill up with petrol before she set out, but had let the matter slip and the gauge was now pointing unpleasantly close to zero.

She took a quick look round her.

On both sides stretched flat bare fields with very few bushes or trees on them, mostly clumps of rushes between potholes that threw back the light of the moon. A night on the marshes might be romantic, but the idea was not really attractive even to her adventurous spirit.

She had been driving for a full twenty minutes after the road fork. Surely it couldn't be far now to Upton.

Then, as the road swung to the left, she saw a light. Hurrah! A human habitation and someone still awake. And a further stroke of luck. The building was, as she saw when she drove up to it, a garage. Not a pretentious place. A single pump stood, like a lone sentinel, in the forecourt.

When she slid up alongside it and turned off her engine, the silence was almost complete. But there was a noise somewhere in the background, behind the squat building, which seemed to serve as both dwelling house and shop. There was an uncurtained living-room window on one side of the front door, a bulging casement on the other side through the dim panes of which she could see what looked like tins of fruit or sweets.

She pulled the bell and followed up with a sharp rat-tat on the knocker. Nothing happened. However, she could still hear the hopeful sound of activity, which seemed to be coming from the back of the building, so she followed the stone-flagged path until she could see that the light she had spotted came from a sizeable annexe. It was clearly some sort of workshop.

As she was wondering what to do next, the door of the annexe opened and a man came out.

The light being behind him she could not see him clearly. Not a dwarf, but a man of below average height. The proprietor, she supposed.

He listened in silence until Elizabeth had explained, with suitable apologies, how she had got there and what she wanted. When she had finished the man said, 'Taking a bit of a chance, weren't you? Coming out at night, with all that finery on.'

It was not spoken in a threatening way, but she felt that she would have been happier in broad daylight with a friend beside her.

Since the man seemed to expect an answer, she said, 'Yes. I suppose it was rather stupid of me.'

When clients came to consult him, Francis Fearne, the senior partner of Fearne & Bracknell, Solicitors of Little Bethel by the Tower, normally preferred to see them alone. But on this occasion his visitors were clearly important and, equally clearly, disturbed, and he thought he would ask his managing clerk, Horace Piggin, to sit in with him. Mr Piggin would not be expected to say much, but his sagacious face and venerable bearing had often proved comforting to the distressed.

Also, he would take careful notes and would be available for discussion and action afterwards. Of recent years Fearne had found himself shifting more and more work onto the shoulders of his clerk.

Mr Piggin did not complain. He enjoyed responsibility.

Lady Fiennes had come accompanied by her nephew, Martin Metcalfe, who appeared, from his flashes and shoulder titles, to be a captain in the Sixtieth.

'His colonel has given him compassionate leave,' she explained, 'so that he can help me.'

Fearne made a non-committal noise and wondered what precise help this upper-class pair might be looking for.

He was not kept long in doubt.

'It's my goddaughter, Elizabeth Tallis. Her father and mother were killed in that terrible car ferry accident. I expect you remember it.'

Fearne did remember it. A number of his clients had been on the ill-fated *Queen Wilhelmina*.

'You'll understand that I feel responsible for her. In fact, I have become a sort of proxy mother. Which makes it even more worrying when I tell you that she has disappeared.'

'Disappeared?'

'Absolutely and completely. She *and* her car. They have vanished off the face of the earth.'

'When did this happen?'

'More than a month ago.'

'Six weeks,' growled the captain.

'And the police haven't been able to do anything about it?'

'Oh yes. They did something. They put her name on the missing persons list. And informed Interpol.'

'Anything effective, I mean.'

Lady Fiennes said, 'You see, the trouble was they'd got hold of this ridiculous story—'

'Let's get this straight,' said the captain. 'It's not a story. That's the trouble. It's the truth. Eighteen months ago, when she was driving back to town, after a weekend at Honey Hill, she changed her mind. Suddenly, and unexpectedly. Turned back in her tracks and headed for Dover. Found a car ferry waiting. Went aboard with her car. Arrived at Calais and drove south.'

'Did she explain?'

'The only explanation she ever gave was that she suddenly had a feeling that her luck was in and she wanted to gamble.'

'And she told no one?'

'On that occasion she did condescend to telephone her godmother, from Monaco.'

The way in which he said this demonstrated his disapproval of Elizabeth's whims and fancies.

'And was she? Was she successful, I mean.'

'Inside a week she had lost most of the very considerable sum of money she always carried with her and was thinking about raising a loan. Which she could very easily have done, on the security of her diamond bracelets and her diamond choker. But as it happened, this wasn't necessary. On the sixth evening she placed all the money she had left on black. And when it came up she left her stake there. It came up six times running. After which, having doubled her stake each time she very wisely withdrew it.'

Fearne, who had been doing some mental arithmetic said, 'So she multiplied her original stake sixty-four times.'

'Correct. And it provoked a story in the local paper – "The Girl who Broke the Bank at Monte Carlo". Which was a complete exaggeration. Unfortunately the police got hold of the story. Immediate conclusion. Elizabeth had repeated her previous escapade. We should be certain to hear from her soon. Probably from somewhere in Europe.'

'I understand that,' said Fearne. He knew that speed with which an unsatisfactory file could sink to the bottom of the pending tray and get covered by more immediate and pressing matters. 'But there's one thing I'm not clear about. If the police of Britain and Europe have failed to locate her, just what do you think that a small firm of solicitors can do?'

Lady Fiennes said, in a voice that a thousand organizers of charitable events would have recognized, 'I know I'm being unreasonable, Mr Fearne, but I'm sure you can help. My sister, Mrs Metcalfe, told me how wonderful you were about her father's will—'

'What we're really suggesting,' said the captain, 'is that you get hold of a firm of private detectives – you'd know the best firms to go to – and put them onto the case.'

Fearne said, 'The only private detective I know personally is Captain Smedley, an ex-gunner.'

The captain nodded his approval of this. An infantry man, in difficulties, always turned to the artillery.

'But as for putting him on the right track, if I'm going to do that, I shall have to start with an assumption that you won't enjoy. Now that six weeks have gone by without a sign of your goddaughter or her car, we must suppose that either she managed to get abroad with it – or that she, and it, have been' – he paused for a moment – 'have been disposed of in this country. I must warn you that Smedley isn't cheap.'

'Money is no object,' said Lady Fiennes.

The captain said, 'If someone has harmed Elizabeth, let us catch the bastard and nail his hide to the barn door. Cost what it may.'

It seemed wise to let Smedley do his stint first. Having been paid a sizeable retainer he set his employees to work; personable young men, able to conduct house-to-house enquiries without upsetting the householders.

They worked their way along the two inland routes that the car might have taken.

North of the Downs from Rochester to Faversham and then, because they had been told to leave no stone unturned, south of the Downs from Aylesford, through Harrietsham to Challock. The two lines converged at the Boughton turning which led to

Blean and then to Lady Fiennes's house at Honey Hill.

It was the northern line that produced the most positive results.

Smedley reported that there was a reasonable body of evidence that the car, fortunately an uncommon make and of a vivid scarlet colour, had been seen on the A2 up to a point south of Teynham and a mile or two short of Faversham.

The results from Faversham itself were negative.

'Bearing in mind,' said the report, 'that it was a night of full moon and that Faversham is not a place where people retire particularly early to bed, this lack of observation becomes significant. It looks as though the car, *before* reaching Harrietsham, may have diverted into the area of marshland and small villages south of the River Swale.'

'That's where my boat may come in useful,' said Hugo. 'It's an interesting part of the world. And I'd been meaning, for some time, to see whether I could circumnavigate Sheppey. It wouldn't be possible under sail alone. The wind would be too fluky and some of those currents are pretty treacherous. But with an outboard motor—'

'Don't be too long about it,' said his father. 'We've got the Rumpole Estate sales this afternoon and the reinvestment of the proceeds to think about.'

'One full morning,' said Hugo. 'If I can't find something in that time I'll be ready to assume that she didn't come that way.'

Accordingly, on the following morning, he made a very early start and was round the Leysdown end of the Isle of Sheppey by midday.

He had taken his time, penetrating each navigable creek and inlet, encountering a number of semi-wild cattle, but no human beings of any sort. It had not occurred to him before how deserted the southern half of Sheppey was. The two-thirds of the island, south of the B2231, was a desolate area of field and swamp.

The maps named the right-hand end of it as the Isle of Harty and the left-hand end as Elmley Island, but these were courtesy titles for two pieces of wasteland divided from the rest by larger dykes or ditches.

Afterwards, discussing events with his father, Hugo said, 'I've never liked or trusted that stretch of water. There's something uncanny about it. If the tide is making, as it was on this occasion, it should push the boat along easily enough. Hardly necessary to use the motor. But all the time one feels that there is some hostile force at work. Not the current of the Swale, which is being held up by the tide, but a lateral movement, from north to south, almost as though something was coming in under the surface.'

His father, having listened to this with interest, said, 'According to the great geologist, Christopherson, that is the sort of thing that happens when you have a stretch of land with a strong fresh current on one side of it and a weak one on the other. If the land in between is soft – sand or gravel – then you will get an open inlet which will, in time, wash the earth away entirely. Where, however, the intervening soil is clay, as here, the water can only penetrate by forming a pipe. Christopherson calls it a subterranean counter-flow.'

Hugo thought that something of this sort must be happening to him at that moment.

He found that at half speed and with the rudder hard over, he was being forced, do what he would, onto the southern bank.

When he gave a fretful jerk to the rudder he felt it go suddenly slack. His final effort had fractured the linkage. Out of control, the boat sidled in among the rushes and grounded on the clay.

Irritating, but in no way dangerous. He found, in fact, that he could step ashore without even getting his feet wet. What was really worrying him was a question of time.

He had planned to have finished his inspection of the coast line of Sheppey by midday. Then to run down to Whitstable, leave his boat with a friend and catch a bus along the A290 into

Canterbury, where he had a date with the manager of the National Provincial Bank at three o'clock.

Whether he could fulfil this programme was now questionable. However, it seemed that his luck was in. It was what he was hoping for, but had despaired of finding.

It was a stout, two-storey building, part dwelling house, part shop. Its name, painted in straggling letters on the fascia board, was Halfway House. It had a substantial annexe at the back. Someone was at work in it. He could hear the sound of metal on metal and the purring of an electric motor. Just the place to attend to his broken linkage.

His knocking on the door must have been drowned by the workshop noises, because it produced no reaction. He opened the door cautiously and peered inside.

Someone who had been attending to a lathe looked up, switched off the current and turned towards him; a man of rather under medium height, with broad shoulders, dressed in oil-stained denims.

Hugo was glad to see that he was smiling.

He said, 'George Lampe at your service. What can I do for you?'

Hugo explained what had happened and the sort of help he needed.

'Doesn't sound too difficult,' said Lampe. 'Let's walk down and have a look at it.' And when they had reached the boat and lifted the base boards, 'Yes. I could make a temporary attachment out of wire – triple wire. A bit of welding at each end. Should be strong enough to do the job. It won't be perfect. You'll need a blacksmith for that.'

'As long as it gets me out and back.'

'Out and back?'

'Down to Whitstable and back upriver as far as the Tower. That's where I hang out.'

'You've come a fair distance. Bold of you to come all this way

154

on your own. There are places round here where it pays to have another man with you. Tricky currents and no help at hand if you do hit trouble.'

'Right on both counts,' said Hugo. 'I asked for trouble and I hit it. I haven't seen a living soul since I turned the north-west corner of the island an hour ago.'

'Aye. It's a lonely place,' the man agreed. He had taken a steel rule from his pocket and was making some measurements.

'Right,' he said. 'I think that's all I need to see. If you'll come back with me while I cut and shape the attachment. Then the two of us should be able to push you off the bank and send you on your way.'

'I'm really very much obliged,' said Hugo. He might have added that he was also very much surprised to find a fully-equipped workshop in this desolation. He was watching Lampe twisting wire into a two-ended hook. His broad brown hands worked with professional certainty.

Thinking of this turned his mind to the question of payment.

When he stepped ashore he had brought two things with him: a bulging briefcase and a canvas satchel. Opening the briefcase he said, 'I'd like to pay you now, if I may, for your labour and materials.'

'A fiver will cover the lot,' said Lampe.

'I'm ashamed to do this,' said Roger. He was fumbling in the briefcase as he spoke. 'I'm afraid I look like one of those American multi-millionaires you see in films. You know the type. When they pay for anything they extract a great wad of dollar bills from their vest pocket and peel off two or three of them.'

Lampe, who had suspended operations to watch him, said, 'Do you always travel round with hundreds of pounds in your case?'

'Not hundreds. Thousands, I'm afraid. Yesterday afternoon we completed the sales of a number of plots on the Rumpole Estate. Normally we'd have expected a certified cheque, or a bank draft, but in this case the purchaser insisted on paying in cash. My father wasn't keen, but all the deeds had been signed and the cash was on the table.'

Lampe, who had finished what he was doing to the improvised hook, said, 'Why wasn't he keen? If I was offered the choice, cheque or cash, I'd take cash every time.'

'It's his experience that people who want to pay large sums in cash are usually operating some sort of tax fiddle.'

The idea seemed to amuse Lampe, who smiled as he gave the wires a final twist and tucked in a loose end, using the largest pair of pliers Hugo had ever seen.

'That should do the job,' he said. He moved to a cupboard in the corner and extracted two glasses and a bottle.

'Let's wet our whistles before we fix her up,' he said. He poured out a generous tot from the bottle. 'Good Scotch. Best drunk neat. But you can have a drop of water in it if you like.'

'Neat for me,' said Hugo valiantly.

'Down the hatch, then.'

Hugo had the glass actually raised to his lips when a thought occurred to him. He said, 'I'd better tell the office what I'm up to.'

Lampe, who seemed to be watching every move he made with unnerving closeness, saw him dip into the satchel and extract the mobile telephone that always accompanied him when he left the office. After listening for a moment, he said, 'Is that you, Piggy? I've run into a bit of trouble, but fortunately I've also run into a good Samaritan. What's that? No. I didn't say his name was Samaritan. It's Lampe. Spelt with an "E". That's right. Hangs out in a garage called, I think, Halfway House. It's between Connington and Upton. My steering fractured itself, but he's mended it a treat and I should be in time – just – to do the business at the bank. Perhaps you could give them a ring and tell them I might be a little late.'

As he replaced the receiver he said, 'What in the world?'

Lampe had taken his full glass to the sink, tipped the contents out and was washing it carefully under the cold tap. He said, 'It was a moth. Attracted by the light, no doubt. Decided to have a bathe in your drink. Filthy little beast.'

He returned to the cupboard, fiddled for a moment with the bottles and came back with two full glasses. Then he said, 'Good luck,' and raised his glass and drank.

Hugo echoed the sentiment.

His luck had, indeed, been good.

'So I just made it,' he said to the partners and Mr Piggin, assembled as was their custom, to open the post next morning. 'It was a close thing, but thanks to Mr Lampe I did it.' He explained, in some detail, what had happened to him.

But no one seemed greatly interested in Hugo's adventures. Coming in late to the meeting he had interrupted what Fearne was telling them. It was a great deal more exciting than anything that had happened to him.

'Thinking things over,' Fearne was saying, 'I came to the conclusion that although it was in order for us to pursue our own investigations, it was wiser to let the police know what we were up to. We didn't want to appear to be working behind their backs. So I called on Chief Inspector Mayburgh at Cable Street. And when I had finished passing on to him what Lady Fiennes and Captain Metcalfe had told us, do you know what he said?'

'Something pretty rude I imagine,' suggested Bob Bracknell, who knew the inspector.

'No. This time he wasn't offensive, but he was clearly interested. When he'd thought it over carefully he said, "I don't suppose you realize that Miss Tallis was number five on the list. Might be number six or seven for all we know".'

There was a moment of aghast silence. Then Bob said, 'Do you mean that five or more people have disappeared?'

'Yes. In the last eighteen months, all of them connected in some way with the north Kent area between London and Dover.'

He looked at the notes he had scribbled down while Mayburgh was talking.

'The first was an old darling called Marjorie Hartshorn, who lived near Canterbury. A touch eccentric, her family said, but not in any way certifiable. Although she was over seventy she insisted on driving herself everywhere, alone, and was known to keep a large sum of money in the car. Didn't trust banks, she said. Preferred to keep her money with her. She drove off one morning and could have ended up anywhere in England, Scotland or Wales. In fact, she had mentioned that she had a date with her solicitor in Lincoln's Inn, but it seems he saw nothing of her. The only other possibility is that she had a married daughter at Oare who she visited from time to time. Turning up without any prior warning.'

'Oare,' said Bob thoughtfully. 'Then she would have gone off the A2 at Faversham.'

'It's possible. The second one was Rudolf Neligmann.'

'The swindler?' said Mr Piggin.

'The alleged swindler. Since he never came to trial nothing was proved. When he drove off from London he took with him, according to his fellow directors, a lot of the firm's money. He was thought to be heading for France, or northern Europe.'

'If he was heading for France,' said Bob, 'it would be Folkestone, Dover or Newhaven. If for northern Europe, then it could be Sheerness.'

'Whichever way he was planning to go,' said Fearne, 'one thing is clear: neither he nor his car has been seen since.'

'But surely—' said Bob.

'We'll think of the difficulties when I've told you about the other cases. The third one was a little like Elizabeth Tallis. An independent-minded young lady called Joanne Terry. She had a flat in London that she'd disposed of, and a number of friends in the north Sheppey area where she was negotiating for a house. It might have been with the idea of putting down a cash deposit on the house that she was carrying the proceeds of the flat sale with her. In any event, she was traced as far as Teynham and then drove off the map.'

'Teynham,' murmured Mr Piggin, who was examining the map spread on the table in front of him.

'Number four,' said Fearne, 'is, in many ways, the most straightforward. Tom Trescot, owner and manager of Trescot Holidays. Had an office, garage and boatyard at Reculver. He liked to take a prospective client out, in his boat, to show him the best fishing and camping areas, and get him well hooked. On this occasion he was intending to pick up a Mr Cann at Queenborough. There was a storm in the offing and local weather prophets had advised him against setting out, but he thought he knew better. He had been originally intending, no doubt, to go north of Sheppey, but at some point, with the weather deteriorating, he must have changed his mind, because a fisherman saw him in the mouth of the Swale, heading west.'

'Running for shelter,' suggested Bob.

'I think that's right,' said Fearne. 'Anyway that's the last that was seen of Trescot or his boat.'

There was a long silence. All four of Fearne's listeners had been taking notes and Mr Piggin had been drawing quite an elaborate plan.

It was Tara Fearne, Francis Fearne's daughter, the youngest of the four partners, who broke the silence.

'When I was a girl at school,' she said.

'Not all that long ago,' said Bob.

Tara awarded him a brief smile, but was not to be diverted.

'When we had a mathematical problem we were always told to look for the LCD otherwise the lowest common denominator. If the four cases the inspector mentioned are all part of the same series – and I think that must be so, or he wouldn't have drawn our attention to them – then it follows that if we are to work out what happened to Elizabeth Tallis, the best way to start would be to work out what points the four earlier cases had in common.'

Hugo noted the look of approval of Mr Piggin's face. This was exactly the mathematical way in which he liked to approach a problem.

'The most persistent common factor,' said Fearne, 'is the shoulder of land south of the Island of Sheppey, between the Swale and the A2. An uninhabited area protected from development, and set aside as a nature reserve. Marjorie Hartshorn, if making for Oare, would be driving straight up into it. There's a tangle of roads north of Faversham. She could very easily have taken the wrong one. Rudolf Neligmann, heading for Sheerness and very possibly trying to escape observation by choosing minor roads, was making for the same area when last seen. Joanne Terry, also was heading for North Sheppey. Tom Trescot is the most interesting of the lot. He was last seen proceeding up the Swale, no doubt with the idea, in view of the bad weather, of by-passing the Chetney Marshes and reaching Queenborough from the south.'

'And I can assure you, from my own experience,' said Hugo, 'that the lateral current at that point would have landed him in that particular area whether he'd wanted to or not. It takes charge of you in the most uncanny way.'

Fearne said, 'All right. We have deduced to our own satisfaction, that these four people *could* quite well have been in that particular area at one time or another. But does that help us to decide what happened to Elizabeth Tallis? It's quite a sizeable piece of North Kent. It contains two villages, Connington and Upton, and a dozen or more isolated houses and farms.'

'With respect,' said Mr Piggin; there was something in his voice that brought all their heads round, 'are we not perhaps forgetting one point? Have we not six rather than five journeys to consider?'

'Six?' said Bob.

'Certainly. Allow me to outline journey number six. It has all the hallmarks of the other five. In it we have a young man entering the *locus in quo*, encountering a stranger and, in the course of conversation, disclosing two matters to him. First, that he has encountered no one for some time past so that no one knows exactly where he is and second, that he happens to be carrying a very large sum of ready money.'

'I suppose you're talking about Hugo,' said Fearne. 'And I must agree that there are similarities in his case. But is there not one important difference? Neither he nor his boat has disappeared.'

'That is indeed an important distinction,' agreed Mr Piggin. 'And its rationale seems to depend on what Sherlock Holmes might have described as "The Mystery of the Mythical Moth". I am referring, of course, to the moth that landed in your glass, Hugo, and prevented you from drinking the contents. Tell us. Did you, in fact, see it?'

'See what? The moth? No. I was too busy telephoning the office. I assumed it existed. Do you mean—'

'I mean,' said Mr Piggin, 'that it was exceedingly lucky that you did telephone. Once you had explained where you were and who you were with, you were in no further danger. But the drink had to be disposed of. Hence the opportune moth. And you say the glass was then rinsed. A pity. It would have been interesting to discover what was in it – apart from whisky.'

Mr Piggin had been speaking slowly and by this time the others were beginning to understand what he was suggesting.

'You may be right,' said Fearne. 'And if you are, the answers to all our questions could lie with Mr Lampe at Halfway House.'

'It's well situated,' said Bob, 'going from east to west, halfway between London and Dover. And halfway from south to north, between the A2 and the river.'

'And halfway,' said Mr Piggin softly, 'between life and death.'

There was a lot more thinking and talking to be done, and further enquiries to be made. It was three days later that Fearne reconvened the meeting.

He invited Mr Piggin to speak first.

He said, 'I had a word with an old friend of mine.' Mr Piggin seemed to have an astonishing number of old friends. 'He's the petrol and oil wholesaler for this district. He tells me that the total amount of his products that Mr Lampe buys and sells, in any quarter, could hardly generate enough profit, even if you add in fees for small services to the occasional customer, to pay his electric light bills. It was supposed that he must enjoy a private income and that he maintained the premises at Halfway House to give him an excuse to pursue his hobby of metal-working.'

'It's a wonderfully well-equipped workshop,' agreed Bob, who had called on Mr Lampe on some pretext and had been shown round. 'The sort of place a grown-up schoolboy could be happy pottering about in all day.'

'And if our suppositions are correct,' said Fearne, 'he did indeed have a private income. It came to him at irregular intervals, tax free, whenever someone, who was on their own, called at his isolated garage. The visitor had to fulfil a number of prerequisites before he could be ranked as what you might call a prospect. First, and most important, it had to transpire that no one knew precisely where he was. That he had, as you might say, wandered off the map. A common example would be a driver who had lost his way in the tangle of roads between the A2 and the coast. Another possibility was that the man had been forced onto the bank of the river by that underground current that Hugo has mentioned. He'd need help to push the boat off and would come inland to find it. The second, and equally important point was that the visitor was either carrying money or was, as in the case of Elizabeth Tallis, wearing valuable jewellery. If all these matters were in due order, the procedure could swing into action. The prospect is offered a drink. If he is a man, grateful for Lampe's help, he will probably accept it. If a girl, the chances are she may say "no" – but a girl could be dealt with by more straightforward means. After which – always bearing in mind that Lampe had no near neighbours – the wooden parts of the boat or car could be burned and the metal parts, cut into manageable chunks in his excellent workshop, could be sunk in the river, and rolled down by it, in time, to the North Sea.'

When he had finished there was a silence, broken only by the cries of a sea bird who appeared to be screaming in protest – 'No, no, no.'

Then Fearne said, 'I passed on the gist of that to Chief Inspector Mayburgh. He was interested, but not totally convinced. He made it clear that he could not move against Lampe without some concrete evidence.'

'Then it all depends on one point,' said Mr Piggin.

'On what?' said Bob.

'On what he did with the bodies.'

'Would he not have thrown them, also, into the river?'

'It's possible,' said Fearne, 'but I'm not convinced of it. A body is not inert, like a piece of metal. However securely it has been weighted, sooner or later it will wriggle out of its attachment and surface on a reef or a sandbank. No, I feel certain that Lampe, being a careful man, would have taken the safer option and buried them somewhere in the wide expanse of water-meadows available to him around his garage. He had all the time he needed and no inquisitive neighbours.'

'In that case,' said Hugo, 'why don't we call in the army? Captain Metcalfe would, I am sure, be only too willing to help us. And a number of his friends are sappers. They'd lend a hand. He mentioned that they've developed a detector – very useful when scanning a suspect minefield – it tells them if the soil has been disturbed.'

Captain Metcalfe needed no persuasion. It took him only three days to organize his team.

On the third night, whilst the rind of a moon peeped over the gaunt outline of Halfway House, and its owner slept, a number of men were at work. The breezes from the sea, blowing through the rushes, drowned any small sounds they made.

The first body they unearthed was Tim Trescot. The second was Joanne Terry.

Thereafter, with Lampe now in custody, the search could be extended to his workshop where an enthusiastic young detective extracted, from the teeth of a metal saw, minute fragments which could be microscopically identified as coming from the bodywork of a scarlet motor car.

This caused less excitement than the discovery of two more bodies. The second of them was Elizabeth Tallis.

Like the others she had been strangled.

9

Police Business

Fearne & Bracknell, Solicitors of Little Bethel, by the Tower of London, was a family firm and, like all the best families, it was a benevolent despotism.

The two senior partners, Francis Fearne and Robert Bracknell, conducted most of the routine business, but if an important question arose for decision it was dealt with on democratic lines. Fearne's daughter, Tara, Bracknell's son, Hugo, and their managing clerk, Mr Piggin, all had an equal vote.

The matter they faced that spring morning was important.

It had been introduced by Tara, who had put forward a new client for their consideration. This was Detective Inspector Quinn.

'A detective inspector,' said Bob Bracknell. 'I don't think we've ever acted for a policeman before.'

Tara said, 'Why do you speak of policemen as though they were a lower form of animal life?'

'You're exaggerating.'

'No I'm not. There was a distinct curl to your lips when you said, "detective inspector".'

'Stop quarrelling,' said Fearne. 'What Bob meant was that it's fatally easy for a firm of solicitors to acquire a reputation for being pro or anti-police. Both reputations can be equally harmful and equally difficult to throw off.'

He was examining a plan which showed the new arrangement of police authorities. Being, postally, E1 they had fallen into the southern half of what had recently been defined as No. 2 Area East.

This was served by three sub-stations – Cable Street, Leaman Street and the Isle of Dogs. The nearest and best known to them was Cable Street, which was within sight of their upper-storey windows.

This was the kingdom of Chief Inspector Mayburgh, who had once been described by Mr Piggin as an old-fashioned rhinoceros, who tried to arrive at the truth by butting it head first. He regarded solicitors as obstructive nuisances and was particularly suspicious of Fearne & Bracknell who, it seemed to him, interfered in matters which ought to be left to the police.

Leaman Street, on the other hand, had proved helpful in many ways. It had originally been occupied by the Water Guard, who controlled the barge and lighter traffic on the reaches between Surrey Docks and Lavender Pond. The Metropolitan Police had taken it over as a contact point with the River Police. When it had seemed that the current economy drive might result in its closure, it had been saved by that great thief-taker, Inspector Wensley.

'Close Leaman Street,' he said. 'A mad idea. It controls all the road traffic coming south into the docks and east to the Essex coast. It's the cork in the bottle. Take it out and the people who'll bless you are the folk who use the ships in those parts to carry off stolen goods – and wanted men – to the Continent.'

Wensley was already a man of mark and his words had been listened to.

So Leaman Street had not been closed. Rather it had been enlarged and its present incumbent, Chief Inspector Whyman, had been given peremptory orders by Area to seal the cracks through which a stream of illicit merchandise seemed to leak out to Belgium and Holland. He had scored a number of successes, though they had, on the whole, been against the smaller characters, the carriers. The man who was organizing the traffic seemed to stay tantalizingly out of his reach.

It was Whyman's second-in-command, Detective Inspector Quinn, who now sought the help of Fearne & Bracknell.

Tara said, 'It was Frank Quinn's wife, Melissa, who came to see me. She's been worried, for some time, about Frank. It's some special job he's been on. She couldn't tell me much about it, because he hasn't told her anything. Which is unusual. Before this he'd always been prepared to discuss his work with her. Recently he's been keeping his mouth tight shut. And it took a lot of persuading before he'd agree to consult us.'

Fearne looked round the table. He was not happy. He loathed the thought of dissension.

Before he could speak, Mr Piggin had cleared his throat in a way which meant that he had something important to contribute to the discussion.

'My knowledge of the law,' he opened with customary solemnity, 'is far from profound—'

'A good deal profounder than mine,' murmured Hugo.

'But it is true that I do, perhaps, keep my ear closer to the ground than any of you. And if I might summarize my feelings about Inspector Quinn, I'd say that he needs help and is worth helping.'

Tara looked at him gratefully.

'I think we should accept that view of the matter,' said Bob. 'I've never known Mr Piggin wrong in his evaluation of a person or a situation.'

'Very well,' said Fearne, glad that the matter had been taken out of his hands. 'If that's unanimous—'

Four heads were nodded.

'Then I'll see him tomorrow afternoon. I was going to suggest that he might speak more freely if I saw him alone, but I feel that it would be sensible to ask Mr Piggin to sit in with me.'

Three nods.

Fearne looked at his diary and said, 'Four o'clock, then.' And to Tara, 'Don't give him any promises. Just say we'll listen to what he has to tell us and will see if we can help him.'

At first sight Detective Inspector Quinn looked quite unlike the normal burly and self-confident policeman. He was tall and thin and, at the start, spoke hesitantly. However, when Fearne looked at him more closely he could see that he was not physically weak. Rather wiry and indestructible, like a wing forward who could go down on the ball and emerge unharmed from a pile of struggling bodies.

'Let me begin at the beginning,' he said.

'Please do,' said Fearne, 'most of my clients start halfway through their story.'

'Very well, then. I'm sure I don't need to tell you that a success-ful jewel thief is lucky if he can realize a tenth of the value of what he's stolen. The stuff is well known to the police and is on every pawnbroker's list. It will have to be broken up and disguised before he can hope to dispose of it. And that won't increase its value. But if he can export it to Belgium or Holland, and happens to be in touch with one of the big buyers, then he'll get a fair price.'

'And it's your idea that the men who steal the jewellery and the smugglers who carry it abroad are now working together?'

'Under common management, you might say. And I know who the head manager is.'

'Know? And can prove it?'

'Yes. It wasn't an easy job. But I think I could put my hand on his collar now.'

He laid his right hand on the desk. It was a working-man's hand. Rough and well muscled.

'I only began to get results when I realized that I'd been approaching the matter from the wrong end. As I sat in my office at Leaman Street and watched the stream of private cars and vans heading east up the Whitechapel Road, I used to think about the dozens – maybe hundreds – of men who would help the thieves—'

'Are we universally dishonest?'

'Not universally, perhaps. But I guess that half the farmers in Essex and most of the fishermen on the eastern seaboard are on the side of the smugglers, as they have been for centuries.'

'Difficult,' agreed Fearne. 'So—?'

'That was when I realized that I had to start at the other end. My holiday trips to Zeebrugge formed a useful cover for visits to Ghent. I managed to get in touch with one of the leading diamond merchants. He had suffered a good deal in his legitimate trade from this illicit competition and he was only too willing to help me put a stop to it. So he gave me such names as he knew of the operators at the English end. The skippers of boats who used the smaller Essex ports at Walton-on-the-Naze and Clacton and private docks and slipways in the mouth of the Colne river. Once I had these names I was able to work back to the man they were controlled by. A real professional at the top of an amateur network. A man called Samuels. Roper Samuels.'

Quinn had lost his initial hesitancy and his words were now starting to flow rapidly. Almost too rapidly for the articled clerk who was taking it down in shorthand.

'Hold your horses for a moment,' said Fearne, 'and tell me this. To what extent were your superior officers – Chief Inspector Whyman at your station and Superintendent Oliphant at Area – in the picture?'

'If you want the truth, I knew that I was onto something good and I didn't want to share the credit. When I had gathered everything up it would, of course, have gone up to Area. That would be the level at which action would be initiated.'

'But until you had it all neatly tied up and packaged you preferred to keep it to yourself. Right?'

'Yes.'

'But why? Your superiors would certainly have approved of what you were doing and could have helped you in a number of ways. Why did you prefer to conduct it as a private crusade?'

This produced a long pause.

Then Quinn said, with evident reluctance, 'I was afraid that if I let too many people in on my plans, they'd be leaked back to Samuels who would take steps to wriggle out of the net. We knew there was a leak, somewhere. What I'd failed to realize was that Samuels already knew what I was up to and had concluded that attack was the best form of defence. I realized this all right on the day I got back from Zeebrugge, when I was told to report to Superintendent Oliphant. He didn't waste any time over attempts to sugar the pill. Simply told me that I was to be suspended, pending the hearing by the court of the charges against me.'

'Slowly,' said Fearne. 'Take it slowly. What were the charges and who was preferring them?'

'The matter had been handed over to A.10. They had advised that on the evidence I should be charged with accepting money corruptly, in order to pervert the course of justice.'

'What evidence?'

'On the evidence of my own bank account and a statement made by a small-time crook called Stevens.'

'So. Then let's deal with the bank first, shall we?'

'My current account is with the National Provincial Bank, at their Limehouse branch. I had a standing arrangement that they were authorized to answer questions about this account, provided they came from the Receiver.'

'Good,' said Fearne. 'And sensible.'

'Well, I knew that if they wanted to look into my account they could always get an order from the court. I was simply saving them trouble.'

'And when they looked, what did they find?'

For the first time Quinn showed some evidence of the bitterness behind his self-control. He said, 'They found that on the day

I departed on holiday for Zeebrugge the sum of one thousand pounds had been paid into my account, in cash.'

'Who by?'

'According to A.10, by this man Stevens. And it's true that I'd been getting a certain amount of help from him. He'd been involved in that Hatton Garden jewel heist – the one where the private detective who was guarding the Dutch jewel merchant got badly knocked about. Stevens had taken no part in the actual robbery. He was driving one of the getaway cars. In a typical piece of carelessness he'd left an identifiable print – a single finger-print – on the car when it was abandoned. He was now, apparently, saying that he'd pay me a thousand if I'd fix things so that he was left out of the matter. Or if that wasn't possible, that his part in it was played right down.'

'Was that true?'

'Absolutely untrue. He'd made no approach to me of any sort. Even if he had there was nothing I could do to help him. The matter was being handled by the Central Robbery Squad. I only came into it because the getaway car had been abandoned in my manor and was under my care at that time.'

'So why did he make this statement?'

'You've got to realize that he's a poor creature, without back-bone or guts. His only accomplishment is that he can drive a car. Apart from that he's a worm.'

'And does what Samuels tells him.'

'Exactly. When the payment to me of a thousand came out – which it did with surprising speed – he was ordered, by Samuels, to make a clean breast of the whole matter. The worst that could happen to him was a minor penalty for his part in the heist and he was booked for that already. It would be mitigated by the fact that he'd helped the police in the past and was prepared to come clean with this statement now. His story was to be that he'd had a successful day at the races and thought he could use the money to buy, through me, police assistance and forgetfulness.'

'Yes,' said Fearne. 'I see. And how far have A.10 got with the charge?'

'It comes up before the Stepney Bench on Monday.'

'Doesn't give us much time. We may have to ask for an adjournment. Meanwhile, I suggest that you stay at home and keep quiet.'

When Quinn had departed, not greatly encouraged, Fearne turned to Mr Piggin.

'You told me that Quinn needed help and was worth helping. The first proposition is true. He surely does need help. It's the second one I'm doubtful about.'

'You realize,' said Mr Piggin, 'that if Quinn is found guilty, the evidence he has so carefully accumulated will be tainted. His work will be discredited and Samuels will, very likely, go free. Which will be a gross miscarriage of justice.'

'Provided that Quinn is telling us the truth.'

'I believe that he is. If it comes to a straight choice between him and Stevens – about whom the general view is that he is a poor-spirited sneak and a liar, who jumps in whatever direction Samuels tells him – then I know which of the two I should go for.'

Fearne thought about it. He appreciated the force of what Mr Piggin had said, but was still unhappy about it.

He said, 'The first thing to do will be to brief counsel. A junior for the police court. A leader for the higher court, if it goes that far. He'll need money. I suppose he could get legal aid.'

'It did occur to me to wonder whether he needed it. The opposition has paid him a thousand in an effort to discredit him. Why should he not use it for his defence?'

'Something in that,' said Fearne. He sounded happier. He always liked to have his costs covered.

Having taken on the job, Fearne decided to aim for the top.

One of the best known and most effective members of the criminal bar at that period was Bernard Ericsson. His teddy-bear figure, cautious delivery and warm smile had combined to make him – so his rivals maintained – undeservedly successful.

'The judges all love him,' they complained. 'They let him get away with things that anyone else would be hauled over the coals for.'

He listened, without interruption, making only an occasional note, to what Fearne had to tell him. Then he said, 'Yes. I see. Having this creature, Stevens, under his thumb – he'd nothing to lose. He was going down for his part in the heist anyway – Samuels says to him, "Here's a thousand in notes. Pay it into the inspector's account. How? Get a paying-in slip at the counter. Do it quite openly. Suppose the bank clerk does identify you. What does it matter? It's all part of your story, isn't it? You've had a bit of luck on the races and decide to use the money to buy Quinn. A little later you experience a change of heart and decide to come clean".'

He thought about it a bit more, then added, 'Incidentally I expect you spotted why he paid the money in on the day Quinn departed on holiday. No? The reason surely is that when he got back he'd find a number of bills that needed paying. And he'd write out cheques for the more pressing of them without bothering to see how his account stood. Actually I see it was quite healthy. Over eight hundred before the unwanted thousand arrived. Yes. A very carefully worked out scheme. Simple, but dangerous because of its simplicity. There's only one thing to do.'

A pigeon that had volplaned down onto the window sill stood, with its head on one side, as though it, too, waited for the oracle to speak.

'When you're up against a manufactured case, you have to look for a crack. Maybe quite a small crack. Then you take a wedge and hammer it in. And go on hammering. And in the end the most watertight case will spring a leak. Here's where I'm going to need some help. Isn't one of your staff a man called Piggin?'

'Effectively, he's almost the whole of our staff.'

'A useful man, I'm told. Send him along. I'd like a word with him as soon as possible. There's a lot of work to do.'

The preliminary hearing before the magistrate caused little excitement. There had been so many cases in the past year of alleged dishonesty by members of the CID that this one caused no more than a routine wrinkling of the lips.

'Another bent copper?'

Junior counsel instructed by the Director of Public Prosecutions, presented the case against Detective Inspector Quinn fairly and without rancour. He made no attempt to side-step the fact that the principal witness for the prosecution was himself charged with participating in a serious jewel theft, if only in a subordinate capacity. He did not try to justify what Stevens had done. The way he put it was that he had got into a hole and was anxious to climb out of it. So he had paid, out of his own resources, the sum of £1,000 into the defendant's bank account and the defendant had, in fact, drawn against it to pay some of his own debts.

For the defence, an equally white-wigged counsel seemed anxious to get the facts on record.

He said, 'Is it correct that you had won a considerable sum of money – in round figures one thousand pounds – at the mid-week race meeting at Frimpton Park? Please address your replies to the Bench.'

'That's right, Your Honour.'

'And that having this unexpected sum available, you decided to use it to purchase the support of this police officer?'

'That's right.'

'And did the suggestion come from the accuser, or from you?'

Faced with this direct question the witness hesitated for a moment and then said, 'It was sort of mutual.'

'Explain that.'

'Well, he said that we might have a little talk, about matters that concerned us both, and that the back room at the Queen's Head would be a convenient place for us to meet.'

'And it was at this meeting that you offered him a thousand pounds.'

'That's right.'

'And what did you expect him to do in return for the money?'

'I looked to him to play down anything I'd done.'

'Present it in a favourable light, you mean?'

'That's the long and short of it.'

The witness seemed gratified at having his evidence neatly summarized for him by counsel for the defence, who asked a few more harmless questions before resuming his seat.

The senior of the three magistrates, after collecting nods from the other two, announced that they found that there was a case to answer and that the matter would be remitted to the Central Criminal Court.

Hugo Bracknell said to his father, 'I don't know what we were paying counsel for. He didn't attack the case for the prosecution. Simply underlined it.'

'He was doing what he was told to do,' said Bob.

'Allow me to clarify a few points,' said Ericsson.

Stevens, having survived the preliminary hearing without a scratch, was not unduly overawed by the solemnity of the Old Bailey. He said, with a smile, 'Ask anything you like.'

Ericsson was studying the thick sheaf of papers that formed part of his brief. He said, after a long pause, 'When you attended this race meeting – at Frimpton Park wasn't it—?'

Stevens nodded.

'Did you operate on the rails, or did you actually go into the meeting?'

'I went in.'

'Then you placed your bets in person?'

'Of course.'

'In the Cheap Ring, or in the Tattersall Ring?'

'Not the Tattersall Ring. That's for the nobs.'

'Then it was the Cheap Ring.'

'That's right.'

Having got this answer Counsel dived back into his notes.

Hugo, who was in court with orders from his father to make a record of all that occurred, found, suddenly and inexplicably, that the atmosphere had changed. Ericsson's voice was still quiet and friendly, but the change was there.

'Let us go a little further. Can we have the name of the book-maker with whom you placed this fortunate bet?'

'I'm not sure. There were so many of them.'

'Then let me help you. I have here a list of all ten of them.'

One copy was handed to the witness, another to the judge. Whilst they were being examined, Counsel said, 'Your Lordship will appreciate that it has not been difficult to compile a list of all the bookmakers who were present. They could only operate if they held permits from the Bookmakers Protection Association. It is from them that this list has been obtained. Should a further check be necessary it can be obtained from the local court, since a bookmaker has also to hold a three-year permit from a magis-trate.'

The judge had been examining the list with interest. He said, 'Most of the people in it appear to have two names.'

'That is so, My Lord. In the column on the left you will see their real names. In the next column the names under which they operate on the course.'

'So Honest Mike is, in fact, Mr Michaelson.'

'That is correct. And the third column contains the names of their clerks. They accompany their principles to the scene of action and, once there, do most of the real work.'

'Just like my clerk,' said the judge. 'Very interesting. Has the witness managed to identify the bookmaker with whom he placed his bet?'

Stevens, who had been studying the list in a bemused way, said, 'I can't be quite certain. But I think it was one of those two. "The Old Firm", or "Masterman Ready".'

'If it had been "Masterman Ready" you would have had no difficulty in recognizing her. She is one of the only women book-makers. She inherited the business from her father and runs it with two assistants. Both women.'

'Then it must have been "The Old Firm". Yes. Come to think of it I *do* remember that name. It was painted on a board, propped up beside the desk.'

'And this was the man who took your bet? Or was it his clerk, Mr Riddle?'

'It could have been either of them.'

'And the horse you were backing?'

'Palladian Hero.'

'An outsider?'

'A 25-1 outsider.'

'And what led you to select this particular horse?'

'That's always a difficult thing to say.'

From time to time, as he answered, the witness had allowed his gaze to leave the courtroom and stray up towards the public gallery, focusing on a stout and comfortable-looking character seated in the middle of the front row.

'Then are we to understand that you chose this horse at random?'

The witness appeared to be gaining assurance from the stout man, who smiled at him encouragingly.

'Not entirely at random,' he said. 'I had got into conversation with a man in the carriage on the way to Frimpton. He advised me that Palladian Hero was a promising outsider.'

'And you felt his advice to be so reliable that you were prepared to venture a bet of – let me see – it must have been forty pounds on this particular animal.'

'Yes. I did.'

'In cash?'

'Of course.' The witness seemed amused by Counsel's ignorance of the fact that bookmakers dealt in cash.

The judge, having concluded his study of the list of names, turned to Counsel and said, 'Without wishing to shorten your interesting excursion into race-course bookmaking, I would like to know where, exactly, it is leading us.'

'Certainly, My Lord.' Counsel was suddenly speaking in a voice from which all vestige of good humour had departed. 'I may have to ask for a short adjournment because I propose, if Your Lordship agrees, to bring before you all ten of these bookmakers, *and* their clerks. If they repeat, in court, the information that they have already given to my instructing solicitors you will learn that none of them has any recollection of this witness. And, moreover, that a study of the records kept by their clerks will show that the only bets placed on Palladian Hero at that meeting were two of five pounds for a win and one of ten pounds for a place.'

Everyone had been concentrating on the figure of the witness, but at this point a disturbance in the public gallery drew their eyes upwards. The stout character was leaving his seat. Had he done so alone he might have squeezed past his neighbours without attracting much attention, but the big men on either side of him were moving with him. Their departure seemed to knock any remaining confidence out of the witness who was grasping the rail in front of him like a non-swimmer facing a rising tide.

The judge said, 'In view of the observations made by Counsel, I must ask you to repeat now, as part of your evidence, an oath, that you did, in fact, place a bet of forty pounds on the horse, Palladian Hero, with a bookmaker at Frimpton Park whom you cannot now positively identify and were paid by him the sum of one thousand pounds.'

The witness's mouth opened and shut, but no sound came out of it. The stout man, having reached the exit door of the gallery had paused. He, too, seemed to be waiting for the answer.

Finally, in a voice which was a mixture of bravado and desperation, Stevens croaked out, 'Yes, I did.'

The judge made a careful note, turned to Counsel for the prosecution and said, 'You have heard the further evidence which the defence intends to bring. If I adjourn the hearing for seven days, I trust that this will give you sufficient time to consider it.'

'Yes, My Lord,' said Counsel, impassively.

'Very well. Adjourned until this day week.'

'He's between the devil and the deep sea,' said Fearne. He was in conference with his partners, with Mr Piggin in attendance.

'He doesn't dare to retract his evidence and tell the truth – which is becoming clear to everyone – that he didn't win this money at the races, but that it was given to him by Samuels, to be used to blacken Quinn and discredit his discoveries. But if he *did* say anything like that, he knew what would happen to him. I imagine you saw Samuels in the gallery?'

'And the two goons with him,' said Hugo.

'So much for the devil,' said Bob. 'The deep sea is the charge of perjury which he faces every time he repeats, on oath, that he won the money on this horse, at that race meeting.'

'And since,' said Tara, with evident pleasure, 'we can prove that he can't have won the money in the way he says he did, how's he going to avoid an open and shut charge?'

'If I might make a suggestion,' said Mr Piggin.

The partners looked at him hopefully. Mr Piggin's suggestions, although they did not always run on strictly legal lines, were always helpful.

'For what I have in mind,' he said, 'we shall need the support of the police. For they are more anxious even than we are to put Samuels behind bars. I've been having a word with Whyman, who is rather more friendly to us than Mayburgh. He has already made some progress in tackling the minor members of the Samuels theft-and-export organization. What he would now give his belt and buttons to be able to do, is to land Samuels.'

'So what precisely would you suggest to him?'

'That if he could offer Stevens effective police protection and support he might be induced to change sides. To admit that the money came from Samuels and was to be used to discredit our client. Such an admission could do him nothing but good. He can see the sharks circling round and would give a lot to get back onto dry land.'

'Very well,' said Fearne. 'It's worth trying. But you'll have to take great care that the opposition don't get to know what you're planning.'

'I can assure you,' said Mr Piggin, 'that I shall take the greatest possible care.'

And so he did.

But he was not careful enough.

Three days later Stevens was found, face down in the mud, by two boys who were out in their cockleshell boat fishing, at the point where the River Crouch runs out to sea under Foulness Point.

Mr Piggin, who was never sentimental about criminals, said, 'He lived a muddy life and has ended face down in the mud.'

'An excellent result,' said Fearne. 'Deprived of their only witness A.10 have been forced to abandon the prosecution.'

The partnership had met in a mood of self-congratulation.

Tara said, 'Melissa is over the moon about it. She thinks that Fearne and Bracknell are the best solicitors in England and she's been going round saying so. She's a leading light in the Women's Institute and I guess we'll be getting a lot of new clients.'

'Women?' said Fearne doubtfully.

'Come off it,' said Hugo. 'You started by disliking the idea of having policemen as clients, are you now extending your veto to women?'

Before the argument could develop, Mr Piggin intervened.

He said, 'There has been a further unexpected result that you may not yet have heard about. In the past, as you know, Samuels has always managed to keep clear of any personal involvement. He'd got plenty of time to make suitable arrangements for the theft of the jewels and their transport abroad to be carried out by third parties. The proceeds could be paid into a Dutch bank account and transferred to Samuels through two or three inter-mediaries. Now, suddenly, the situation had changed. He was forced to move quickly and personally to shut Stevens's mouth before he could give him away. And moving quickly and trying to handle the matter himself, led to carelessness. I understand that Whyman has got two good witnesses already. One who saw Stevens being driven off from his house. And another, a fisher-man, who saw his body being loaded aboard a dinghy for disposal. He feels confident enough to bring a charge of murder against Samuels.'

'That's excellent,' said Fearne. 'Why are you looking so worried, Bob?'

'I'm not worried,' said Bob. 'Just puzzled. When the case started I remember you saying that it was equally unsatisfactory for a firm of solicitors to gain a reputation for being pro or anti-police. Which reputation have we come out of the case with?'

Fearne said, 'If you consider the matter carefully, I think you'll find that we have managed to achieve an admirable balance.'

10
High Finance

To become a client of Fearne & Bracknell, Solicitors, of Little Bethel in the City of London, you had to secure a positive vote from all four of the partners; Francis Fearne, his daughter, Tara, Robert Bracknell and his son, Hugo. This was not always easy, since a quarter of a century divided the two older from the two younger partners, and twenty-five years was a wide gap at a time when ideas and standards were changing so rapidly.

Francis Fearne who, as senior partner, had the final say in the matter was, normally, unwilling to accept a majority vote.

'When we take on a new client, he used to say, 'they become one of the family. We can only support them wholeheartedly if we all approve of them.'

'So tell us all about this lady you're putting up to us.'

'Monica Farlowe,' said Tara. 'I've known her for some years. It started as what you might call a catty friendship. She has a very lovely blue Persian called Shahbanu. I got one of its kittens from her. She used to write to me, about once a month, to see how it was getting on.'

'Good marks for that,' said Fearne.

'Certainly. But it didn't leave her much time to deal with business matters. While her husband, Tim, was alive she was happy to leave all that sort of thing to him. Now that he's gone, she doesn't really know which way to turn.'

'Tim Farlowe,' said Hugo. 'I remember the name, vaguely.'

Bob said, 'Wasn't he one of the partners in the firm of brokers who dealt with the Hackwood estate?'

'Toplady, Farlowe and Day,' said Mr Piggin. Though not a partner he attended most partners' meetings. 'They carried out all the valuations and sales. Efficiently, I thought.'

'I remember him,' said Fearne. 'Quite a sound sort of man, I thought. For a stockbroker.'

Nobody seemed to dispute this.

Hugo said, 'When you told us she didn't know which way to turn, did you mean that she's got into some sort of trouble?'

'Not exactly trouble,' said Tara. 'More a tiresome sort of difficulty. Barely a fortnight after Tim's death, when she was just beginning to get over it, she was upset all over again by the intrusion of a West Country financier called Hyde. Harry Hyde.'

'Never heard of him,' said Fearne. His partners shook their heads.

Mr Piggin said, 'I've heard of him. But nothing much to his credit.'

'I think we ought to look after Monica,' said Fearne. 'Bring her round, Tara. I'll have a word with her. I won't commit us to anything until I've found out exactly what the problem is.'

When Monica turned up, two days later, it was Mr Piggin who brought her into Fearne's room. Although Fearne usually liked to see his clients alone he realized, on this occasion, the advantage of having Mr Piggin there. His evident kindness and sagacity had clearly made a favourable impression already on a troubled lady.

'When I tell you about it,' she said, 'I'm afraid you'll think I was being feeble, and that I should have been able to deal with Mr Hyde myself. But he was such a – such a positive sort of person.'

'Had he telephoned to make an appointment?'

'No. He simply walked in and introduced himself as one of Tim's oldest friends. He said, "I expect you'll have seen a number of references to me in his correspondence".'

'And had you?'

'I've not really had a chance to look through Tim's letters. For all I know there may be a lot about him in them. But I can't remember Tim ever talking about him.'

'Seems a pushing sort of chap. What exactly did he want?'

'He wanted to buy all of Tim's stocks and shares. He was offering a handsome sum, in cash. More than their total market value as he more than once pointed out to me.'

'Then do I gather that you've had a number of letters from him?'

'No. It's all been on the telephone. He was ringing me up several times a day. Now he's threatening to come and see me. Which is the last thing I want.'

'If you don't want to see him,' said Fearne, 'then, of course, you needn't. If he harasses you, let us have the details. We'll choke him off quickly enough. But two things first. Who looked after Tim's tax affairs?'

'That's Angus Robertson. An accountant and a golfing friend. He's always been friendly and helpful.'

'Good. He'll be able to tell us exactly what securities your husband did hold. Next, and even more important, who were Tim's solicitors?'

'The only ones he had much to do with was a firm called Sympersons. I think Tim went to them because they acted for the two companies he had a large holding in. A chemical company and a publisher. I can't remember the names.'

'No problem. We'll get the details from Robertson. However, if they were acting for those companies it makes it rather difficult for them to give independent advice if you want to dispose of the holdings.'

'Then couldn't you act for me – please?'

'If my partners agree, I'd be happy to do so. I'll have a letter typed now, for your signature, simply saying that you're changing your legal advisers, but I won't post it until my partners have concurred in the arrangement.'

'How I hope they will,' said Monica fervently.

She, like many people, found the deliberately old-fashioned atmosphere of Fearne & Bracknell a source of comfort.

'By this time,' Fearne reported to his partners, 'she was practically holding Horace Piggin's hand.'

'If Piggy says she's all right,' said Hugo, 'that's good enough for me. I've never known him wrong about anyone yet.'

'In that case—' said Fearne.

Robert Bracknell and Tara nodded.

'I'll send this letter to Dale Symperson, the senior partner. He won't be best pleased.'

To say that Mr Symperson wasn't best pleased proved to be the understatement of the year.

He started by talking about solicitors who poached other solicitors' clients, moved on to ambulance-chasing and when these comments failed to do more than amuse Fearne, he fired his final shot.

'If Mrs Farlowe really wishes to take her work elsewhere we can't stop her, but she'll have to discharge her husband's outstanding liabilities.'

'You mean pay your bill. Of course. I'll see to that. Send it along.'

He knew that, in addition to the securities that Harry Hyde seemed so anxious to get hold of, the Farlows had a substantial balance in the bank. This was in a joint account, which meant that, on Tim's death, the money automatically became available to Monica.

'I wish all married men were sensible enough to do that,' said Bob. 'If he hadn't, there'd have been endless delays over probate and old Symperson would have been dunning us for his costs, and enjoying every moment of it. Now, as soon as his bill's paid, he'll have to hand over Farlowe's papers and fade quietly away.' He added, to Hugo, 'You can collect his papers. I don't suppose he'll actually assault you. Anyway, you can stand up for yourself.'

'Take a recorder with you,' said Tara. 'If he blows his top it'll be useful to have it all on tape.'

'Meanwhile,' said Fearne, 'I'll have a word with that accountant, Angus Robertson. Then we may get some idea what it's all about.'

'Speaking as an accountant,' said Angus Robertson, 'I find it very difficult to see what this chap Hyde is after. It isn't as though Farlowe held a lot of unquoted shares. It's really an open-and-shut two-horse race. Five thousand ten-pound shares in Anglo-British Chemicals and six thousand ten-pound shares in Community Press Limited. Two very sound, middle-of-the-road holding companies, put together by the careful buying up of smaller outfits. Farlowe bought into both, at par, when they were first quoted. His ABC holding has more than doubled in value. The CP shares haven't done badly, either. Starting at sixty thousand their most recent quotation was one hundred and five thousand pounds. The rest are tiddlers. I concluded that he must have bought them for their attractive share certificates. Particularly the French ones. He had shares in three different French wine growers and one or two Italian art firms. I haven't bothered about them because none of them produced any dividends. And there were two British companies. Ten shares in West Country Tinstone. They regularly produced the magnificent sum of twenty-four pence per share. And five shares in Welsh Holidays, which once announced a dividend of five per cent, but never, I think, actually paid it.'

'So that anyone purchasing the portfolio must have his eyes on ABC and CP.'

'Right. Both healthy outfits and going up steadily in value.

Either of them might be due any day for a big leap forward, and Harry Hyde, with his ear to the ground, could have predicted this.'

'But if he really wanted these shares, couldn't he have bought them in the open market?'

'Certainly.'

'Then why pester Monica?'

'Perhaps he enjoys pestering women. Some men do. If he tries again we'll send Tara round. He won't get much change out of her.'

'No change at all,' said Tara. 'Surely all we have to do is dig our toes in. I've had a word with Mr Robertson about the income side of it. ABC has been producing a steady five per cent, CP between six and seven. That brings in seven thousand five hundred a year. And you have to remember that Toplady's always insisted on partners setting aside a portion of their annual income into a personal pension fund. This was sixteen thousand a year for Tim and half, on his death, for Monica. All in all, quite adequate for a flat in Kensington and a daily woman.'

'Where she can exist happily.'

'Quite happily, I'd say.'

'Then your advice to her is clear. Stick your toes in and tell Hyde to take a running jump at himself. You look worried, Bob.'

'I'm always worried by something I don't understand,' said Bracknell. 'We've missed something somewhere.'

When Mr Hyde did, eventually, put in an appearance and found that his audience was two women, both apparently willing to listen to the pearls of wisdom which fell from his lips, he was at his most avuncular.

He said, 'I can't give you more than a rough estimate, Mrs Farlowe, of what your late husband's estate will amount to, but if you add the value of this house to his cash balances at the bank and the shareholdings that we've discussed, it can't be less than half a million pounds. Estate duty will be payable at fifty per cent at least, and you will have to find the money or suffer a heavy interest charge. The cash offer which I – which my client – is making will take care of all that and leave you a fair balance.' He switched his attention to Tara, who must, he supposed, be a personal friend. 'I trust,' he said, 'that I have made the position clear.'

'Quite clear,' said Tara, who had been sitting with her hands folded demurely in her lap. 'However there are certain facts which you seem to have overlooked, and one important question to which we would like an answer before we finally make up our minds. Surely Mr Farlowe's gross estate was not nearly as valuable as you suggested. His house is leasehold and the lease is, and always has been, in Mrs Farlowe's name. The bank deposits are in joint names, so that the most that will rank as Mr Farlowe's is fifty per cent of them. Also, of course, they will come to his widow without the delay of obtaining probate.'

As she spoke Hyde had first gone red, now a purplish scarlet. 'Do I gather,' he croaked out, 'that you're a lawyer?'

'A solicitor,' said Tara. 'You can see my practising certificate if you wish. We intend to apply for probate – no hurry – so that Mrs Farlowe will be able to deal in due course with the shares you mentioned.'

'I'm glad of that,' said Hyde in a stifled voice.

'But before you go' – Hyde had, in fact, shown no sign of moving, he seemed to be glued to his chair – 'perhaps you would answer the important question which I referred to. Why are you so interested in these particular shareholdings that you are prepared to tell lies to obtain them? You must be aware, as a financier and a businessman, that Tim Farlowe's estate will come to his surviving spouse free of all estate duty. So why did you postulate the payment of duty and the need for borrowing to pay it? Well?'

On this last word, delivered by Tara in her sharpest voice, Hyde succeeded in climbing to his feet. Now he made his way to the door, opened it and said, 'I am under no obligation to answer impertinent questions.' Then he went out and they heard his footsteps clattering down the stairs and the banging of the front door.

When Tara reported all this – with some pleasure – to her father, he said, 'Well done. But it still doesn't answer the real question. Why did Hyde make his offer? If he had paid us more than the shares were worth – to say nothing of attendant costs – he'd have been very considerably out of pocket. Moreover, as you say, if he wanted the ABC and CP shares he could have bought an identical holding in the open market. So why was he doing it?'

'I've got a feeling,' said Tara, 'that he'll be back. He isn't a very nice sort of man – a hot temper. Kept under control with difficulty, and obstinate as hell.'

'And he didn't like being taught law by a woman?'

'Hated it,' said Tara with a grin. 'But I tell you, he'll be back. He wanted those holdings, and he's determined to get them.'

'If he turns up again, and starts to throw his weight around, we'll arrange for Hugo to be on hand. He's been taking judo lessons.'

But the approach, when it did come, was impersonal, and by correspondence. An extremely correct letter arrived, addressed to Fearne & Bracknell, and marked 'For the attention of F. Fearne, Esq'. The operative part of the letter ran – *On behalf of the client who is instructing us in this matter we are prepared to make the following unconditional offer for the portfolio of shares held by the late T.B. Farlowe. We will pay the full market price for all the holdings, ignoring only for this purpose the foreign ones in which we are not interested. Moreover, we will discharge any capital gains tax that will fall on the vendor on account of her carrying out these sales. This offer will remain open for fifteen days.*

'You realize,' said Fearne, 'that, by making this formal offer, Hyde has put us on the spot. It is, on the face of it, an extraordinarily generous one. Both those two major holdings were acquired at par and both have roughly doubled in value. If Mrs Farlowe did need the cash and made the sales herself she would be faced by a very steep charge of capital gains tax, which Hyde is offering to pay for her. Are we entitled to say "No"?'

Bob said, 'We must, at least, inform her of the offer. It would be totally wrong to withhold it.'

'And we know,' said Tara, 'exactly what she'll say when we do tell her. She'll say, "What do you advise?" '

Mr Piggin said, 'The position is an awkward one. But this letter does, in a way, focus the problem. You'll have noticed that while the offer doesn't include the foreign shares – the French and Italian holdings – it does, by implication, include the small English ones. So far we've ignored them, because the holdings are so trivial. Ten shares in West Country Tinstone and five in Welsh Holidays. I can't suppose that the Welsh Holidays are going to turn in trumps, but West Country Tinstone has possibilities. Suppose Hyde knew that they had struck a new and rich vein of cassiterite, that could double or treble the value of the shares.'

'Even that,' said Fearne, 'would produce such a tiny profit to a holder of only ten shares that to acquire it wouldn't be worth all the trouble he's taking, or a hundredth part of the money he seems prepared to spend.'

'Then can you suggest a reason?' said Bob.

Mr Piggin said, 'Lacking the relevant data it is not possible to supply a definite answer. But it did occur to me that the mere fact of holding shares in this Tinstone company – any shares – might entitle the holder to some valuable information or privilege.'

'Well,' said Fearne, 'we've got ten days to find out. Hugo, you'll have to take a Cornish holiday.'

'No objection,' said Hugo. 'Where exactly is this tin mine?'

'It's a few miles south of Boscastle on the Bristol Channel coast of Cornwall. A place called Hellsworth. Not all that easy to get at. Best to take the express to Plymouth and change onto a stopping train to Saltash and Bodmin, get out at Liskeard, and hire a car. The driver will know the way. Judging from the map. I'd say that any road that follows the Fowey stream up to its source should bring you out where you want to go.'

'That sounds easy enough. But how am I supposed to find out anything about the mine, and the company that owns it? If there *is* some vital information to be got hold of, I shan't get it by walking up to the front door and demanding all their secrets.'

'I've been making some enquiries,' said Mr Piggin, 'and I'm told that the man you should get hold of is old Mr Saltmarsh. He lives in Hellsworth and was, for many years, secretary to the company. If I was doing it, I think I'd tell him that I'd had a lucrative offer from an American magazine for a piece about the Cornish tin industry. And that if he could help me, I'd consider him entitled to a share of the fee.'

'I wish it was you who was doing it, Piggy,' said Hugo. 'I've a feeling I shall make a mess of it.'

As his taxi, driven by a black jowled Cornish giant, took Hugo north from Liskeard, he thought that he had rarely crossed a stretch of land so bleak and so unfriendly.

The fair weather of early summer was trying hard, but could do little to lighten an unending series of rugged hillocks, alternating with stretches of greenery, spattered by outcrops of red earth like patches of dried blood.

'Bodmin Moor,' said his driver. 'Not a lot of people come here, even in summer. In winter I wouldn't take you across it, no matter how much you paid me. That piece over there is Linkinhome Marsh. Get into that, and you wouldn't get out of it in a hurry.'

As he deposited Hugo in the main, and only, street of Hellsworth village he said, 'If you don't mind, I'll drop you and turn round quick. Wouldn't want to be caught here after dark.'

When he had driven off, Hugo looked for, and found, the Fox and Geese Inn, where a room had been booked for him for three nights. He deposited his bags and descended to the taproom to get directions to Mr Saltmarsh.

'Top of that lot,' said the landlord, indicating a thin, three-storey building of yellow brick that stood up, like an exclamation mark, on the north edge of the village. 'He'll be home now, I don't doubt, having his tea.'

Before visiting him, Hugo thought he would take a look at West Country Tinstone. This turned out to be a substantial clump of buildings, though surprisingly it possessed none of the cranes and derricks that Hugo associated with a mining enterprise. It looked like a normal factory and office building, with a large boiler house behind it; the whole surrounded by a formidable fence of barbed wire. Inside the gate to the front yard was a guardhouse in which a man was sitting smoking.

In the yard, a new-looking car was parked in one of a number of marked slots. A Mitsubishi Galant, it looked like, no doubt the property of one of the directors. He judged Tinstone, from its appearance, to be a prosperous and go-ahead place.

Having examined all that he could see of it, he turned back into the village. He found old Mr Saltmarsh at home, perched in his tiny third-floor flat like an eagle in its eyrie.

Hugo had planned various conversational openings, but they proved to be quite unnecessary. It was not a question of getting him going; like all solitary men, Mr Saltmarsh was only too willing to talk. The difficulty was stopping him.

'First time you've been here, isn't it?' he said. 'It's a real piece of old England. Hasn't changed a lot in five hundred years. You see those rocks' – he pointed to the wicked coast line behind Port Isaac Bay – 'that's where one of the ships of the Spanish Armada went aground. Planned to sail right round England, Scotland and Ireland and back home to Spain. Some hope.' The old man snorted his derision. 'A few of the men from that ship did succeed in scrambling ashore. Much good it did them. The local people had no use for foreigners who came to take them over. They thought it best to cut their throats and drop the bodies in to one of the pots. You understand about our pots?'

Hugo shook his head.

'They're holes in the rocks. Anything that goes in comes out on the ebb and ends up out to sea. A clean and economical way of getting rid of unwanted rubbish, eh?'

'Oh, very,' said Hugo, mastering his distaste.

'But you didn't come for a history lesson, I'm sure. Our tin mine. That's what you want to hear about, isn't it? I saw you walking down to have a look at it.'

Not much that happened in Hellsworth would escape the eye of Mr Saltmarsh in his eagle's nest.

'I expect you were surprised, weren't you, that you didn't see a lot of hoists and winding gear. Visitors are usually surprised at that. When they hear the word "mine" they think in terms of coal mining, but tin mining isn't like that at all. What they're after is cassiterite. It's valuable stuff and they dig it out slowly and carefully. Then they roast it – you saw the furnaces? – and stir it with green wood poles. That produces the pure metal, highly valuable and mostly used for tinning iron.'

'I didn't know about that,' agreed Hugo, 'but I certainly thought it looked a busy and productive sort of place. The company that owns it—'

'Busy and productive, eh?' Mr Saltmarsh chuckled. An uncanny whinny of sound. 'But not happy. No, sir. Not happy, nor meant to be.'

Hugo looked up at him perched on his high chair. He felt that something important might be about to emerge.

'Why do you say that?'

'It was unhappy, because old Mr Standen, who formed the company, meant it to be unhappy. He had that sort of mind. He'd just the two boys, you see, a son and a step-son. Cyril and Jake. So what does he do? He leaves them a half-share each in the company. He knew that they loathed each other, but being equal shareholders they'd have to work together. No option.'

'According to the last published account,' said Hugo, 'the capital of the company is ten thousand pounds.'

'Correct.'

'Then the sons hold five thousand each?'

'Not so. Four thousand nine hundred and ninety-five pounds each. Before he divided the shares, old Standen had one of his typical ideas. He saw that the explosive situation he'd created needed a safety valve. So he allotted ten shares to his old friend, Tim Farlowe. He exacted a solemn promise from Tim that as long as his sons behaved themselves he wouldn't use his shares to favour either of them. But if one of them did really kick over the traces – they were both wild Cornish men – then he could step in, join forces with the other one and get rid of the wrong'un. You see the idea? Within limits they were masters in their own house. They could run the company, they could increase the capital as high as they liked, they could allot the shares to themselves. But only equally. Ha ha! Only equally. It was like tying two high spirited horses into the same harness. They could buck and kick, but both knew that if he went too far, the other could call in Tim Farlowe and get rid of him. When old Standen was gathered, he must have gone aloft still chuckling, the wicked old creature.'

Mr Saltmarsh chuckled in sympathy with the thought.

Incapable of sitting still, Hugo had moved to the window. From where he stood he could look down into the forecourt of the Tinstone building. Old Mr Saltmarsh hoisted himself to his feet, and stood beside him. As they watched, two men came out of the building and approached the car in the courtyard. Looking down on them Hugo got a clear, but fore-shortened impression.

One of the men was short, with an aggressive red beard. The other was tall and clean-shaven.

'Cyril Standen – the one with the beard. And his professional adviser, Harry Hyde.'

Mr Saltmarsh was whispering, though nothing he said could

possibly have been heard, but the sight of the two men seemed to have upset him. They had got into the car, and sat, for some time, talking, before driving off. Hugo turned back into the room and sat down. He had a question to ask, but he knew what the answer must be.

He said, 'The other son, Jake Standen, has he been away lately?'

'Aye. He's been in America on company business. He's due back at the end of next week.'

All the little pieces fell into place, and the mystery was a mystery no longer.

Tim Farlowe's death might have rated a paragraph or two in the local papers, but not in the national Press. Even less likely to be noted by American papers.

At the moment Cyril was alone in the field, but that happy state of affairs would only last until Jake got back and heard the news.

Which explained why Cyril had clapped a terminal date on his offer.

Whilst he was thinking all this out there was a silence in the little upstairs room. It was broken by Mr Saltmarsh, who, it seemed, had also been thinking.

'You do realize,' he said anxiously, 'that anything I've told you was disclosed in confidence. You're a solicitor yourself. You understand about professional confidence.' He had grabbed Hugo's arm, and was so moved that the latter part of what he was saying was almost unintelligible.

'I'll not say a word,' Hugo promised him, 'to anyone who hasn't got a right to know the truth. When I get back to London I'll have to tell my partners. They're solicitors, too. They won't make any improper use of the information. I can assure you of that.'

Mr Saltmarsh seemed to be more impressed by Hugo's opening words than by his closing promises. He repeated, under his breath, 'When you get back to London. Quite so.' He didn't say

'If you get back to London,' but it seemed possible that he meant it.

When he left, Hugo found that the evening dusk had brought with it a light mist from the sea and visibility was down to a few yards.

What was it that Mr Saltmarsh had said?

"Anything that goes in comes out on the ebb".

The village was so quiet that his footsteps rang with offensive loudness from the cobblestones. When he reached the Fox and Geese the landlord was putting up the shutters.

'Shan't have any more visitors tonight,' he said. 'Strictly speaking I'm told that it's against the law not to stay open until legal closing-time. But in a place like this we mostly make up laws to suit ourselves. Can I get you a drink before you go up?'

'No,' said Hugo. 'I'll be all right. See you in the morning.'

"Goes out on the ebb, and ends up in the sea".

As he sat by the open window in his bedroom the night was so quiet that he could hear the sound of the waves beating against the rocks a full mile away.

He had made his mind up some time ago.

He did not undress, but sat listening to the clocks in the village telling out the hours as they slipped past.

When eleven o'clock struck, he opened the bedroom door quietly and stole downstairs. He was looking for a window that was shuttered, but not barred, and found it in the kitchen. It took a few minutes to get the shutters open and lift the bottom sash. Then he turned on his stomach and slid out, feet first.

He had, he reckoned, more than six hours of darkness, and, measured in a straight line on his map, some twenty-five miles to cover. Put in that way it sounded easy enough, but there were difficulties.

The most serious of these was that he dared not walk straight across a stretch of unknown moorland. He remembered the warning his driver had given him about Linkinhome Marsh. And there were likely to be other similar dangers.

To combine speed with safety would mean sticking to made-up roads, keeping as nearly as possible towards the north-east where alternative paths offered a choice.

A zig-zag, but steady advance.

The luminous hands of his wrist-watch showed four o'clock before he was crossing an upper stretch of the Tamar on a rustic footbridge which lacked a number of slats. But he felt that he had now reached country where the rule of law ran.

Finding a signpost that showed him the way to South Molton he slackened his pace, and a further ninety minutes of steady walking brought him to East Lydford which featured on the map as being a halt on the Exeter line.

The little station, when he reached it, was deserted and sleeping peacefully. Hugo, stretched out on the bench on the up platform, followed its excellent example. The first train to stop woke him and he climbed into one of its many empty carriages and went to sleep again.

On the following morning, in good shape after ten hours' sleep in his own bed, Hugo passed on to his partners the facts which gave such importance and value to the ten shares in the Tinstone company. He concluded his account by saying, 'And then I ran away.'

'Can't blame you,' said Fearne. 'They sound a wild lot down in that corner.'

'I think you did very well,' said Tara.

Bob said, 'I second that, but now that we know the truth, what are we going to do about it?'

'Clearly,' said Fearne, 'we explain the position to our client. Then it will be for her to make up her mind. Since there'll be two people bidding against each other for those shares, they could be worth a lot of money. Seeing that you've done all the work so far, you'd better be the one to go down and explain it to her.'

'I'll take Piggy with me,' said Hugo. 'Monica seems to have fallen for him. I'm sure she'll do anything he suggests.'

Mr Piggin smiled modestly, and said, 'Then the sooner we get going the better. I'll find out if she can see us this afternoon.'

Monica was only too pleased to fall in with this arrangement, and accordingly Hugo and Mr Piggin took the lift up to her South Kensington flat.

Fearne had arranged to sell the house that she and Tim had been living in, and although the sale had not yet been finalized he had, without difficulty, raised a temporary loan to cover all the costs of moving.

The best pieces of furniture had come with Monica, and she had quickly made herself comfortable. Shahbanu, whose name signified 'The Queen', was occupying the deepest chair in a truly regal manner.

When Mr Piggin gave Monica a meticulous explanation of the status and value of her Tinstone shares she was interested, but not greatly excited.

She said, 'Mr Robertson – such a nice man – has been through all the financial side of it. He says that even if I do nothing at all I shall have as much money as I need.'

'A policy, then,' said Hugo, 'of masterly inactivity.'

'There's just one thing that worries me. It seems that now I shall have two of them pestering me. Three, if you count in that terrible Hyde creature.'

'Allow me to make a suggestion,' said Mr Piggin.

'Please do.'

'Which is your favourite charity?'

'Oh, the Royal Society for the Prevention of Cruelty to animals. My favourite by far. They do such splendid work.' Shahbanu had one eye open. She, too, seemed to approve of the RSPCA.

'In that case, since you don't need the money yourself, I suggest that you donate the Tinstone shares to them. Explaining of course, the circumstances that make them so valuable. I'm sure that they'll strike a very satisfactory bargain.'

'Excellent,' said Monica. 'I'll do just that.'

Shahbanu had both of her amber eyes open by now, and was starting, very gently, to purr.

Evidently she, too, thought that it was a very good idea.

11
Enter the Vulture

No. 2 Area (East) of the Metropolitan Police District is served by three sub-stations; Leaman Street, Cable Street and the Isle of Dogs (usually shortened in speech to C.3). The head of C.3 at that time was Detective Inspector Scratton.

'A good man, Toby Scratton,' said Mr Piggin, the managing clerk of Fearne & Bracknell, Solicitors. 'He's been very helpful to me, on more than one occasion.'

'Indeed, yes,' said Francis Fearne. 'And we've had a number of useful clients through him. The Lampards, the Coxes, Major Bessingham and, recently, Edward Freudinger.'

Freudinger was a notable citizen, and wealthy. He had been married twice, each marriage presenting him with one son and one daughter. The eldest of the four Freudinger children was now twenty-four, the youngest ten.

'Edward Freudinger,' said Fearne, 'came to me when his second wife, Amelia, died so unexpectedly last May. I would assume that he was, to start with, in a state of shock. I could picture him, living alone, in that vast house of his in Belgrave Street prowling round the rooms like an unhappy ghost.'

Bob Bracknell said, 'And are his children no help to him?'

'They should be. But I don't know that they are. The son and daughter by his first marriage are in their early twenties, and busy getting on with their own lives. The son and daughter that Amelia produced are both at boarding-school. He sees them in the holidays, but in term time the only other inhabitants of his house are a married couple, who come in daily, to look after the house and garden.'

'Long, lonely evenings,' said Fearne's daughter, Tara. 'A recipe for suicide.'

'No. I'm sure the thought of self-destruction never enters his head. It would be an admission of defeat. He is too strong for that. But it made him start thinking about the future. About what was going to happen when *he* died. Quite a normal reaction at seventy. What did seem unbelievable, to me, was that a man with his considerable fortune, and the family connections arising from two marriages, should never have made a will.'

'I trust,' said Bob, 'that you pointed out to him the difficulties and dangers of intestacy.'

'Of course. He not only agreed with me, but he approved of the will I drew up for him. A simple, straightforward document. A few personal bequests, including, at his insistence, one for me. I am to have the choice of any six books in his library. I must confess that I worded it like that, because there is a beautifully illustrated six-volume work on the birds of South America that I have long coveted. Apart from such bequests his estate is to be divided into four equal parts, to be held in trust for his children.'

'Well, that settles him,' said Mr Piggin. 'And very satisfactorily. Now, there was one other matter I wanted to raise. When I was over at C.3 yesterday Inspector Scratton had another client to offer us.'

'Another Edward Freudinger?'

'Hardly,' said Mr Piggin with a smile. 'This is a man called Dines. Gregory Dines. I said I'd put it up to you. Though he didn't strike me as being a particularly desirable client, I guess he's been getting into Scratton's hair and he wants to get rid of him.'

'So that he could get into our hair,' said Bob Bracknell.

'We're paid to share other people's burdens,' said Fearne.

201

'True,' said Mr Piggin. 'But if we do take him on, we have to realize that he won't be able to pay the smallest bill. He seems to be a little man who lives in a garret on five hundred and twenty pound a year paid to him weekly by a private benefactor. Never having been in regular employment he's made no pension contributions. In fact his main endeavour seems to have been to steer clear of all officialdom.'

Fearne knew that such people did exist. Small animals that contrived to creep through holes in the net of state security, preferring to tuck themselves away, out of sight.

Bob said, 'If he's so careful to keep himself to himself – can't say I blame him – why is he troubling the police?'

'Because, for the last six weeks, people have been trying to kill him.'

'What people?'

'He doesn't know.'

'And why?'

'He doesn't know that either.'

Fearne & Bracknell looked at each other.

'Are we to assume that he is imagining the whole thing?'

'If so, he has a very vivid imagination. He told Scratton the whole story. Apparently there have been three attempts so far. The first was a straightforward attempt to push him under a lorry. The pavement on which he was walking was crowded, the attack was from behind, and he never actually saw the man who pushed him. He rolled clear of the lorry, which fortunately possessed excellent brakes, and he escaped everything except a storm of abuse from the lorry driver. By the time he had been picked up and dusted down, and forcibly told to keep his bloody eyes open and look where he was bloody going, it was far too late to think of identifying the attacker.'

'He's sure that it wasn't his own carelessness?'

'Absolutely sure. He says that he felt a hand in the small of his back propelling him into the traffic.'

'How long ago was this?'

'Five or six weeks. He remembers it clearly, because he has led a very secluded life, and this was the first time that anything like that has happened to him.'

Fearne said, 'And then?'

'The second attempt took place a week later. The garret he lives in is the top storey of an old-fashioned house, divided into four or five flats. Two men broke into the house and forced the door of his attic. He got out of the window – he's an agile little monkey – shinned down a pipe and spent the rest of the night among the bushes.'

'You speak of a door being forced. That is something that can hardly be done quietly. Did none of the people living on the other floors hear anything?'

'Apparently not. Or, anyway, they have not come forward to say so.'

'I see. Well, continue.'

'The third attempt was more elaborate. Nowadays, when he leaves his attic, he is careful to fasten a piece of black cotton between the door and the jamb. Some days later he found the cotton broken and knew that his room had been visited. As you can imagine, he made a very careful search, without being sure what he was looking for. At first it seemed that nothing had been disturbed. The cotton might, he thought, have been broken by a cat, a tabby brute, whose owner starves it, that came scratching at his door for scraps. On the table beside his bed there was a glass of water – like many people he kept it ready to drink at night. It struck him that it had been moved. He dipped his finger into the water and touched the tip of his tongue with it. The bitter taste was quite apparent. He poured some milk into a saucer, added the water from the glass, and went out, leaving the door ajar. He was away for perhaps an hour, doing some shopping. When he came back the cat was on the floor, rigid and stone dead.'

'Only strychnine would work as fast as that.'

'So he assumed.'

'And no doubt he had the milk and water analyzed.'

'No doubt he should have done. In fact he emptied the mixture down the drain and carefully washed out both the glass and the saucer.'

'Why?'

'He says that it was too dangerous to keep them about the place.'

This produced a thoughtful silence.

'So there is no proof that the three incidents actually happened.'

'None at all.'

Mr Piggin said, 'Surely the most remarkable part of the whole business is what you might call its timing.'

'What do you mean?'

'Assuming, for the moment, that they really occurred, does it not strike you as odd that all three of the attempts should have taken place during the last six weeks? How is it that little Mr Dines, harmless to everyone for many years, should suddenly have become dangerous to people with the money and the muscle to organize his removal? Particularly since he seems, from all accounts, to have no enemies.'

'It's odd,' agreed Fearne, 'but it's clear that he's not a desirable client for us.'

Tara, who had stayed behind when the others departed to get on with the day's work, sat herself down opposite her father, put her plump elbows on the table, and said, 'What are you worrying about, Dad?'

'Who said I was worrying?'

'I always know when you've got something on your mind. You start rearranging everything on the top of your desk.'

'Do I really? I'd never noticed.' He moved a soapstone idol which had got itself isolated behind a pile of law books and put it back in its proper place beside a letterscale. Then he said, 'Very well, Sherlock. I am worried.'

'About Mr Dines?'

'No. About Edward Freudinger.'

'I thought you said that once you'd got his will signed up he was all right.'

'If I said anything like that, it means that I hadn't really thought the matter through.'

'And now that you have?'

Fearne hesitated. It was clear that he was picking his words carefully.

'I think,' he said, 'that I visualized Edward as a sick animal. Sick almost to death. Wandering, lost, on the prairie. In such a case, you may be sure there would be sharp eyes monitoring his stumbling progress. High up in the sky a vulture is hovering. Waiting for the dying animal to go down, try to rise and fail. It will not be long, now, before it can swoop down, and get busy with beak and claws. Do you see the picture?'

'It's a horrible picture,' said Tara. 'Who is your vulture?'

'If I knew that,' said Fearne, 'I could take steps to deal with it. As it is, we shall just have to wait and see.'

They did not have to wait long.

It was less than a month from the time when Tara spoke to her father that the letter arrived. It was from a firm of solicitors, Jocelynn & Zambetta, known to, but not approved by, Fearne. It came over the signature of the senior partner, Cyril Jocelynn. After normal compliments, it said:

Pursuant to the provisions of the Marriage Act, 1931, acting on behalf of Monica Marian Lewin of 20 Ben Jonson Road, Putney, we have given notice to the Superintendent Registrar of that district of the intended marriage between our client and Edward Freudinger of The Old House, Belgrave Street,

'Enter the vulture,' said Tara, to whom, with the other partners in the firm and their clerk, Mr Piggin, Fearne had read out the letter.

'Monica Lewin,' said Fearne. 'Do we know her?' Bob, Hugo and Tara, appealed to separately, all shook their heads.

Mr Piggin said, apologetically, 'I only heard the name for the first time yesterday. I was given it by a friend in the Registrar's Office, who knew I was interested in Freudinger, and had spotted the name when the notice arrived. So I have only had twenty-four hours to look into Monica. But I can offer you a few facts which you may find relevant. Her mother was a Welsh girl, who ran away to Brazil, where she encountered a Brazilian businessman called Alfredo Lewin, and married him. He died some years ago, but her mother's still living in Sao Paulo, comfortably off on her husband's money. Monica was their only child. When she reached what you might laughingly call years of discretion, finding life in Sao Paulo a bit dull, she came over to try her luck in this country.'

'Half Welsh, half Brazilian. Sounds a dangerous sort of mixture.'

'You can say that again. Her next few years seem to have been filled with affairs with everyone she met, from a handsome young man who came to clean the windows, and thence onwards and upwards. One of her more recent captures is said to have been a bank manager.'

'Interesting,' said Bob. 'But do we need to worry about her? Edward's an obstinate old cuss and unless she can persuade him to change his will and make another one in her favour, she won't get much out of her manoeuvres.'

Fearne said, 'When you speak of her manoeuvres, is it possible that you have overlooked the real point of them?'

'The real point?' said Bob – then, 'Oh yes. I see what you're getting at. Of course, if she can bring off this marriage, Edward's existing will is automatically revoked.'

'Which takes her halfway to the winning post,' said Fearne. 'If she can't persuade Edward to make a new will in her favour he is, and will remain, intestate, and when he dies Monica gets the generous share of his estate that the Intestates Estate Act awards her. A life interest in half the residue and a lump sum of five thousand pounds.'

'Not forgetting,' said Bob, 'the personal chattels. Not that they will amount to a great deal.'

'You may be surprised to learn – particularly when you consider what an illiterate old pirate Edward is – that by far the most valuable of his possessions is his library. We had a man from Bullits to do the valuation, and he couldn't help chuckling when he demonstrated that half the books were not only unread, but couldn't be read. They were uncut. "Makes them even more valuable", he said. Also the fact that a lot of them are still in their wrappers. Apparently this also adds to their value. I confess I was a bit sad when I saw that the six volumes of South American birds had been priced at fifteen hundred pounds. They offered them to me at that figure. I had to tell them I'd more important things to spend my money on.'

'And when you think,' said Bob, 'that the widow has the right – which I'm sure she'll exercise – to take a lump sum as the capitalized value of her life interest, all in all she'll walk away with at least a quarter of a million pounds.'

'Lucky vulture,' said Tara. 'I suppose there's nothing we can do to scare her off her prey?'

'I've been thinking about that,' said Fearne. 'I don't think there's much chance of frightening her off, but we can, at least, see that things are done in an orderly and unhurried way. If Edward makes no further will and dies intestate, a first and necessary step will be an application to the court to take out

Letters of Administration of his estate. Since we act for Edward, that will, of course, have to be done by us. Jocelynn & Zambetta will be involved on behalf of the widow. In the circumstances the court would, no doubt, favour the appointment of joint administrators, myself and Jocelynn. And since no positive step can be taken in the administration without my agreement, I can at least see that nothing is done over-hastily.'

This produced a smile from Tara, who remembered her father being described, on one occasion, as 'the most obstinate and obstructive solicitor in the City of London'.

'You're assuming,' said Bob, 'that this marriage actually comes off.'

'From what I've heard,' said Mr Piggin, 'I think you can safely make such an assumption. Monica is clearly a most determined young lady. She will, I imagine, have taken that flat in Ben Jonson Road – almost next door to Edward's house – with two objectives. To be, herself, within the jurisdiction of the Putney Registrar and to have a convenient headquarters from which to conduct her campaign. She has already taken the first step, I hear, by installing herself as Edward's housekeeper.'

'Step one, into the kitchen,' said Hugo. 'Step two, into the bedroom.'

'I'm afraid that's right,' said Fearne. 'She's got her hooks into him. She won't let him go now.'

Nor did she.

On 28 March Fearne was notified that a Certificate of Marriage between Edward Freudinger and Monica Marian Lewin had been entered by the Putney Registrar. The requisite twenty-one days had expired since notice was given and no impediment had been recorded.

On 3 June, with the inevitability of something foreseen and unstoppable, Edward Freudinger died. The doctor who was attending him certified the causes of death as cardiac weakness and advanced senility.

Reporting these developments to his partners, Fearne said, 'There is one odd thing, and that is the complete lack of friction between myself and Jocelynne. Joint administrations are never easy, but I must put it on record that my fellow administrator has been exceptionally co-operative. True, our work has been the more or less routine matter of starting to liquidate the assets of the estate. He might, for instance, have asked for an independent valuation of Monica's life interest. But no, he was happy to accept my expert's figure. His one objective seems to have been to get matters tidied up as quickly as possible. Indeed, I think we could have got a better price for Edward's house if we had been prepared to wait a little. There were several people showing an interest, but he agreed to settle with the first prospective purchaser *provided he agreed to an early completion date.*'

Bob said, 'Here's something else that you may find significant. I asked Toby Scratton to keep a discreet eye on Monica's movements. His report has just come to hand. It seems that she has already made an open-date reservation on a trans-Atlantic flight to Brazil.'

Fearne said, 'Clearly her intention is to grab the money and run. Indeed, if I hadn't managed to slow up the distribution on a number of technical grounds, she'd have been back with her mother in Sao Paulo by now, taking her winnings with her.'

'And there's nothing we can do to stop her?'

'I haven't been able to think of anything. All the same I've got a feeling that there is something wrong somewhere, but I'm damned if I can spot what it is.'

He looked round for Mr Piggin whose customary chair was empty that morning.

'It's no use looking for Piggy,' said Hugo. 'He's off on some ploy of his own.'

Although Mr Piggin prided himself on the strict logic of his reasoning, he was capable, at times, of leaping from facts to conclusions with the agility of a grasshopper. If called on to justify this supra-normal activity, he would refer to it as instinct.

He, like Fearne, had a feeling that there was something wrong somewhere. The only point – but it was a significant point – that connected, in his mind, the history of Gregory Dines, as related to him by Inspector Scratton, with the affairs of the Freudinger family, was one of timing.

The vital period in Edward Freudinger's life had been the final weeks when his mental capacity had started to diminish and finally to disappear and he had been awaiting death. This was the six weeks of his entrapment into marriage by Monica. *And it was precisely in those six weeks that repeated attempts had been made to kill little Mr Dines.*

Why?

Coincidence?

Mr Piggin had no use for coincidences. Properly examined a sequence of cause and effect could usually be established.

How was it that little Mr Dines, who had, as far as one knew, lived a life of modest security for some years, had suddenly become a danger that had to be removed? The only possible answer was that he had chanced on some information that threatened the developing schemes of Monica Freudinger.

There was a subsidiary matter to be considered.

Was it not possible – or even likely – if the humble and parsimonious Mr Dines lived almost entirely on his savings supplemented by a periodical payment from a private source – that this payment was connected with the secret he had discovered?

Mr Piggin's instinct imperiously directed him to find out.

A first step was to discover who the messenger was who brought Mr Dines the money each week. With this in mind he had set out to ingratiate himself with the other tenants of 20 Barlands Road, in the top storey of which little Mr Dines roosted.

Fortunately Mrs Blazer, the tenant of the ground floor, on the left side of the main staircase, turned out to be a middle-aged and garrulous widow. Mr Piggin had a faultless technique for dealing with people of this sort, and was soon enjoying a cup of tea and a heart-to-heart talk with Mrs Blazer. It was not necessary to offer her money. She was lonely and found Mr Piggin an agreeable conversationalist and an appreciative listener. She was only too willing to discuss Mr Dines and the mystery which seemed to surround him.

'Every Friday morning this young man arrives, regular as clockwork. Of course we were curious. We did try to get him to tell us where he was from and what he was doing, but talk about oysters!'

Mr Piggin saw that professional help was needed. Fortunately it was to hand in the person of Captain Smedley, a private enquiry agent who had assisted Mr Piggin on a number of occasions in the past. He agreed to put one of his best men onto the job.

'He'll be there first thing Friday,' said Smedley, 'that's the day after tomorrow. He'll follow the man after he's delivered the cash. It doesn't make a lot of sense to me, but when we find out where he comes from and who's putting up the money, we may be able to see what's behind it. Seems to me it's got a smell of the old black about it.'

Mr Piggin agreed. He, too, had been thinking of blackmail.

At noon on the Friday, Captain Smedley telephoned.

'No problem,' he said. 'My man followed this chap straight back to his office.'

'His office?'

'Well, not exactly his, but the one he works for. A firm of solicitors. Jocelynne & Zambetta.'

Mr Piggin experienced a modest feeling of triumph.

He said, 'I *knew* there was some link between the two cases. This proves it. Jocelynn & Zambetta are Monica's solicitors. It seems clear that Dines has lighted on some information – some document – that threatens Monica. Something he can use to get money out of her.'

'Odd sort of blackmail,' said Smedley. 'Most people on that game grab a lump sum and clear off with it. They don't organize themselves an annuity. What do you want me to do now?'

'What do you suggest?'

'Direct action. Shake down Mr Dines. From what you tell me he doesn't seem to be of much account. I expect we can scare him into telling us what we want to know.'

'Then don't let's waste any time. He hangs out at the top of 20 Barlands Road, with umpteen other tenants.'

When they reached the house they found Mrs Blazer hanging round in the hall. She seemed relieved to see them. She said, 'We were beginning to wonder what Mr Dines was up to. Usually he's up and down the stairs half-a-dozen times a day. With his groceries, and his milk and the papers and all that.'

'And nobody's seen him today?'

'That's right. Nor heard him neither. Not a sound.'

Mr Piggin and Captain Smedley looked at each other. The same thought was in both their minds.

'Could be asleep, I suppose,' said Mr Piggin as they climbed up four flights of stairs.

'I don't think so,' said the captain. 'Nor do you.'

The door of the attic flat was not locked. It swung open to the touch.

Mr Dines was face down in the middle of the floor. The people who had killed him had not thought him worth pistol or knife. They had simply hit him, at the base of his skull, hard enough to break his neck and left him lying. Their attention, it seemed, had been concentrated on making a very careful and thorough search of his room.

In the next hour, before they summoned the police – which they should, of course, have done at once – Captain Smedley and Mr Piggin traced the course of that search. It had left a sea of documents scattered over the floor.

'They started by turning out his pockets,' said Mr Piggin.

'Not turning them out,' Smedley amended. 'Tearing them out of his coat and his trousers.'

The wrecked and emptied pockets lay among the papers on the floor. After which, it seemed, the intruders had started on the drawers of his writing-table. The same treatment had been applied to them as to the pockets.

Smedley said, 'I expect they'd heard of drawers with false backs and a hidden space behind them.'

The ruthless use of a knife had explored this possibility, but apparently without the results that the searchers had been hoping for. When they had finished with the living-room, they had moved over to the annexe where Mr Dines had kept his bed. Equal violence had been employed there.

Examination of the papers that had been extracted and scattered produced only unimportant documents, bills and invoices and a few personal letters. These were from Mr Dines's one regular correspondent, a lady who signed her letters 'Letitia' and filled them with Biblical quotations.

'I'll have a word with her,' said Smedley. 'She lives just round the corner. But I don't imagine she'll be much help. Judging from her letters she's halfway round the bend herself.'

'Whilst you're at it,' said Mr Piggin, 'I suppose you'd better alert the police. Inspector Scratton at the Isle of Dogs sub-station knows about Dines. In fact, he once offered him to us as a client. I'm glad we didn't take him on.'

When Smedley had departed on this double errand Mr Piggin stood for long minutes beside the body of Mr Dines.

Trivial in life, insignificant in death.

Captain Smedley, he reflected, was a professional. If the paper they were looking for had been there, he would surely have found it.

He cast a final eye round the room.

Its arrangement was as starkly simple as had been the life of its owner. He thought of rooms he had read about, exciting rooms, with hiding places concealed behind panels. Here the walls were brickwork, coated with roughcast. No secret panels here. The floors were boards, securely nailed to the joists below. He supposed that a carpenter, armed with the appropriate tools could have raised them, but not without leaving clear signs of his work. The ceiling sneered down at him, blank and unhelpful.

The furniture was as simple as the room.

On the right, as you came through the door, there was a shelf, on which stood two vases of artificial flowers and a table lamp. Along the right-hand wall, ran a two-tier bookcase holding few books, but several bundles of old newspapers and a number of magazines, most of which seemed to be devoted to physical culture. Did Mr Dines spend his off hours developing his puny muscles, or did he get a kick out of looking at the photographs of young men stripped for action?

Up against the far wall was a table, and on it a second lamp. To the left of that table a door leading to the annexe which contained the sleeping and washing arrangements.

The fourth wall contained a fireplace, which had clearly not been used for some time, being full of dust-covered debris. Its over-mantel was crowned by a mirror and held a few cards, the latest, seemingly, from last Christmas.

'Oh dear,' said Mr Piggin to himself. And again, 'Oh dear.'

He was convinced that the room was trying to tell him something but its message was as difficult to read as the riddle of the Sphinx.

What was it his old instructor in secret work, the celebrated Dr Rabagliati, had once told him?

'Look for irregularity. Something odd. Something missing. Something out of place.'

The only irregularity, if you could so describe it, was the fact that the heap of scattered papers was a great deal thicker on three sides of the room than on the fourth, or fireplace side. Was that, perhaps, because the illumination, which would have helped a searcher, was more satisfactory on those three sides, coming from the two large table lamps, one on the shelf and the other on the table? Smedley who had turned both of them on had left them alight.

There was a third lamp on the mantelshelf over the fireplace. Smedley had not turned this one on. When Mr Piggin tried the switch the reason became evident. The lamp was not working.

Was the bulb possibly defective?

Mr Piggin exchanged it with one of the bulbs from lamp number two. But lamp number three remained obstinately dark.

'Something odd, something missing.'

Feeling that he might be getting warm, he unplugged the third lamp, took off the shade, laid it on the table and set about examining it.

When he had it stripped down it became clear why it was offering no illumination. One of its interior wires had been disengaged from its socket, and folded carefully back.

It was at this interesting moment that Captain Smedley reappeared. He looked curiously at what Mr Piggin was doing, and said, 'I don't know what you're up to, but I've got some news for you. I found Letitia – she's a widow, a Mrs Lovejoy – and she produced some useful stuff. She couldn't tell me much about Mr Dines – except that he was a darling man, and was clearly the object of her affections. But when she got onto Monica – "that woman" as she called her – then she really let herself go! She gave me some succulent details of her last few exploits, before she spotted old Edward Freudinger and got her hooks into him. Unfortunately when my informant reached this point she diverted into a string of Biblical quotations, bearing on what was due to happen to a wicked woman in her next life. She promised me several further chapters on this interesting topic, but I felt it was time to leave, and I slid out. I wanted to find out if you'd had any luck here.'

'Up to the point where you came in, I'd have said, "nothing much". But it's just possible that I may have got onto something.'

'Something to do with that lamp you're disembowelling?'

'Indeed. I was wondering why this was the only lamp that had been made inoperative. You can see the way the interior wire has been disconnected, and folded back. Quite deliberate.'

But Captain Smedley was not looking at the lamp. He was examining the shade that Mr Piggin had removed and placed on the table.

'Odd sort of affair,' he said. 'Not parchment like the other two. Strong white paper, folded and stitched. Lend me your knife.'

He cut the stitches carefully, unrolled the shade and smoothed the paper out on the table. Then he turned it over.

The outside was white, plain and uncommunicative. The inside was lime green in colour and contained typed words arranged in boxes. More interesting even than the typing was a circular red seal which could be seen now that the paper was reversed. The lion and the unicorn of the royal arms filled the circle. Round it they read the words – 'The General Register Office – England'.

After examining the seal with growing interest they turned their attention to the typescript, faded, but still easily readable. As they studied it, a number of matters that had been hidden before became clear to them. The document was a certified copy of an entry in the Marriage Register. The parties were Gregory Dines and Monica Marian Lewin, and it was dated almost exactly twenty years previously.

'Do you mean to tell us,' said Tara, 'that little Mr Dines had been married to Monica for twenty years, and had said nothing about it?'

Mr Piggin said, 'The picture is, indeed, a curious one. We must assume that as a young man Gregory Dines was attractive to the other sex. Letitia Lovejoy certainly found him so. Had she not been swept off her feet by the fiery Mr Lovejoy she would, she assured me, have married him herself. However, it cannot have been long before Monica, who was pursuing a relentless course of seducing anyone in trousers who crossed her path, found a husband a tiresome and unwanted encumbrance. The trouble was that she had no grounds for divorcing him and he had no incentive to divorce her. So she removed him from the scene quite simply by buying him off. By that time she could well afford it. Provided he kept his mouth shut, she would pay him a modest annuity. At that time he represented no particular danger to her. If anyone did happen to discover that she had a husband tucked away in the background, they might have been sorry for the little man, or they might have laughed at him. Nothing more. But when it became plain to her that she could only secure Edward Freudinger's money by actually marrying him, *then* the situation was totally changed. Then it became essential to Monica's plans – and, indeed to her continued well-being – to get rid of him.'

'She did her best,' said Bracknell. 'Where did her assistants come from?'

'Almost certainly from her last boyfriend, Syd Coleman. Or that's what Scratton thinks. She was, you see, in a cleft stick. Either she had to give up all thought of marrying Edward and securing a share of his money, or she had to take the highly risky step of going through a form of marriage with him, with a husband of her own still in existence. No doubt she was counting, cold-bloodedly, on Edward's imminent death. When that happened she could grab her entitlement and get out of the country with it before the truth came to light.'

Bracknell said, 'To Sao Paulo, you mean. To join her mother.'

'Certainly. No extradition treaty with Brazil. Once she was safely there we could whistle for a return of the money. But the embarrassing existence of Mr Dines was fatal to her in another way. If he came to light it rendered her purported marriage to Edward a nullity. And being a nullity, *it would not be effective to cancel Edward's will.*'

The partners considered the position. The ripples caused by the continual existence of little Mr Dines seemed to spread ever wider. Hugo said, 'Then if Edward didn't, in fact, die intestate, everything that you and Jocelynne did when you thought you were administering his estate will have to be undone.'

'Certainly. There is now only one person responsible for dealing with Edward's estate and that is myself, as executor appointed by his will.' And to Mr Piggin, 'You agree?'

'I've been thinking about it, ever since that marriage certificate came to light. You will have to see how far you can cancel what you have done. Preferably without invoking the assistance of the court. Will that be possible?'

Fearne said, 'Contracts for the sale of Edward's house have been agreed, but not actually exchanged. I'm sure the purchaser will accept a new contract with me as executor. Apart from that there is only the matter of a certain small sales that have been made for cash. No need to disturb them. The cash is still in hand.'

'And no distributions have been made?'

'Not a penny. Fortunate that the matter should have been handled in such a careful and unhurried way. And what are you grinning about, Tara?'

'Just a thought,' said his daughter dutifully.

'The first step now will be to obtain probate of the will. Then to organize the four shares for the children.'

Bob said, 'So Monica gets nothing.'

'Poor vulture,' said Tara.

'On the contrary, lucky vulture. She has escaped at least two charges. One, of knowingly entering into a bigamous marriage. The second, possibly even more serious, of conspiring to murder Gregory Dines. Coleman's thugs, when Scratton catches up with them, will certainly try to incriminate her. But all in all I'd say that we've come well out of a situation that might have been embarrassing.'

Tara said, 'Is that your only reason for looking so happy? Isn't there another reason?'

'Another reason?'

'Now that the will is re-established you get your South American bird books, don't you?'

'So I do,' said Fearne. 'I'd quite forgotten.'

12
Ranulph Hall

The Reverend Sebastian Stoddart, headmaster of Ranulph Hall Preparatory School for Boys, stirred uneasily in his bed.

In normal times he would have attributed the sound that had woken him to the efforts of the wind that irrupted from across the North Sea and made the shutters on the east side of the house rattle on their ancient hinges.

But the times were not normal.

Two weeks before, shortly after the start of the Easter term, Troop-Sergeant-Major Bailey ("Trooper" to the boys) had reported what he called an attempted break-in. The shutter that covered one of the ground-floor windows had been, he said, lifted from its hinges and laid against the wall.

'Next thing they were planning to do, sir, or so I'd guess, was attend to the window. Simple little catch. Slip it with a knife. No trouble. Only luckily they didn't have time.'

At that moment a particularly violent gust had lifted the shutter from where it had been propped and sent it crashing across the courtyard and smack into the wall of the newly erected squash court. In its headlong career it had picked up a rubbish bin and carried that along with it.

The noise had roused the school more effectively than any getting-up bell. It had taken Stoddart, helped by his second-in-command Simon Truefortt, and the sergeant-major half an hour to round up the excited boys and get them back into their dormitories. After which they had managed to lift the heavy shutter back onto its hinges, had replaced the bar and returned, thankfully, to their beds.

It was on the following morning, after breakfast, that Bailey had first offered the headmaster his considered opinion that it was human hands, not the wind, that had lifted the shutter.

'No wind could have done it, sir, however strong,' he said. 'And look here.' He pointed to two freshly made indentations in the bottom of the shutter. 'Could only have been made by, say, a couple of jemmies. Push the points in here, see, then press down on the ends. Both together – and up she comes.'

'Yes,' said Stoddart, 'I can see the marks. Mightn't they have been made when the shutters were being installed?'

'Look quite fresh to me, sir,' said Bailey. 'The blessing was they didn't have time to get the window open. You can see the scratches where they were trying to slip the catch. That was when the wind did us a good turn. Sent the shutter bowling across the courtyard, yanking up the dustbin, and making enough noise to wake the dead. So they didn't get anything for their trouble.'

'End of story,' said Stoddart thankfully. He didn't want to believe in burglars. Unfortunately Bailey must have talked and the exciting theory that he was propounding had become common knowledge. It also formed a welcome topic to enliven the traditionally dull Easter term. Stoddart couldn't ban discussion, but he censored their letters home. The last thing he wanted was visits from anxious parents.

After a short time, interest had died down and had been replaced by other more immediate and important topics, such as the romance that was believed to be blooming between Simon Truefortt and the matron, Miss Hellaby, who was young and unusually attractive as matrons went, a considerable improvement on her predecessor who had had a hooked nose and prominent teeth and had earned, and justified, her nickname, of 'the Hag'.

'The Hellaby's all right,' said Colin Smedley, a precocious thirteen year old to his two particular friends, Ivo Fisher and Drew Bastable. 'Not exactly my idea of a glamour girl, but she sticks out in the right places.'

'You're swanking,' said Ivo. 'You don't know a damn thing about girls.'

Drew said, 'Can't blame Mr Truefortt. Just suppose he'd had to make love to the Hag.'

The idea made all three of them laugh consumedly.

'All the same,' said Colin, 'since no one seems to be taking these burglars seriously, it's up to the CID to do something about them.'

He was not, as his listeners understood, referring to the Criminal Investigation Department at New Scotland Yard, but to their own, more modest, organization made up of the initials of Colin, Ivo and Drew. They had already notched up a number of minor successes, such as enforcing the departure of one of the temporary maids who had been stealing and selling part of their meagre sugar ration and they were primed for further exciting action.

'So what are we going to do?' said Ivo.

Colin said, 'I had a word with Trooper. He's seen a man hanging about in the market place. He thought he recognized him as a criminal called Dandy Davis. And, sure enough, Dad had a picture of him in his album.'

Colin's father was Captain Smedley who headed a private detective agency in the City. When Colin was home on weekend leave his father had allowed him to look through what he called his Black Bible and it was there that Colin had located a character who closely resembled the man the sergeant-major had described.

He must have acquired his name 'Dandy', Colin thought, in the same way that someone six foot high and broad in proportion would be nick-named 'Tiny', for he was an ugly-looking hunk, with a nose that had been broken more than once. His record included assault, housebreaking and theft.

'Shouldn't care to tangle with him,' his father had said. 'You'd better warn that headmaster of yours that this man has been seen hanging round.'

'Violent, I suppose,' said Drew, when Colin reported all this to his lieutenants.

They seemed more interested than alarmed.

'Very,' said Colin. 'So are the pair he works with Dad told me, Ikey Barnstow and a man called Celly James on account of him being able to force locks with a strip of celluloid.'

'Three of them,' said Ivo thoughtfully. 'Rather a handful for the three of us to tackle.'

'I've been thinking about one way we might level the odds,' said Colin.

He talked for some time. His two assistants listened, doubtfully at first, but in the end they agreed with him. It was clear who was boss of the CID in that district.

As may be supposed the boy's warning, duly delivered, did nothing to calm the headmaster's fears. He had fifty boys to look after, he and a houseful of women. The sergeant-major slept out – he had a cottage in the garden. The only man on the premises was Simon Truefortt – an enthusiastic member of the local Territorial Army, and a useful ally, but could the two of them tackle three professional criminals?

It was this thought that had kept him from falling asleep. Lying uncomfortably in bed, he had heard midnight strike from Westbury parish church. As the sound of the chimes died away, he heard something else. Difficult to say what it was, but there was definitely movement somewhere in the house.

Though a sixty-year-old academic, Sebastian Stoddart was no

sort of coward, and he had all of the Englishman's dislike of people who invaded his privacy. He got out of bed, pulled on a sweater, armed himself with a steel fire-rake, and started out to investigate.

Dandy Davis and his two accomplices had, on this occasion, made a more discreet entry leaving the window shutters alone and opening a basement door with their own set of keys before proceeding upstairs towards their goal, which seemed to be the headmaster's study.

Here they encountered a militant group, consisting of Colin, Ivo and Drew. Unarmed they would have had small chance of opposing the intruders, but they were not unarmed and the night's proceedings opened to the sound of a rattling volley of small arms' fire. It stopped Dandy Davis and his party dead, but it didn't check Mr Stoddart, who continued to advance, with considerable courage but extreme caution.

What he saw brought him finally to a startled halt.

The boys had apparently visited the miniature rifle range, and each had armed himself with a .22 rifle.

'What's all this?' Shock had sent his voice up several octaves. 'What in the world are you playing at?'

'Defending the premises,' said Colin. He seemed unperturbed.

'Did you hit anyone?'

'Don't think so,' said Drew. 'But they didn't stop to find out. We heard them crunching off down the drive.' He, too, seemed quite satisfied with what they had achieved.

'If you had hit them, you'd be in very serious trouble.'

'Why?' said Colin. 'Isn't a householder entitled to defend his house?'

This brought a temporary halt to the headmaster's indignation. Might there be something in what the boy said? He appealed to Simon, who had arrived in dressing-gown and slippers.

'Tell the young idiots that they can't go round shooting people.'

'I'm not sure,' said Simon. 'I'm not really a lawyer. Not yet.

Only a student. I've started on Contract and Tort. I haven't got onto Crime yet. But I understand that you are entitled to use reasonable force in the protection of your property.'

'Are guns reasonable?'

'Bearing in mind that they are boys, who could scarcely be expected to tackle grown men without the help of some sort of weapon, it might be argued that what they did was reasonable. However, I do remember one case where a man waited inside an open window with a shot-gun, and potted a burglar who tried to climb through. That was held to be unreasonable. Clearly what we need here is professional advice.'

'Right,' said Stoddart. He seemed to get comfort from the word 'professional', which he repeated. 'So how do we get professional advice?'

'There's a young friend of mine, Hugo Bracknell. He's a junior partner in the firm of Fearne & Bracknell, City solicitors. Perhaps you could ask him down here for the night? He might want to bring his clerk, Mr Piggin, with him. An excellent man, I'm told, who has advised him in a number of tricky situations.'

'I can think of no one better. They acted for me when I bought this place. And I remember Mr Piggin, who did much of the work. Invite them both. Touch wood, no invalids yet, so we've plenty of spare beds in the sick-room. We can explain the whole situation to your friend and he'll let us know what we can do. And' – he turned to the boys who had reluctantly grounded their arms – '*what we can't do.*'

Some days later, when the rifles had been securely locked up, as they should have been before, and a sequence of peaceful nights had somewhat calmed Mr Stoddart's immediate fears, he and Simon were in conference with the two newcomers. He was glad that Hugo Bracknell should have brought his clerk, a Mr Piggin, with him. Hugo was young, and likely to be rash; Mr Piggin, on the other hand, was of a sensible age, in fact, almost exactly the same that he was himself. And he seemed to be eminently sound in his views.

It was he who finally said, 'I'm sorry that neither of us has been able to give you a definite answer. Self-defence is certainly allowed to all citizens. The only question is whether it is reasonable. The dicta on this point are many, and largely contradictory. It is clear that the age and physical condition of the victim are both to be taken into account, but on the whole I should advise you against the use of knives or firearms. It would be preferable that the defenders should be armed with sticks or clubs and, more important, that they should be in telephonic communication with the police. However,' he continued, 'there is one line of enquiry that we ought to be pursuing and which might go a long way to answering the important question of what lies behind these visitations. Ought we not to be asking ourselves *what are these criminals looking for?*'

Mr Stoddart said, with evident approval, 'I have been thinking on the same lines. When I purchased this place from the squire, Roger Ranulph, I made some enquiries about his past and his background. I was surprised to find that he was by no means an estimable character. In fact, if he had not been killed in the gun battle which immediately preceded the sale, he might well have ended up in prison himself.'

He indicated the pile of books on the table, each one flagged with a number of markers.

'These are reminiscences and memorials of Ranulph's contemporaries. They were, for the most part, written before his decease and are, understandably, circumspect. The more recent ones less so. There is really no doubt that Ranulph was a bad man.'

'Morally bad,' said Hugo, 'or criminally?'

'The records tell us very little about his morals, but a criminal, certainly. He seems to have been a notable fence, a receiver of stolen goods of all sorts. And one man speaks of hidden paths which lead down from the eastern end of what is now one of the playing fields – it was then under plough – to a secluded beach under the cliff where a small boat could be hidden. This could be rowed out, at night, to the mouth of the Yare, where the water was deep enough for a sea-going craft to lie at anchor. You see the idea?'

'An excellent arrangement,' said Mr Piggin. He appreciated neatness, even in his adversaries. 'The stolen goods, destined no doubt for the Low Countries, would have been stored in Ranulph Hall, in perfect safety, since Ranulph was a magistrate. You mentioned a gun battle—?'

'Indeed. It must have taken place shortly before I purchased the property. I can only surmise that there had been a falling-out of thieves over the cargo they were running. It must have been an exceptionally valuable one, which gave rise to a difference of opinion about the sharing of the proceeds between the parties concerned. These were, on the one side, Ranulph and his steward, Hopcraft – who seems to have been as black a villain as his master. On the other side the three smugglers, a dangerous trio. Dandy Davis, Tom Cotton and Micky Marden, all known – only too well known – to the police. The gun fight ended in a draw – though a far from bloodless one.'

Through the open window they could hear what seemed to be a rehearsal of the 'Hallelujah Chorus', the boys' clear voices forming an incongruous background to the dark tale that was being unrolled.

'Ranulph and his steward were both killed, as were two of the robbers, Crofton and Marden. Davis was wounded, but survived. Subsequently he was charged with taking part in an armed affray by night – a very serious offence, for which he received a sentence of fifteen years penal servitude.'

Mr Piggin had been making careful notes as the headmaster spoke. He said, 'One point, Headmaster, if you please. Do you happen to know how Davis behaved himself in prison?'

'When I spoke to Superintendent Holbeach, of the Norfolk

227

Police, he told me that Davis was a violent and implacable prisoner. He was guilty of more than one assault on the warders who were guarding him, as a result of which he forfeited all remission of his sentence.'

'And so served his full term of fifteen years?'

'Certainly. He might even have been charged on account of his conduct in prison and received an additional sentence, but this is not often done. He must, in fact, have been released in the early months of this year.'

'Precisely,' said Mr Piggin, whose eyes had been glued to the calendar, 'and does that not constitute a possible answer to your question? An answer that may appear even clearer when I add certain facts that have recently come my way.'

Although he spoke as though he sat still while facts came flocking round him like homing pigeons, Hugo knew that they were usually the result of enquiries made by Mr Piggin among his wide circle of friends and acquaintances.

'Who have you been talking to now, Piggy?' he said.

'I have been discussing some aspects of the matter with a man who should be better known than he is. I will refer to him, if I may, as Mr X. But for his modesty, understandable in the circumstances, his would be a household name. He has made a lifelong study of the origins and subsequent movement of crystalline carbon in tetrahedral and in octahedral or dodecahedral form.'

Noting the blank looks on the faces of his audience, he kindly explained, 'I mean, of course, stones which are commonly referred to, by a species of incorrect shorthand, as diamonds.'

Diamonds.

Whilst the word was still echoing round the room the voices outside reached the climax of their singing with a triumphant shout of Hallelujah!

In the silence which ensued, Mr Piggin continued with his report. He said, 'There was one other piece of information he gave me that interested me greatly. It seems that when the Low

Countries were invaded by the Germans, machinery and skilled craftsmen in the diamond field were hurriedly extracted and transferred to the comparative safety of this country.'

'Comparative,' murmured Mr Stoddart, himself a survivor of the London blitz.

'Sufficient was brought across to set up a diamond cutting and polishing industry here. Many famous stones came to rest here. Not, of course, the most famous of all, the Cullinan diamond. That has been part of the British regalia for some years, but a number of lesser stones, smaller, but extremely valuable. The Cape Blue, the Mortimer and the Brazilian Vargas. All such stones are well documented, and their ultimate destination is known, with one major exception. A hundred-carat stone, known as the October diamond after the date of its arrival in Belgium. It was in the State Museum in Brussels and was extracted ahead of the arrival of the Germans – wisely, in view of Goering's known weakness for precious stones – and it was planned to bring it to England. The courier who was carrying it would appear to have been inefficiently guarded – though one must bear in mind the confusion and disorganization of the times – and his body was subsequently discovered in a thicket in the New Forest. His throat had been cut. Since then the October diamond has vanished.'

'Surely that is unusual,' said Mr Stoddart. 'Such stones do not usually hide their light under a bushel.'

Hugo could contain himself no longer.

'What you're suggesting, Piggy, is that this stone, the October diamond was brought across here and entrusted to Ranulph to dispose of.'

'I am suggesting nothing,' said Mr Piggin coldly. 'I am simply exploring possibilities. A man who laid hands dishonestly, on such a prize, would he concerned, first of all, to hide it. As soon as the war was over, and the European market opened again, one of the people he could certainly have approached would have been Ranulph. His experience and expertise in disposing of stolen goods was widely known. And, to take the matter one step further, yes, it is possible that it was in a quarrel over this extremely valuable prize that the four deaths we have heard about took place. If that is the truth, it does explain a number of points which have been, so far, in doubt.'

'But surely,' said Hugo, who was finding Mr Piggin's step-by-step approach infuriating, 'surely it explains everything. Davis and his friends come here with the stone. They commission Ranulph to arrange for its disposal. There is a dispute over the division of the profits – a dispute which ended in violence. Four of the five men concerned are killed. Davis is wounded, and arrested. *And he alone knows for certain that Ranulph was entrusted with the stone.*'

'But not where he concealed it,' said Simon, who had been following Mr Piggin's exposition with equally close attention.

'Right. So the stone is back where Ranulph hid it. Davis bides his time. Fifteen years later – if he had been able to control his temper it would have been ten years – he comes out of prison and takes on two new assistants.'

'Probably men encountered in prison,' Simon suggested.

'Very likely. And comes to Ranulph Hall with them to get his hands on the stone.'

'To find,' said Mr Stoddart with a smile, 'that it is no longer a private residence, but a flourishing preparatory school. Tell me, how can he have been sure that the stone had not come to light and been disposed of long since?'

'His allies in the diamond disposal field would have told him. My friend Mr X would certainly have known of it at once.'

'Then the possibility you have been exploring,' Mr Stoddart chose his words carefully, 'is that the October diamond could still be somewhere here.' The idea seemed to interest more than alarm him.

'And all we have to do,' said Simon, 'is to find it. We return it, openly, to the museum, and our troubles are at an end.'

'That is all,' agreed Mr Piggin.

'It would help,' said Mr Stoddart, 'if we knew more precisely what we were looking for.'

'According to the records it is a stone of one hundred carats. It is octahedral and its overall measurements are between twenty-five and thirty millimetres in diameter and ten to fifteen millimetres in depth. I suggest that you make a model, in soft wood and paint it white. That will give us a target to set our sights on.'

'I'm not much of a hand at carving. But Captain Smedley's son, Colin, is, as I know an accomplished practitioner. No doubt his father has kept him fully informed of what we've been up to. I'll set him to work at once.'

'Believe it or not,' said Colin, to the other members of the CID, 'this is what they're looking for.'

He indicated the neat little eight-sided model.

'Have they got any idea where to start?'

'Not the slightest,' said Colin.

'Then it'll take them months and months,' said Drew.

'Years,' said Ivo.

But fortunately Mr Piggin was able to narrow the field.

In conference with Simon and Mr Stoddart he said, 'What we have to bear in mind is that the school was not in existence when the stone was hidden. We can, therefore, ignore all scholastic additions: the squash court, the gymnasium and the two pavilions. What we must concentrate on are the original pieces of Ranulph Hall that now form part of the school. And such of its contents as have come down here with it.'

Mr Stoddart said, 'I can give you a reasonably accurate account of the contents. I have looked up the schedules that were prepared at the time of the sale to me. I agreed to purchase the furniture, pictures and books – Ranulph had inherited an excellent library, though I doubt if he ever opened a book. The contents were listed individually along with the more important items of furniture.'

'Excellent,' said Mr Piggin. 'Then you have a record of everything that was in the building at that time.'

'Everything except a few items that were disposed of earlier. A week or so before the main sale the executors – short of cash I imagine – organized a local sale. Not of any of the major items. Small objects which it had not been worth the trouble to add to the schedules.'

'Yes,' said Mr Piggin. 'I see.' He did not sound happy about this. 'But let us concentrate, for the moment, on what you call the major items. You would have purchased them, I take it, to furnish the private part of your school.'

'Quite so. My study and library, and my private dining-room and drawing-room.'

'Then we've only really got four rooms to examine,' said Simon.

Mr Piggin still seemed to be worried. He said, 'I suppose you haven't by any chance got a list of the small items that were disposed of locally.'

'I'll see if I can find one, but I doubt it.'

'There must be people living round here who were at the local sale. They will remember who was there. They may even remember what they and other people bought.'

'They might,' said Mr Stoddart. 'But bear in mind that it was more than fifteen years ago.'

The Junior CID had ideas of their own.

Ivo said to Colin, 'What we ought to do is have a word with your great-aunt.'

'Great-aunt Beatrice? She's supposed to be a witch.'

'Tells fortunes, doesn't she?' said Drew. 'Why couldn't she look into that magic globe of hers and tell us where this diamond is?'

Colin thought about it. Beatrice Smedley, nearly ninety, was

not a reputable member of the family. People avoided mentioning her, as much as they could. Also they avoided offending her.

'You ask her,' said Ivo. 'We all know she's potty about you.'

'Marry you if you gave her half a chance,' said Drew.

Colin disregarded this persiflage, all of which he had heard
many times before. All the same, there was a substratum of truth
in it.

'She might help us,' he said. 'It's true she seems to like me a lot,
for some reason, but if I get the wrong side of her, she might turn
me into a toad.'

'We'll look after you,' said Ivo.

'Feed you slugs,' said Drew.

'Your kindness overwhelms me,' said Colin. 'Very well. I'll
have a shot at it.'

Meanwhile the senior researchers had done a great deal of work
with, so far, disappointing results. But that morning a ray of light
appeared. The headmaster, making a final examination of his
records, unearthed, from under a pile of printed papers, two
photographs that had been taken at the time of his purchase. One
of them showed the drawing-room of Ranulph Hall, the other the
study, both in fair detail.

The study was unhelpful, being furnished with one large table
and half-a-dozen steel filing cabinets.

'When I took it over,' said Stoddart, 'I emptied the papers out.
They were mostly catalogues, and a few bills and accounts. I made
a bonfire of the lot.'

'Oh dear,' said Mr Piggin.

'The table had two drawers in it. You can see them in the
photograph. I emptied them too.'

'And burned the contents,' said Mr Piggin sadly.

'It's all very well being wise after the event. How were we to
know that we'd be hunting round for clues to the whereabouts of
a priceless diamond?'

'You weren't, of course,' said Mr Piggin. 'But I agree that we can disregard the office; the drawing-room looks much more promising.'

'A typical Victorian set-up,' said Hugo, voicing the massive intolerance of youth. 'How could people ever be happy with ghastly stuff like that all round them?'

There was a lot of Benares brass; there were vases of dried grass and palm leaves; there were anti-macassars on the chairs and knitted pictures on the walls in frames of brightly coloured beads.

'I can't see anyone giving twopence for the lot,' said Simon. He cast an eye down the list of people known, or thought to have attended the private sale. Some were dead, others had left the neighbourhood. There seemed to be a lot of hard work ahead of them, without much chance of success at the end of it.

Great-aunt Beatrice welcomed Colin to her den, a dark and crowded pair of attic rooms overlooking the river. She listened fondly to Colin's explanations, interrupting them only by cackling from time to time.

When he had finished, she said, 'I'm not a magician, and I can't tell you anything about the diamond. I didn't even know it existed. But I do remember the sale.' She studied the list of names. 'Mostly they bought vases and pictures. And my goodness, those pictures!' She seemed to be overcome by the remembrance of them. '*Knitted* pictures. Yes, actually knitted in different coloured wools. Can you imagine it?'

Colin could imagine it, and he shuddered sympathetically.

'I only bought one thing myself, and I've still got it, though I've sometimes been tempted to throw it away. It's a girandole. You wouldn't understand what that means.'

Colin shook his head. The warm and crowded room was beginning to overpower him.

'They come in different shapes and forms. Mine, as you can see,

is a plain mirror, with two candle-holders in front of it. Not everyone's taste, I agree, but there must have been something about it
that appealed to me at the time.'

Colin had got up to look at it. What interested him was not the
mirror or the candlesticks: it was the thick border of beads round
the mirror. As he examined them he put his thin, strong fingers
through them.

Then he said, 'I think it's lovely. Would you sell it to me?'

'For God's sake,' said Ivo. 'What do you want a thing like that
for?'

'Just an idea I had.'

'How much was she asking for it?'

'It cost her two pounds. I had to offer the same.'

'Had you got two pounds?'

'Actually all I had was sixty pence. I promised to raise the
balance as quickly as I could. I thought you might help.'

Drew said, 'I've got one pound.' Ivo said, 'And I can make up
the other forty pence. I hope you know what you're doing.'

'I hope so,' said Colin.

He had placed the mirror of the girandole on the table, under
the light.

'All right,' said Ivo. 'What happens next?'

'I didn't want to mess about with it until Dad and Mr Piggin
were here. I think that's them now. I told them what I'd been up
to and they seemed to think I might be on the right track.'

Drew said, 'For God's sake, let's get going. The suspense is
killing me.'

When they had made room at the table for the two newcomers, Colin took out a pair of nail scissors, and began, very
carefully, to cut the threads which held the beads. As these came
away the layer behind them was revealed: a dozen small, but
perfectly cut octahedrons, which fitted neatly into a slot in the
woodwork.

Mr Piggin lifted one of them out. Under the electric light it seemed to be self-luminous, with an adamantine lustre of its own.

'You see,' said Colin modestly. 'It occurred to me that you might perhaps have been looking for the wrong thing. With a famous stone on his hands, I thought, surely the first thing Ranulph would do, would be to have it cut up.'

'So what we should have been looking for,' said Mr Piggin, 'was not one diamond about the size of a billiard ball, but ten or twelve diamonds each the size of a large bead.' He laid the one he had picked up back on the table.

'How much did you pay for them?' said Mr Piggin.

When Colin had told him how much he had paid, Mr Piggin said to Captain Smedley, 'I'd advise you to retain, at all cost, the services of your son. I feel sure that he'll be worth his keep.'

13
A Problem in Ethics

'Suppose,' said Tara, 'that if we followed the instructions of a client we should seriously harm a third party. In such a case, what would our duty be?'

The four partners of Fearne & Bracknell, Solicitors of Little Bethel by the Tower, used to meet at ten o'clock on most mornings in the room of Francis Fearne, the senior partner, to review current matters. When these had been dealt with, they would allow themselves a few minutes for the discussion of general topics.

As often as not it was one of the two younger partners, Hugo Bracknell or Tara Fearne, who initiated these discussions.

'Can I assume,' said Francis Fearne, 'that the instructions you refer to are legal and practicable?'

'Certainly.'

'Then the interests of our client must naturally override the interests of outside persons.'

'Why?' said Hugo. 'Your client is only one person. Why should he be more important than the rest of the world?'

'Because he's paying your fees,' said his father, Bob Bracknell, drily.

'So money is more important than morality,' said Tara.

This was the traditional parting of the ways. Youth for idealism: age for common sense and practicality.

Fearne said, 'Had you got some actual case in mind?'

'Nothing specific,' his daughter admitted. 'But it's the sort of point that might easily arise, and I'd like to know which road one was meant to take. What do you think, Piggy?'

Horace Piggin, their managing clerk who attended most of the partners' meetings, said, 'If you thought it out carefully you could probably find a way to help both parties.'

Fearne said, 'I expect you could. And since the question is both theoretical and unlikely to arise, might I suggest that we turn our minds to something of more immediate importance. You will all have seen what *The Times* has to say about the proposed changes in VAT.'

Two years after this conversation had taken place, and certainly long after it had been forgotten by the four partners, though not by Mr Piggin (who had a facility for storing up odd items of information and producing them at unexpected moments), the firm was approached by the Randall family.

The arrival of old Sebastian Randall, with his son Aubrey and his son's wife Antonia, had been prefaced by an urgent telephone call. Antonia, speaking in tones which panic had raised an octave above normal, had not only asked for but had demanded immediate attention.

Fearne knew Sebastian well. He had first met him when Sebastian was starting his financial advisory business, and he had formed for him the small company which was to handle it. When it had twice increased its capital and had finally obtained a public quotation, Fearne had handed over corporate matters to one of the firms in the City that specialized in that field. He had, however, continued as Sebastian's personal adviser, had made and remade his will, and had dealt with the sad formalities that needed attention when Sebastian's wife had died – a victim of an incurable disease. He knew their only son, Aubrey, less well, and could only recall one occasion of meeting Aubrey's wife, Antonia.

He had retained an impression of a sharp and tolerably attractive female. As soon as the three Randalls, Fearne, and Mr Piggin were seated, Aubrey extracted a single sheet of white paper from his briefcase. The message on it had been formed by single words and groups of words cut from printed pages and pasted on the paper. After Fearne had had time to read and digest the message he fully understood the Randall family's distress.

The note read: *TO SEE MARK AGAIN WILL COST YOU 10,000. ACKNOWLEDGE THIS MESSAGE IN TIMES SOONEST, SIGNING A.B.R. IF YOU INFORM THE POLICE HIS THROAT WILL BE CUT.*

Fearne stared at the words as he tried to collect his thoughts. Then he said, 'Mark is your son, yes?'

'Our only son,' said Antonia in a choked voice.

'Tell me what happened.'

'He went out last Friday,' said Aubrey, 'on some ploy of his own. We were worried when he was not back by lunchtime. More than worried when he missed supper. It was after supper that this message arrived.'

'By post?'

'No. It was slipped into our letter box. In a plain, unstamped envelope.

'Three days ago,' said Fearne. 'And you told no one?'

'I told my father at once. He agreed that it was better, for the time being, to do what we had been told.' He looked at Sebastian who nodded, but said nothing.

'We sent our reply to *The Times*,' said Aubrey. 'It appeared on the following morning. It said: 'We have your message. We await to hear further.'

'And you have had a further communication?'

'We found this in our letter box this morning.'

A second sheet of paper was laid beside the first.

MAKE A PACKAGE OF THE 10,000 IN USED NOTES AND BRING IT TO THE ENFIELD ARMS HIGHGATE

*NEXT MONDAY AT ELEVEN WHERE YOU WILL
RECEIVE FURTHER INSTRUCTIONS. YOU WILL COME
ALONE AND IF YOU VALUE YOUR SON'S LIFE AND
GOOD LOOKS YOU WILL TELL NO ONE.*

'Monday next,' said Fearne. 'They don't seem to be in any hurry for that money.' He thought for a moment. The question had to be asked. He said, 'If you agreed to this demand, could you find the money?'

Both the younger people looked at Sebastian, who said, 'I could quite easily make the money available, if it seemed the best thing to do.'

'The only thing to do,' said Antonia with passionate conviction.

A long silence followed. Finally Fearne said, 'I assume that you have come to me for my advice.'

'Yes,' said Sebastian. 'I agreed that they should come to see you. If the decision had been left to me, I should have said to go straight to the police.'

'That is my advice also,' said Fearne.

Antonia, who was already picturing her son with his face disfigured and bleeding, said, 'No. No. We can't take a chance. You must see that.'

'Then let me be frank with you,' said Fearne, addressing the couple. 'There's no point in me giving you advice if I know in advance that you won't accept it. On the other hand, your father is an old friend of mine and a former client, and if he wishes to consult me I am happy to offer him my services. He nodded to Sebastian, who nodded back but said nothing.

'However,' Fearne continued, 'when I advise a client, I prefer to advise him on his own.' He rang for his secretary and rose to his feet when she arrived, then moved across the room to hold the door open for Aubrey and Antonia. 'If you care to wait, this young lady will look after you.'

Aubrey got up and moved across to the door. Antonia followed him, but with obvious reluctance. She turned before going out to say, 'I beg of you. Think of Mark. He is more important than any of us.'

Fearne said, 'We won't forget the boy. I promise you that.'

As the door shut behind two very worried people, leaving Fearne and Mr Piggin alone with their client, Sebastian said, 'What next? Telephone the police?'

'Please bear in mind,' said Fearne, 'that I've had a bare thirty minutes to consider the matter. Ultimately, no doubt, my advice will be to go to the police. It's the only sensible thing to do. They have the machinery to follow up a number of lines. For instance, they can identify the publication the words were cut from. It looks like an art magazine, probably with a limited circulation. And the piece of paper . . . .' He picked it up. 'You can tell by the feel that it's not inexpensive. The address has been cut off, but it suggests an enquiry among the firms that go in for personalized stationery. Those are just two lines that could be followed up. No doubt there are more.'

As Fearne spoke, Sebastian had been sitting in his chair tilting it backwards. Now he brought it forward with a snap and placed both hands flat on the desk.

He said, 'Very well. We've been given a week. If you can't get a line on these people in that time, I'll hand over to the police.'

It was an unwilling compromise.

Fearne said, 'We're solicitors, not policemen. We'll do our best, of course.'

Mr Piggin said, 'Just one point. Your son says that Mark went out and failed to reappear. How old is he?'

'Fourteen this summer.'

'A strong active boy?'

'More than that. A promising athlete.'

'Then how do you suppose that the people who have taken him managed to grab him? No struggle? No shouts for help?'

'I hadn't thought about it. But now that you mention it, it certainly seems odd.'

'If a stranger in a car had offered him a lift?'

'We've warned him about that sort of thing. He'd never have accepted it. And if they'd tried to grab him, he'd have put up a fight.'

'Unless,' said Mr Piggin, speaking more slowly, 'they happened to be people he knew. His own friends, or friends of the family. Then he might have got in. And once they had him in the car they could deal with him.'

'Suppose you're right . . . .'

'If I'm right it leads to my next suggestion. Get from Aubrey a list of his son's friends, old and new. Acquaintances as well. Spread the net even wider. Rope in the headmaster from his school and the local clergyman. Get them to compile a list as well.'

'It seems a distant hope,' said Sebastian. 'Better than doing nothing, I suppose.'

'And one thing more. When you consult these people, you can make up whatever story you like. Since it's the start of the summer holidays, the school won't have missed Mark. And the church would only if he was a member of the choir or something like that.'

'He wasn't.'

'Right. Then the thing you must be careful about is to get independent views. Don't let the schoolmaster know what the parson is doing – or either of them what Aubrey is doing.'

'They'll be longish lists.'

'The longer the better,' said Mr Piggin. 'But please be as quick as you can.'

The lists arrived three days later. During that time Mr Piggin had not been idle.

Since he had helped Chief Inspector Whyman of the Leaman Street Station to land Roper Samuels – the thief and exporter of stolen jewellery – Piggin had found Whyman to be friendly and co-operative. So much so that he had agreed to allocate two of his men to keeping an eye, from time to time, on Aubrey Randall's house in the Chattenden suburb of North Rochester. It had been possible to carry this out, without too much wasted manpower, by periodic visits to Beacon Hill.

'It won't be permanent surveillance,' Whyman had said. 'But if any doubtful characters are hanging round they'll be able to spot them. I'll put Sergeant Whitely on the job.'

This achieved one immediate and unexpected result.

'Two men,' Whyman reported, 'seem to be showing an interest in the Randalls. The Frey brothers – Charlie and Tim. Debt collectors for Sam Turlough.'

'Bookmakers' bullies, you mean.'

'Yes.'

'They haven't attacked Aubrey or his wife?'

'Not yet.'

'Do you think they will?'

'Not now,' said Whyman. 'They've got eyes in the back of their heads, these types. Whilst they've been watching the Randalls they must certainly have found out that we were watching them.'

Mr Piggin thanked him but offered no further comments to either Inspector Whyman or to Fearne, who was also in the room. When the inspector had left, Piggin and Fearne turned their attention to the lists which had just then arrived.

Aubrey's was, naturally, the longest of the three lists. It contained thirteen names of individuals and families. The headmaster had produced ten, the parson only seven – but he had added notes which helped them to identify the individuals concerned.

'Very satisfactory,' said Mr Piggin. 'Narrows the field nicely.'

'I'd hardly describe it as narrow,' said Fearne. 'It gives us, let me see, thirty people Mark might have known well enough to accept a lift from.'

'True. But you haven't cancelled out the names that are common to more than one list. It isn't all that easy, I agree, as they are sometimes called by first names, sometimes by surnames or even, in the case of boys, by nicknames. But with a little thought and investigation, it can be done. It will, I think, help to clarify the situation if I start by allotting a letter of the alphabet to each name. So, I call the first group of four on the parson's list *A*, *B*, *C* and *D*. They are personal and village acquaintances. The other three, all from the church, I call *P*, *Q* and *R*.'

Fearne marked his own copy of the list obediently. He was aware of Mr Piggin's liking for turning people into arithmetical symbols and then juggling them.

'Now let us examine the headmaster's list. His first three, though differently described, clearly correspond to the first four on the parson's list, so we will call them *A*, *B*, *C* and *D* as well. *A* is a local poacher and scallywag called Jim, who helps stock the Randalls' larder, and taught Mark the art of setting snares. *B* is the village policeman, Constable Perry, who would dearly like to catch Jim – who is always too slippery for him. *C* is a fisherman who takes Mark fishing. Known as Ben. Surname unstated. *D* is a junior master who is fond of Mark and visits him at home.'

'That'll be David Grieg,' said Fearne. 'It says here he thinks a lot of Mark, both as an athlete and a scholar.'

'Very well,' said Mr Piggin happily. 'To proceed – *P*, *Q* and R on the parson's list are all connected with the church. Yes? *P* is the organist and choirmaster, Dr Philpott. *Q* and *R* are tenor and bass choristers, Michael Seven and Ronald Truman. So much for the parson. Turning back to the headmaster, we have identified *A*, *B*, *C* and *D* from the parson's list. *G* and *H* are members of the school staff who know and like Mark, Mr Crowne and Mr Westall.'

'Mark is a popular boy, with a host of friends. But the names on the list are confined, I take it, to those who visit him at home.'

'Quite so,' *M*, *N* and *O* are boys who are Mark's particular friends. They, too, come to his house, and he visits them. I think we can ignore them as possible kidnappers. But the final letter on this list, *P*, is important.'

'Dr Philpott,' said Fearne. 'Yes. A man I never really liked or trusted.'

'Very well. Then, to round the matter off, let us look at Aubrey's list. Among the first six names (*A*, *B*, *D*, *E*, *G* and *H*) the only floater is *E*, who is the school sergeant, Hector McAndrew. I don't think we need waste much time on that valiant warrior. Three of the next six are boys from the head-master's list (a little group of Mark's friends) with one boy added, *L*, *P*, *Q* and *R* we know about from the parson's list. And that's the total.'

'It is indeed the total,' said Fearne, scanning his own lists. 'But what does it add up to?'

'Logically,' said Mr Piggin (it was a favourite word of his), 'the next step is to consider the names that appear in all three lists. What you might call the threesomes. They represent the most favourable field for further exploration.'

'Very well,' said Fearne. He had marked his own list with the red ink pen that he used for marking exam papers. 'We have *A* and *B* of course ... and we have *D*. Those stick out a mile. After that the only one I can see is *P*.'

'Correct.'

'Which gives us Jim the poacher, Constable Perry, David Grieg and Dr Philpott. Three possibles, one improbable.'

'An excellent trawl,' said Mr Piggin. 'And here, if you agree, is where we hand off to the professionals.'

'You mean bring in the police?'

'Not yet, no. We have four days left of the seven that Sebastian allowed us. I was referring to Captain Smedley's organization. He and his detective agency have helped us more than once in the past. We will give him the four names that appeared on all three lists. If any of them have taken part in removing and concealing Mark, Smedley's group will be sure to find them out.'

'We must give our client some idea of what we're up to,' said Fearne. He didn't say it very hopefully.

Neither was Sebastian impressed with the alphabetical juggling.

Mark, meanwhile, was frightened, but not as frightened as he might have been.

He was in the ground level room of a converted barge. The door – a stout piece of oak – was locked at night, and this had been alarming to start with. On the other hand it was comforting to know where he was. The barge was at anchor in the middle of a backwater in the wilderness of small streams and tidal inlets known as the Castle Point District. He had derived that knowledge from a glimpse through the barred porthole in the northern wall of his prison which revealed the distinctive outline of Two Tree Island. He guessed also, from the sounds and smells of cooking, that his captors were occupying the corresponding room in the stern of the barge.

He had studied their routine. On most mornings one or other of them departed in the dinghy which was attached to the barge. He guessed, from the meals they produced for him, that these were shopping expeditions. They were good meals. A lot better than the stodgy food at his boarding-school – exciting fry-ups of eggs, sausage, and bacon, with occasional tidbits such as mushrooms and kidneys.

An additional pleasure was that he was allowed one swim a day. This usually took place in the early morning when the sun was starting to disperse the mist that blanketed the river.

'No clothes,' was the order, and Mark dived into the water and swam about whilst his gaoler sat in the dinghy and watched him. He was a fast swimmer but it was clear that if he tried to escape, the dinghy would catch up with him before he had hauled himself out of the water. The thought of being pursued, naked and barefooted, across the rocks that lined the bank was unappetising enough for him to abandon any thought of flight.

Taken all in all, he thought, it was not such a bad life. Not nearly as unpleasant as his first term at boarding-school.

When he was lying in his bunk at night, before sleep overtook him, his thoughts turned to his father and mother. No doubt demands for ransom had reached them. His mother would be worrying herself silly, of that he was sure. His father would be taking things more calmly.

If a ransom were demanded he knew that his father, however willing to pay it, had very little money, and that recently, in an effort to repair the family fortunes, had been betting heavily – and not very successfully – on horses and greyhounds.

Any money would have to come from his grandfather, who might be disposed to help, but might not.

Mark considered, as calmly as he could, what his real captor would do if no money was forthcoming. His gaolers, he was convinced, were not the principals. They were acting under orders. Mark visualized his real captor as a tall, black-haired man who wore glasses. This was based on the villain in a television series he had been watching. In this, as in all other television dramas, the baddies were always, eventually, defeated and the good people came out on top. With this comforting thought in his mind he rolled over and went to sleep.

On the following morning, when he was standing on the deck, drying himself after his swim, Mark saw it. From the very top of the opposite bank, among a thicket of thorn and alder, a pair of round yellow eyes were looking down at him. The rays of the rising sun had caught – and were being reflected by – the lenses of a pair of binoculars.

When Captain Smedley's reports on Jim the poacher, Constable Perry, David Greig and Philpott the organist came in – all firmly negative – Mr Piggin should, by rights, have been downhearted. But it simply caused him to redouble his efforts. He said, 'The truth is hidden somewhere in those lists. I'm sure of it. It may be that we've been looking in the wrong place. Perhaps it was a mistake to concentrate on the threesomes. The truth may be in the twos. And if it is, I'll extract it. I promise you that.'

He retired early to his own room, and his light burned late into the night. On the following morning, after the regular meeting, the others departed but Mr Piggin stayed behind with Fearne. He said, 'I thought that I should let you have this alone. I know where Mark is being held.'

Fearne was, for a moment, incapable of speech.

'I worked the answer out last night and telephoned Captain Smedley. I got him at home before he left for work. He agreed that I was probably on the right track, and that he would put one of his best men on it – a retired burglar who has a way with locked doors. The man spotted Mark this morning. He'd just had a swim, and was looking very fit and happy.'

Fearne had gotten his breath back. 'Will you be good enough to tell me just exactly what you have discovered? Start at the beginning and talk slowly.'

'There's an old saying,' Mr Piggin began, 'and like many old sayings it has more than a grain of truth in it.'

Fearne, listening to him, was trying to pin down a recollection. The way Mr Piggin spoke, the way he sat in his chair, reminded him of something.

'All right,' he said, 'let's have this pearl of ancient wisdom.'

'If you encounter one improbability, that is all that it amounts to. An improbability. If you encounter two improbabilities they add up to a possibility. If you then meet with a third improbability, add them all together and you have a certainty.'

That was it! It was Fearne's old Balliol tutor speaking. Ready to tear one of his essays to pieces and scatter the pieces on the winds of scholarship. Obscurely comforted, he said, 'Proceed please.'

'Very well. The first improbability was the demand itself – ten thousand pounds. Think of it! The penalty for kidnapping is a minimum of ten years penal servitude. Some judges would hand down fifteen. And ten thousand pounds! Chicken feed! The least one would expect would be half a million – to be reduced, by bargaining, to a quarter. That would make the possible gain more or less worth the risk.'

'Yes,' said Fearne slowly. 'Now that you mention it, it does seem a little ... what should I say? ... amateurish.'

'The exact word that I should have used. And now for the second, and even greater improbability. The second letter Aubrey received was delivered by hand. Like the first it had, as he put it, been slipped into his letter box. The kidnapper had no reason to suppose that Aubrey had not gone straight to the police. Most men would have done so. In which case his house would have been closely watched, night and day. If a letter had to be sent, what was wrong with the postal service? Safe and perfectly secure.'

'A second amateur touch,' agreed Fearne. 'But neither of them contain any indication of who the sender was.'

'To discover that we have to turn to the lists which we obtained. It is written there, quite plainly. You remember the first four entries? A, B, C and D we called them?'

'Certainly,' said Fearne. He extracted his copies from a file and spread them on the table. 'Please go on.'

'The parson has all four of them. So has the headmaster. But what is curious, and indeed inexplicable, is the omission from Aubrey's list of C.'

'Ben the fisherman?'

'Right. He turns out, on further investigation, to be Ben Schooling; Aubrey must have known that Ben is a particular friend of Mark's. They often go fishing together. The parson and the headmaster certainly knew about him and put him near the head of their lists. So tell me this. Why did Aubrey leave him out?'

'And that showed you the truth?'

'The whole truth,' said Mr Piggin sadly. 'Aubrey Randall, being dunned by Sam Turlough for money he can't raise, and faced with the possibility of violence from Turlough's bullies, seemingly unable – or unwilling – to apply to his father, of whom he is in considerable awe, devised this little pantomime and used Ben to carry it out. I was certain that this was the answer, and Captain Smedley has confirmed it.'

Fearne looked bleakly at his managing clerk. After a silence, heavy with unspoken apprehension, he said, 'So what do we do about it?'

'I have suggested to Smedley that his man bring Mark straight to your house. It will then be for you to break the good news to his parents.'

'And then?'

'Most of the parties concerned will be very happy with the outcome. Antonia, of course, will be overjoyed at getting her son back unharmed. To her, nothing else is important. Mark will see himself as the hero of an adventure story.'

'And Sebastian?'

'I suggest that you present the whole thing to him as matter of finance. He understands money. He has been saved the possibility of having to pay out ten thousand pounds. I have every confidence that, if he leaves it to Smedley, Turlough can be settled for five or less. He knows that he cannot exact payment by legal means, and demanding money with menaces is a criminal offence. The fisherman, Ben, has no doubt, been funded by Aubrey. One might suggest, perhaps, a further five hundred for him, which still leaves Aubrey substantially in credit.'

Fearne thought about it for a long minute. Then he said, 'This is not something I can decide unilaterally. I shall have to have a word with my partners.'

'I suppose so,' said Mr Piggin sadly.

When his partners heard the news they were, to start with, simply delighted. They joined in congratulating Mr Piggin and praising Captain Smedley. It was only when they had exhausted their first demonstration of pleasure that they began to be aware of the rocks and cross-currents ahead.

Tara, in her usual common-sense way, said, 'I don't see the problem. We've got Mark back. He'll have to be persuaded to keep his mouth shut about the part played by Ben.'

'No difficulty there, I'm sure,' said Mr Piggin. 'Now that it's all over the last thing he'll want is to get Ben into trouble. He's an intelligent boy. I'm sure he'll be convinced that he was simply doing what he was told and that if anyone is to be punished, it should be the man who was giving him orders.'

'Just so,' said Fearne. '*And when he finds out that the man in question was his own father?*'

This produced a lengthy and thoughtful silence. Finally Tara said, 'Why should he find out? If we don't tell him, no one will.'

Hugo said, 'Yes, that's right. Suppose we tell Sebastian that we've had to pay ten thousand pounds to get Mark back. He'll certainly reimburse us. And when we have the money we can use part of it to pay off Turlough. I'm sure he'd accept much less than the full sum to clear his account. Right, Piggy?'

'I expect so,' said Mr Piggin shortly.

'Right,' said Tara. She seemed delighted by the way her idea was working out. 'Then we can use part of the balance, as you suggest, as a tip for Ben. Even if his expenses have been covered by Aubrey, an extra payment won't be amiss.'

Hugo said, 'After taking part of the remaining money to pay our bill, we return the balance to Sebastian, telling him that we were able to beat down the kidnappers. He'll be several thousand better off than he thought he was going to be, and he'll have his grandson back.'

'Everyone happy,' said Tara.

Apart from explaining the steps which he had taken to discover Mark, Mr Piggin had refrained from taking part in the discussion. Fearne had also been silent. When he continued to say nothing, Mr Piggin was constrained to break what had become an awkward silence.

He said, 'I seem to remember us discussing, a few years ago, a situation in which the truth would please one party, but could badly hurt another. Isn't that precisely the situation that has arisen?'

'Yes, I remember it,' said Tara. 'And I remember you said that if we thought the matter out carefully we could devise a way to make all parties happy. If we adopt my plan that's exactly what we're doing.'

There was a further long silence. Then Fearne said, 'It's ingenious, but unfortunately it's quite impossible.'

'Oh. Why?' said Tara, sharply. She was clearly preparing to lose her temper.

'Because it involves deceiving our client – in this case, Sebastian – which is one of the things a solicitor must never do.'

'I have to agree with that,' said Bob Bracknell. 'It would be a breach of legal ethics.'

'What's so special about legal ethics?' said Tara.

'They happen to be the rules of conduct that respectable solicitors observe.'

'Fiddlesticks,' said Tara. Hugo nodded his agreement with her. It was the old division, only deeper and sharper.

'There's only one honourable course open to us,' said Fearne slowly. 'Sebastian must be told the whole truth. If he then – being cognisant of all the facts – agrees to the ingenious solution you have propounded, well and good.'

'He'll blow his top,' said Tara.

'And refuse to disgorge a penny,' said Hugo.

'If I might say something,' said Mr Piggin, 'the decision is, of course, yours and yours alone. The only thing I would venture to suggest is that you may be misreading Sebastian's character. May I tell you what I think he'll do when he learns the truth? I don't think he'll blow his top. I think he's more likely to split his sides laughing. And he'll pay off Turlough – which he would have done anyway if the matter had been squarely put to him. I'm sure that if we let Captain Smedley conduct the negotiations, five thousand pounds will be more than enough for that. Even if he doesn't feel kindly enough towards Ben to want to tip him, I'm sure that he won't want any action taken against him. This way the boy need never know the truth. And, if I'm right, it will lead to one further good result. Sebastian has, unfortunately, got used to dismissing Aubrey as a child. This affair will, at least, cause him to take more notice of his son. Surely a desirable relationship between any parent and child.'

Like many of Mr Piggin's predictions this, happily, turned out to be the result.

14
Locard's Principle

Francis Fearne, the senior partner of Fearne & Bracknell, Solicitors, of Little Bethel by the Tower was not feeling at his best. In fact, as he told his daughter, Tara, a junior partner, (and the best theoretical lawyer in the firm) he was feeling bloody.

Tara was unsympathetic.

She said, 'It's your fault, Dad. You should have had your flu jabs, like we all did.'

'I can't see that flu jabs have anything to be said for them. Most people get flu once a year, whether they are inoculated or not. I remember when there was all that fuss about T.A.B. It was in the first year of the war—'

He meant *his* war. The one that started in 1939 and ended six years later.

'What was T.A.B?' said Hugo, the son of Fearne's partner, Robert Bracknell.

'I can't exactly remember,' said Fearne. 'I think that "T" stood for tetanus. What I do remember is that our MO took the whole thing very seriously. He armed himself with this huge syringe, we lined up, with our trousers down, and he injected us all in our bottoms. Next day – it really was pathetic – everybody was creeping round like paralyzed monkeys. If Hitler had launched his threatened invasion he'd have had a walk-over.'

'And were you one of the ones who was punctured?' said Tara.

'Fortunately I was on leave, and escaped this futile injection, and was none the worse for missing it.'

'And the end result is that you have lost your faith in science, and as a result have had a well-deserved bout of flu.'

'Science,' said Fearne complacently, 'is all right in its place. But we mustn't allow it to rule our lives.'

Tara said, 'He's talking nonsense, isn't he, Piggy? I'm sure *you* believe in science.'

Mr Piggin, who was their managing clerk, and attended all conferences, said, 'Since I have no idea what you mean by science – and I don't believe that you have any clear idea either – I can't produce a useful answer to your question. Certainly medical science is advancing steadily. And, though I'm not so certain about this, the scientific investigation of crime does seem to be becoming a little more precise than it was.'

The report in front of them was the account in the local papers of the inquest on a girl called Eileen Blaine which had terminated in a not unexpected verdict of murder against Eileen's husband, Julian Timberley.

The facts, so far as they had been reported, were not really in dispute.

The three people concerned were all members of a local dramatic society, the Blackheath Thespians. Most of their productions to date had been modern comedies and thrillers, performed with success on a number of local stages, but recently a more attractive possibility had presented itself. Their president, Colonel Watchett, had friends at Broadcasting House, and as a result of his advocacy, the BBC were planning a television performance of *Twelfth Night* in which a number of the Thespians had been considered for parts.

In one case a firm offer had been made.

Julian Timberley, youngish, blond and good-looking, was evident television material. Two other offers were subject to preliminary trials. Eileen Blaine, though married to Julian had retained, and was usually referred to, by the maiden name in which she had scored a few small successes on the fringe of the professional stage. She was dark, heavily built and by no means ill-looking, but subject to fits of breathlessness and depression.

In almost total contrast was Angela Millison, light, quick-moving and competent, with the self-assurance that success had brought with it.

The result of what might have seemed, in retrospect, an uneven contest had just been announced. It was Angela who had secured the coveted role of Viola. Eileen had been offered the much smaller part of the servant, Maria, which she had been tempted to reject out of hand. She had had second thoughts when her agent had said, 'Don't put people's backs up. If you do, you'll be black-listed and never get another engagement.'

This turned out to be an accurate prediction – she never did get another engagement – but not for the reasons her agent had given. Two days after he had proffered this advice Eileen had been found hanging from a beam in the kitchen at the back of the Timberleys' bungalow in Culloden Street.

It was Julian who, according to his own account, had discovered her when returning home at four o'clock in the morning.

'Four o'clock!' said Hugo. 'What *had* he been up to?'

'He had been at a rehearsal – a prolonged dress rehearsal – of *Twelfth Night*. But wait for it. We get more about that rehearsal, from other witnesses, later. First we have the evidence of the pathologist, Dr Basil Bredwin, who arrived on the scene with Chief Inspector Lovell at around half past four in the morning.'

'No time wasted there,' said Bracknell.

'No, indeed. And the prosecution certainly seem to have placed great reliance on the medical evidence. Which was crucial on two points. The time and cause of Eileen's death and the sequence of events leading up to it. Dr Bredwin's view, based largely on a bruise at the back of her neck, was that

Eileen was first stunned and then strung up to simulate suicide. As to the time of death he had been equally definite. 'Not less than eight and not more than nine hours prior to when he saw the body.'

'Which means,' said Bracknell, 'that he timed the death as having taken place at some time between seven-thirty and eight-thirty on the previous evening.'

'Exactly. And you will appreciate the importance of this when you find that the other members of the Thespians have given evidence, supported by their producer, Tom Guilford, that Julian arrived at the rehearsal at around eight-fifteen.'

'If that's right,' said Hugo, 'he must be a cold-blooded fish. Leaving his wife hanging in the kitchen and toddling off to a rehearsal.'

'Not just toddling off to a rehearsal. The prosecution version is that he was making straight for the arms of Angela Millison, designed by him to be his second wife.'

'If they've got any proof of that,' said Bob, 'surely it's an open and shut case. Who's acting for Timberley?'

'No one. He insisted on acting for himself.'

'Then it would seem,' said Fearne, 'that he is not only a murderer but a fool into the bargain. In any event, not a suitable client for us.'

The other partners nodded their agreement.

After snubbing Tara, Mr Piggin had refrained from contributing any further to the discussion. Where the four partners were in agreement it was almost unheard of for Mr Piggin to oppose them. On this occasion, however, he seemed to be unhappy. His views were valued sufficiently for them to wait for him.

At length he said, 'If it had been anyone but Bredwin, I'd have gone along with you. Speaking for myself, I distrust him. He seems, recently, to have been making strenuous efforts to promote himself as the successor to Bernard Spilsbury – the infallible oracle – you remember the Thorne case—'

They did indeed remember the case of Norman Thorne in which five experts had said 'suicide', Spilsbury alone had said 'murder' and his view had sent Thorne to the gallows.

'I'm not saying that Julian Timberley is innocent. He may have done exactly what the prosecution alleges. What I'm unhappy about is that Dr Bredwin's evidence was accepted without it having been tested in cross-examination. You all know, I'm sure, what's been happening. Until recently the universities and the great teaching hospitals have provided a forensic pathology service which the Home Office found useful and adequate. Then the old bogey of finance raised its head. Hospitals and universities which were both being squeezed for money, argued that they should not be expected to provide a pathologist to be at the beck and call of the police when the funding of forensic pathology should be the responsibility of the Home Office. Seeing the way things were going, one or two ambitious pathologists, like Bredwin, seem to have thought that it would pay them to go freelance—'

'Sounds dangerous to me,' agreed Bracknell. 'Without the solid professional backing of the university or hospital, they'd just be a one-man show. Expressing a personal view.'

'So what do you suggest we should do?' said Fearne.

'I think we should obtain Timberley's agreement for us to act for him. If he accepts our help, then we should make an application for legal aid, which would certainly be granted if he was properly represented.'

Tara, who seemed to be enjoying the turn the discussion had taken said, 'Let's brief Maxwell Gracey. Expert witnesses are meat and drink to him.'

Fearne, speaking slowly, and with a reluctance that may have been based more on his recent influenza than on logic, said, 'Very well. If that's what you all wish I won't stand in your way. And if we do enter the lists, it's certainly sensible to choose the champion with the sharpest sword.'

'I'm all for that,' said Hugo. 'The only time I heard Bredwin in court I thought he was a self-satisfied prick.'

'I hear that we've been promoted to the Central Criminal Court, the Old Bailey,' said Julian.

Fearne looked at him curiously. The young man had spoken as though he was discussing a play in which he was acting. A play that had opened in some unimportant provincial theatre and had now been transferred to the national stage.

'You don't seem unduly alarmed,' he said.

'Why should I be alarmed? I had nothing to do with Eileen's death. I wasn't even in the house at the time.'

'The other members of the company agree that the dress rehearsal was a lengthy one. They are equally clear that it finished by two-thirty a.m. Yet you seem not to have got back to your house until four a.m. Have you offered any explanation of how you spent the intervening period?'

'If anyone had troubled to ask me,' said Julian, clicking on his well-known and much-admired smile, 'I should have been happy to tell them that I spent more than an hour with Angela in the garden – the public garden that runs down from behind our house to the river. It was a fine night, and we were both too excited to think about going to bed.'

'Excited? At what in particular?'

'Why, because at the end of the rehearsal our producer, Tom Guilford, had made a firm offer to Angela of the part she badly wanted, the part of Viola. It's one of the finest parts in the whole Shakespearean canon. Elizabethan audiences had become used to seeing girls' parts acted by boys. This went even further. It's a boy acting as a girl acting as a boy.'

'And whilst you were discussing this exciting project, did anyone else come into the garden?'

'No. Fortunately we were undisturbed. We had so much to talk about.' The smile flashed out again.

259

'You hardly seem to realize the strength of the case against you,' said Fearne, crossly. 'Let me put it in plain words. Their medical expert is prepared to swear that Eileen was first stunned by a blow on the back of her neck, and then had a noose placed round her neck. The end of the rope was, he says, thrown over the rafter in the kitchen, the unconscious girl was then hauled up and the end of the rope was attached to a hook in the wall. None of this would have taken more than five or ten minutes, which allows you ample time to pick up Angela and depart with her to your rehearsal.'

'Which fits in, incidentally,' said Bracknell, 'with Bredwin's calculation of the time of death. Eight or nine hours, he says, before he examined the body at half past four that morning.'

'Quite so,' said Julian, unperturbed. 'Fortunately it will be for the court – the judge and the twelve members of the jury – to decide whether to believe the truth, as I shall speak it, or to believe the half truths and lies produced by this charlatan who calls himself a pathologist and has no real scientific background and training.'

This was spoken with apparent seriousness, but sounded to Fearne a bit like a speech that had been made up and learned by heart.

'Anyway,' added Julian, his face once more crumbling into a smile, 'it's a well-known rule of the theatre that, in the end, the good shall prosper and the bad be defeated.'

'I hope you're right,' said Fearne. He made no attempt to hide his irritation at an impossible young man who, disregarding the peril in which he stood, seemed determined to believe that he was starring in a dramatic production.

At the Central Criminal Court, two weeks later, the attorney general had presented the case for the prosecution with dispassionate care and had been listened to with equal care by Mr Justice Singleton and the jury.

His first witness was a Mrs Forrestier, who lived in the bungalow next door to the Timberleys and shared a front garden with
them. She knew Angela Millison by sight, and had observed her
hanging about outside the Timberley front gate. She had seen
Julian emerge from his front door, proceed down the path, greet
Angela, and walk off with her; presumably, she thought, to the
rehearsal room. Eileen had not been around at the time. She had
seen her earlier in the day doing something in the back garden.
She was a keen gardener.

No questions.

Next came the producer, Tom Guilford. He timed the arrival of
Julian and Angela at the rehearsal room as 20.05. He had had his
eye on the time, being anxious to get going, particularly because,
owing to the irritating absence of Eileen Blaine, he had been
forced to alter the running order of the rehearsal. Maria, though
a minor part, featured in two of the early scenes in Act 1. He had
despatched his assistant, Dan Raybould, to look for her.

No questions.

Dan, an eager, fresh-faced young man, glad to have attracted
some of the limelight, told the court that he had knocked several
times at the Timberley front door and rung the bell, and although
he could see that there was a light on in the hallway there had
been no answer to his assault on the door.

'Wake Duncan with thy knocking, would thou couldst', said
Bracknell to himself.

'And for all you knew,' said Counsel, 'the deceased was at that
time hanging in the back room.'

'For all I knew, yes.'

No questions from Gracey, who seemed to have fallen asleep.

Then came Inspector Lovell. He had been summoned by telephone at 04.27 – so his log recorded. Fortunately Dr Bredwin had
been in the office when the call came through, discussing a case
they were jointly involved in, and they had proceeded together,
in a police car, to the Timberley residence, arriving at 04.35.

When the inspector had finished, Gracey opened his eyes and murmured, 'A couple of small points, please, Inspector. When the body was taken to the mortuary, it will have been stripped for examination. What became of the deceased's clothing?'

'The normal routine was observed. Different items were packed away in cellophane bags. If you require any item for further examination it is, of course, available to you.'

Gracey thanked him, and as the inspector made ready to depart, he said, 'You did not, I imagine, confine your attention to the room in which the body was found. You will have searched the whole bungalow?'

'Of course.'

'And I expect you made notes.'

'Full notes. And a plan, to scale, of the room in which the body was found. I have made extra copies of the plan and the notes in case you think it would be helpful to have them exhibited.'

'Certainly. Exhibits B.1. and B.2. if you please.' Gracey was examining the plan with evident appreciation. Meticulous measurements showed the distance of the body from the door, the length of rope round its neck, and the precise point at which it had been passed over the beam before being attached to the hook in the wall. 'Very good and very clear,' he said. 'One last question, Inspector. In the course of your search did you find a ladder?'

The inspector, surprised by the unexpectedness of the question, took a moment to think out his answer. Then he said, 'Yes. There had been a number of break-ins in the neighbourhood, and we had circularized householders warning them to keep their ladders locked up. I was gratified to find that in this case the only ladder, which was in an out-house, was not only chained to the wall, but the door of the out-house was locked, too.'

'Excellent,' said Gracey. He seemed as pleased as the inspector by this evidence of the co-operation of the public with the police, and indicated that he had no further questions.

Like a skilful producer, the attorney general had kept his most important witness to the last, and Dr Bredwin, conscious of his own importance, took the stand and prepared to drive the final nails firmly into Julian's coffin.

He divided his evidence into three parts, exactly as he had done when giving evidence at the inquest. The cause and the time of death, and the events leading up to it.

When he had answered the last of the attorney general's careful questions, Maxwell Gracey hauled himself up onto his feet. He allowed almost a full minute of silence to elapse before he spoke.

A typical piece of theatre, said Fearne to himself.

'It will be helpful, I think, if I adopt the same division of his evidence as the witness did, and deal first with the cause of death. If you please, Doctor Bredwin-'

'In my view, death was due to strangulation. There was a clearly marked hanging groove on the neck, and even without this, the fact that the epiglottis was congested, and that there were marks of interior bleeding, allowed us to arrive at no other conclusion.'

'Your attention was drawn, was it not, to a bruise on the back of the neck? Could this have been a contributory cause of death? I mean, in the sense put forward by the prosecution, that the deceased was first stunned, and then had a noose placed round her neck, by means of which she was hauled up to the rafter.'

'Yes. This theory has been propounded to me. In my view it is tenable, and not contradicted by the medical evidence.'

Mr Justice Singleton, who had refrained so far from interrupting the proceedings, now leaned forward courteously and said, 'Would you explain, for my benefit, and for the benefit of the jury, exactly how you arrived at that conclusion? Some of the medical evidence appears to contradict it.'

'That is so, My Lord. It has been suggested that had this bruise been caused by a blow forceful enough to render the deceased unconscious, it must certainly have left some other external marks on the neck. And that no such marks were visible. I do not regard this as in any way conclusive. It is perfectly possible, as has been shown only too many times in this court that a single blow, well placed, will produce unconsciousness without leaving any more mark than the single bruise that was found in this case.'

'You mentioned two points?'

'Further, My Lord, it has, I know, been suggested that a violent blow would have fractured the hyoid bone in the neck of the deceased girl. Which it did not do. I do not regard that as conclusive either. The hyoid bone, though admittedly brittle is normally only broken by direct pressure, as in cases of manual strangulation.'

'In short, Doctor, I understand you to say that there is nothing in the medical evidence to contravene the theory put forward by the prosecution.'

'That is so, My Lord.'

Maxwell Gracey, who had resumed his seat during these exchanges rose once more to his feet.

He said, 'I am happy to leave this first point, and to say that my learned friend and myself are in agreement that death was due to strangulation. The precise circumstances in which it took place are, of course, a matter for further elucidation. So let us move on to the second point. You stated in evidence before the coroner that you estimated the time of death as being – I quote from the report of your evidence in the papers – "not less than eight and not more than nine hours prior to the time when you saw the body".'

'That is what I said, and that is what I meant,' said Dr Bredwin truculently.

'When you consider that most authorities on this matter – I have here a book entitled *The Scientific Investigation of Crime* by Stuart Kind – you know it I'm sure.'

'It is one of many works on the subject.'

'Certainly. I can refer you also to *Crime Detection* by Arne Svenssen and Otto Wendal, or the equally well-known work by L.C. Nickolls, the Director of the Police Laboratory at New Scotland Yard – you would agree that they are all reliable authorities.'

'Oh, certainly,' said Bredwin, in a voice of calculated indifference as though he was wondering what these questions could possibly be leading to.

'You will remember that Dr Kind at page 218 – I have a copy for His Lordship, if you please, Usher, thank you – the centre paragraph on that page which runs, "In a murder investigation the fixing of the time of death is a very important, but very difficult problem". It goes on to list, in order of importance, the factors that have to be considered: that is to say, body temperature, post-mortem lividity and rigor mortis. The one point on which the authorities are unanimous is that the simplest and the only reliable test of the time of death is the taking of the temperature, at stated intervals, both of the body and of the surrounding atmosphere.'

Since this did not lead to a question, Dr Bredwin said nothing, but it was clear that he knew what was coming and did not like it.

Gracey continued, in the same level tone of voice.

'To be fair, the authorities add that this particular procedure may not be possible where a substantial period has intervened between death and the time that the pathologist is called – three days is mentioned as an example of such delay – but in this case, most fortunately, you were summoned within a matter of hours. Correct?'

'Yes.'

'So perhaps you would explain to the court why you neglected the accepted and accurate method of calculating the time of death, and would appear to have based your estimate on such a notoriously incorrect indicator as the progress of rigor mortis.'

The witness, who seemed to be shrinking under this implacable assault, hesitated, and then started, 'Well—'

Counsel intervened, before he could formulate a sentence, to say, 'You may think it unfair to quote the theoretical views of scientists, so may I add that your own handbook, *The Practical Police Surgeon*, published under the auspices of the Association of the Police Surgeons of Great Britain – a copy for His Lordship, please – lists at page 145 six matters which have to be considered: lividity, hypostasis, jaundice, cyanosis, pallor and, sixthly and lastly, rigor mortis.'

'I must confess,' said the judge, 'that I have myself been puzzled to know why, in a matter so clearly important, you discarded the reliable test of body and atmospheric temperatures.'

The witness said, with a show of confidence which deceived no one, 'I have had, My Lord, considerable experience of cases such as the present one, and have always found that the onset of rigor mortis was the best and simplest guide to estimating the time of death.'

'Although,' interposed Gracey smoothly, 'the law books to which I have referred all agree that the onset of rigor mortis, *particularly where death occurs from strangulation*, can be irregular and imprecise. I can quote a number of statements bearing on this subject if Your Lordship thinks that they would be of assistance.'

'Perhaps we might leave it at that for the moment,' said the judge. 'You have other questions for this witness?'

'Yes, My Lord. My next questions relate to the precise circumstances in which death occurred. You will, no doubt, have considered the significance of the stool that was found lying near the body.'

'Certainly I considered it.' The witness appeared to be recovering some of his confidence. 'It was the only movable item of furniture in the out-house, and since the hook to which the end of the rope was attached – please see my sketch, Exhibit B.1. – was seven feet six inches from the floor, and since, as Inspector Lovell has told us the only available ladder had been carefully locked away, it was clear to me that the accused must have stood on the stool when he attached one end of the rope to the hook. He could not have reached it otherwise.'

'You say that the accused must have done so?'

'That seemed to me to be probable.'

'But if one accepts the view put forward by the defence that death was the result of suicide, then the deceased, not the accused, would have used the stool when attaching one end of the rope to the hook before slipping the noose, which she had formed at the other end, round her own neck and kicking the stool away. Is that not so?'

'I suppose it is possible,' said the witness grudgingly.

'So, being faced with two opposed theories, did it not seem to you that the matter could be finally, and decisively, set at rest by the application of Locard's principle?'

This produced an uncomfortable silence in which the witness seemed to be trying to formulate an answer, but could get no further than, 'I'm afraid that, at the moment, the precise application of that particular principle escapes me—'

That's sunk him, thought Fearne.

He had been reminded of the point in the burning car case at which Norman Birkett had finally destroyed Rouse's witness, a mechanical engineer, by inviting him to discuss the coefficient of expansion of brass; and the witness had been as hesitant in his answer as Bredwin was now.

The judge decided to take a hand. He said, 'Since you attach importance to the principle you have mentioned, Mr Gracey, and since it appears to puzzle this witness, might we invite you to explain what you have in mind or is it something that will be dealt with by your own witness?'

'I would much prefer to leave the point to that witness who is, as Your Lordship will have observed, the only witness that the defence proposes to call. He is the Official Analyst to the Home Office, Professor Angus Meiklejohn.'

The judge said, 'I have had the pleasure on more than one occasion of listening to Professor Meiklejohn and I have no doubt that what he says will be enlightening. If the attorney general agrees, I suggest that he lets us have his evidence now. If any of the matters he raises prove to be controversial, Dr Bredwin can, of course, he recalled to deal with them.'

The attorney general indicated that he had no objection. In truth, he was anxious to get Dr Bredwin out of the box before he did any more damage to his case. Bredwin, for his part, seemed only too glad to vacate his uncomfortable seat, and hand it over to the bespectacled and heavily bearded Scotsman.

Gracey said, 'You have heard the evidence so far given, and will be able to appreciate that the difference of opinion between the prosecution and the defence has been virtually narrowed down to a dispute as to which of the parties made use of the stool which was found beside the body. Whether it was the deceased herself, in committing suicide, or the accused in an effort to conceal his crime.'

'As a preliminary,' said Meiklejohn, 'I feel I must congratulate Inspector Lovell over the care with which he has preserved certain important items which might otherwise have been disturbed or lost. He was able to supply me with – I have them here, and suggest that they be marked Exhibit "A" – thank you – the shoes which the deceased was wearing at the time of her death and which were taken from her body, along with her clothes, when she was stripped for examination in the mortuary. With these in my possession, together with the top section of the stool in question – Exhibit "B", please – I was in a position to apply the well-known principle first enunciated by Professor Locard, that when two objects come into contact there is *always* a transference of material from the one to the other. Minute, possibly, but visible to the eye of the microscope. So far as the shoes are concerned, I found the soles covered with an uncommon type of red clay and deposits of more normal earth overlapping the clay. I was given an opportunity of examining the small garden behind the residence of the deceased and found that a trench had been dug in it for the planting of roses, but not yet filled in. This revealed the presence of a stratum of that particular clay some twelve inches *under* the garden soil. In my view it was only someone standing at this point who would carry away on his shoes the particular mixture of earth and clay that was found on the soles of the shoes *and* on the surface of the stool. Further microscopic examination of a sample of the earth from the garden showed small fragments of pine needles and decomposed leaves, which were present both on the shoes and on the stool. This demonstrated to me, beyond any possibility of doubt, that the deceased, who had, in fact, been observed by her neighbour working in the garden on the morning of the day she died, must, at some point thereafter, have climbed onto the stool. Nor could I find a trace of any superimposed substance to suggest that the stool had been mounted by any person other than the deceased.'

When Professor Meiklejohn resumed his seat, it was clear that the jury was not only convinced by his evidence, but was glad to be able to acquit the handsome young actor of the charge against him. Directed by the judge, and without withdrawing from their seats, they recorded a verdict that Eileen Timberley, professionally known as Eileen Blaine, had taken her own life; adding, as was conventional in such cases, that she had done so whilst the balance of her mind was disturbed.

Half an hour later, when the formalities of acquittal had been rapidly completed, Julian Timberley left the dock, apparently unmoved by his experience. Fearne watched him walk off among a chattering and congratulatory crowd of his fellow Thespians.

He strolled back slowly from the court to his office in Little Bethel by the Tower. There was no hurry. His clerk would be settling up with Gracey's clerk the financial side of the affair. All that remained was for him to receive, as he was sure that he would in due course, Julian's thanks for his efforts.

What he had not expected was what Julian said when he did arrive. As soon as the door was closed and he was comfortably seated, he observed, 'I'm sorry that I seemed to you to take the matter so calmly. It must have been very provoking.'

'It certainly was. I wondered sometimes if you quite realized the seriousness of your position.'

'I had one good reason for my calmness that you couldn't know about. You see, I knew that Eileen had committed suicide.'

'How did you know it?'

'I knew it because she had told me she was going to do it. I forget exactly what she said, but her meaning was quite clear. Couldn't have been clearer. If she failed to get the part she was yearning for – and, more, if it went to her bitter rival, who would be able to gloat over her – then life would no longer be worth living, and she would be forced to take steps to terminate it.'

'For the Lord's sake,' said Fearne. 'Why did you keep this piece of evidence from us?'

'I thought it out. Of course, I realized the force of it, *if* it was believed. But it seemed more likely that it would be disbelieved. That I should be thought to have made it up, in an effort to save my own skin. Which would have antagonized the jury and turned them against me. And it would have been out of character.'

'So you were prepared to take a chance on the verdict going against you?'

'It was nicely balanced. But I was sure that science would come to my rescue if I gave it a chance.'

As Julian was speaking, Fearne realized that his opinion of him was misjudged. His feckless small-boy attitude was a piece of superficial gloss. The icing on the cake. Underneath, there was a hard man. Maybe hard enough to climb the long and slippery ladder that led to success for the few, or descended to mediocrity for the majority. Might they, in a few years, see his name in lights in Shaftesbury Avenue as audiences crowded in to witness his latest hit? It seemed possible.

Five minutes after Julian had left, without having awarded Fearne a single word of thanks, Bob Bracknell came in.

He said, 'They're starting to queue up already for the extra matinee of *Twelfth Night* that's just been announced. Shall I see if I can get us tickets?'

'Not for me,' said Fearne. 'I've had enough.'

'Well you can always read his book when it comes out.'

'What book are you talking about?'

'Julian's autobiography. Stars always write their autobiographies. We'll all feature in it.'

'Favourably, I hope.'

'Oh yes. We'll be goodies. And what's more, he won't have to ferret round to find a title for it. He's got one ready made: *Saved by Locard.*'